BOUND

KATE HAWTHORNE

Bound
Kate Hawthorne

Copyright © 2023 Kate Hawthorne

Edited by:
Jordan Buchanan

Cover Design:
Samantha Santana - Amai Designs

"The closer I'm bound in love to you, the closer I am to free." - Robert Green Ingersoll

I walked out of Cunningham's without so much as a goodbye, the neatly stapled stack of papers and the manila envelope already softening from my clammy palms. Flynn, Barclay, and the rest of my friends shouted after me, once they'd stopped laughing at the prospect of me getting sued, but I waved them off and stalked out of the bar and into the parking lot.

The crisp evening air didn't do shit to help clear my mind. The cool breeze burned my throat as I sucked in gasping breath after gasping breath. Sweat had already started to bead against my temples and heat rolled over me like endless waves determined to take me down. I made it to the car before the dry heaving commenced, and thanks to a half-drank water bottle in the console, I was able to stave off the impending panic attack.

It had been years since I'd had one. College had been hell for me in about a thousand different ways, one of which being the then-unmedicated anxiety that I'd been struggling with for my entire life. The stress of college with Greek life, and tests, and the ever imposing bar exam only made it worse until, one day, I'd worked myself up into such a frenzy I blacked out in the basement of my frat house and woke up in the medical center.

Once the nurse had ruled out alcohol poisoning and overdose, neither of which I felt would be rampant issues at the overpriced university I attended, she settled on anxiety and recommended I go find a therapist and a prescription for Xanax.

She changed my life.

School got better after that. Balancing fraternity requirements with the expectations of my almost long-term girlfriend and the weight of my senior year class load was finally easy for me. Well, *easier*. I had a lot on my plate, and some of that was by design, some of it from example.

Because my parents had high expectations of me and the career I would make for myself, the life I would build, and the legacy that would provide them. The pressure was a lot, sometimes unbearable, and my one extracurricular had started innocently enough.

My freshman year, I'd joined the coed club sailing team.

I still didn't know what I'd been thinking because I had a full course load and an internship that my dad had been arranging since I was in junior high. Spare time wasn't something that existed on my calendar, but I'd needed an outlet for my stress, and I'd always loved being in or on the water. I'd spent plenty of summers on boats, albeit they were more like yachts where I didn't have to lift a finger, but sailing offered me something I was craving.

A purpose.

Everyone on the team had a job and everyone was integral to the success of the race, and my position as pit was no different. I quickly learned that sailing wasn't for me, but ropes and knots…

That was another story entirely.

Lost in the memories of that first year of college when I'd learned the difference between a handcuff knot and an anchor hitch, I'd also met Genevieve. She had been sailing her entire life, or at least as long as she could remember. She was at school on a sailing scholarship, which was something I didn't even know existed until she told me about it.

I think I fell in love with her the first time I saw her on a boat, her straw blonde hair whipping around her face with the wind as she yelled out to the rest of the team. Genevieve was strong, and she was beautiful, and she was also dating the president of my rival fraternity. I knew better than to poach her because I had a life to build and a legacy to establish, so she and I became friends instead.

It was unavoidable, with our proximity to each other on the boat and on the team, or at least that's what I told myself. Sometime my freshman year, I'd also met Perceval Barclay, who was a little bit older and a little bit meaner than me, and very much in love with his long-term boyfriend, Dennis. As far as I was concerned back then, the two of them were goals. Everything I wanted for my own life, except I wanted it with Genevieve.

"You look lost," Barclay said to me, his shoes making an obnoxiously loud echo as he walked up to my car.

I was in the driver's seat with the door open, legs spread and elbows braced on my knees. My shoes were brand new Tom Ford's and I was very glad I'd managed to *not* throw up all over them. I glanced up at him, the whiskey from our earlier drinks churning in my stomach. Apparently hurling my guts up all over the both of us was still not out of the realm of possibility.

"I feel like I'm in college all over again." I still had the papers in my hand and I threw them up onto the dash with a groan.

"What part?"

"The end of it," I said.

Barclay gestured toward the paperwork.

"Genevieve?" he asked. "Do you have a kid running around somewhere you didn't know about until now?"

My stomach roiled, the thought of that almost sounding more manageable than what the paperwork actually detailed.

"No kids that I'm aware of," I muttered.

"What then?" he asked, dropping down onto the ground at my feet. He bent his legs at the knee and propped his forearms on them, fingers threaded together in the open space between.

Something about seeing him sitting on his ass in a parking lot, knowing that he was wearing pants that probably cost five hundred dollars, made me laugh. It sounded pained and ill-timed, and I scrubbed a hand down my face, wishing I could wipe the past eighteen years of my life away entirely and start over, legacy and success be damned.

"Are you here to get the answer and go back and settle the bet?"

I figured that with my hasty retreat and cold shoulder, my friends would have started taking bets about who was suing me and why. None of them would even come close to guessing the truth of the matter. Hell, it was a revelation to me and it was my fucking life.

"I'm here as your friend," he said, smacking my calf. "Ruining my pants for you."

"You can get in the car if you want."

"Will you drive us both off a cliff if I do?" he asked, not budging from his position on the ground.

I loved him.

I loved him so much, in the most platonic way I'd ever love anyone in my life. Barclay had been there for me through so much, and I'd been there for him. There was a time we'd been near inseparable, even after he'd graduated and started work. I still had a few years left of school then, but he stayed local and we stayed in touch. It was through him that I'd met Rob, Archie, Flynn, the rest of my friends.

It was wild to think how interconnected life was. If I hadn't joined sailing, if I hadn't blacked out in the basement, if I had reacted any differently when Genevieve had dumped me a week before graduation…

"I'd unlock the door so you could bail," I told him.

It was true.

I'd always leave the door unlocked for him. I always had, in many ways.

"And ruin these slacks?" He laughed and stood, dusting gravel and grit off his backside. "Tell me what's happened and tell me if we can fix it."

"It's fixable," I assured him. "Just…unexpected."

"Are you going to tell me or are we going to continue to speak in riddles?" Barclay held out his hand.

"I don't want *them* to know," I muttered. "Not yet."

"Fine, but are you sure it's not a secret baby?"

I snatched the papers from the dash and read through them one more time, then shoved them into his still-waiting hand.

"No baby," I said.

Barclay took the stapled packet, eyes going wide when he read the names in the top left corner of the first page.

"Why on earth is Carter Royce suing you?" he asked.

"Carter Royce the fourth," I corrected, swallowing down the very short-lived nickname that threatened to spill out of my mouth. Royce, as he'd been called for years by almost everyone who knew him, was my best-kept secret, or so I'd thought.

"Are you sure this isn't about Gen?" He kept reading, then choked. "Oh."

I could see how he'd make the stretch, since Carter Emerson Royce IV was the fraternity president in question that Genevieve had been dating until she wasn't. The man she'd been with until she was with me. But that was a whole story in and of itself, and a time I generally preferred to not dwell on for about a hundred different reasons.

"*Oh*," I repeated, lacing the single syllable with all the knowing I could manage. "You remember when Gen broke up with me?"

"Bitch."

He remembered.

"Before I told you about it…" I dragged my tongue across the front of my teeth, the memories from back then all a little hazy. "I went to I…Royce."

"That's honestly ballsy as fuck."

Barclay read through the suit, flipping the pages in silence. They didn't make a sound, once crisp, they were still saturated with the cold sweat from my hands.

"It was, but I knew he'd understand what it was like."

"And I wouldn't have?" Barclay neatly slipped the papers into the envelope, flipped the flap closed, and threaded the brass brad through and locked it all down before giving the envelope back to me.

I tossed it on the dash and thumped my head against the headrest.

Barclay's tone sounded hurt at the implication there was something monumental that had happened to me that I didn't immediately take to him, but it had felt so damn complicated at the time. Everything was hard at twenty-one, with the expectations of a million people circling like vultures at all times. Barclay was still a junior partner at the firm and I should have been studying, even though I knew the legal code as well as I ever would.

"I did tell you about the breakup," I reminded him. "I came to you two days after it happened, when I was in a better headspace to talk about it."

"But you went to Royce first?"

I nodded.

"That doesn't quite explain how—"

I raised a hand and he snapped his mouth shut, raking his hand through his gold highlighted hair. Groaning, I angled my head so I could see him through the door, taking note for the first time of the slight graying around his temple, the crow's feet that had settled in the corners of his dark brown eyes.

Sometimes, I wondered why I couldn't have been romantically interested in him. We were the best of friends and we'd been in bed with each other more than once. Barclay was attractive and he was a very generous lover, but there had never been that violent and necessary kind of spark between us. We both realized it early on, which I think made our friendship stronger in the long run. Barclay and I were able to do a lot of things together while never having to worry about it getting weird, at least not on account of feelings.

He and I had done plenty of weird things in the years we'd known each other.

Even if weird was subjective.

"Are you mad I went to him first?" I asked.

"I'm too old to care about decisions either of us made in college."

"He knew what Gen was like," I said with a weak shrug. There was a lot about her that Barclay didn't know, that I'd never told anyone, but I knew that he would understand. There was no way he wouldn't understand.

"Okay, so all that aside, that doesn't explain how that..." He pointed at the innocuous-looking envelope. "Happened."

"He took one look at me and knew what she'd done." I swallowed, screwing my eyes closed and fighting back a fresh wave of nausea at the memory. "Then he grabbed me, put us both on a plane, and forty-five minutes later we were in Vegas."

"Step one," Barclay mused.

"I don't remember much," I admitted, forcing my eyes back open even if I had no intention of looking him in the eye when I confessed. "We gambled a lot, drank even more, and that first night we were there..."

I trailed off, and Barclay didn't say anything. He walked around to the passenger side of my car and climbed in. Once he closed the door, I swung my legs inside and closed mine too. The soundproof door panels were really worth their money because the hum of outside traffic immediately silenced, leaving only the sound of our mingled breaths and the battering of my heart in my ears.

"I remember that we kissed," I let loose the confession under my breath, but it was impossible he didn't hear me. "We kissed a lot, and we did more than kiss."

"Clearly."

"I...we...I don't remember how any of that got started, but I remember not wanting it to end. It was like..."

"A lightbulb," he offered.

I nodded. "A lightbulb, like...I hadn't ever thought about being with men before him, but—"

Barclay interrupted, "Not even me?"

"Especially not you." I chuckled and then sighed, and then groaned. "I know that he sucked me off. I remember..."

I trailed off again, letting my hand hover in the space between my chest and the steering wheel. If I tried hard enough, I could remember the silky feel of his hair against my fingers and my palm while he bobbed up and down my dick. The room swam when I'd opened my eyes to watch him, but it was only partly from the alcohol.

"I remember being intimate with him," I finally said, rolling my head to the side to find Barclay studying me intently. "But I sure as fuck don't remember marrying him."

CHAPTER 2
IVEY

THE GIN TASTED LIKE PAINT THINNER, STRIPPING AWAY THE INNER lining of my throat before setting to the same task in my stomach. It had been nearly fifteen years since the last time I'd tasted the abhorrent liquor and, honestly, I struggled to find why I'd ever enjoyed it in the first place.

But college Carter was a different person from real-life adult Carter. College Carter had fraternity responsibilities and obligations, school to deal with, and of course…years of therapy in the wake of everything that revolved around Genevieve St. Charles.

That included Dalton Fox, but the gin had been strong back then, and I didn't realize just how much he'd unintentionally ingrained himself into my life until I put my application in for a penthouse at a co-op in the city. Imagine my surprise when the board called me in for a second interview to ask why I'd lied about my marital status.

I assured them I had done no such thing, but they had evidence to the contrary. They produced a nearly two decades-old marriage license from Nevada, my initials scrawled across the bottom, right beside Dalton's scratchy signature that trailed off the far edge of the page. My first instinct had been to tell them I had absolutely no recollection of the union—which was the truth—but I didn't want to cast myself in a less than savory light.

I really wanted that goddamn penthouse. My whole life, I'd always considered a birds-eye view of New York had always been the pinnacle of success. Every career decision I'd made had been with the singular focus of a future in a skyscraper. It was a kind of prize that was different from what my father had planned for me, but not so different that it would get me in trouble. It was branching out and making his name my own. That next check box was so close now, well within reach, and the last thing I needed for the board to think of me was that I'd ever been the kind of man who got drunk enough to get married in Las Vegas and then promptly forget about it.

"Where is your husband, Mr. Royce?" they'd asked me. "We can't approve the application if this can't be explained or remedied in a morally agreeable manner."

"Can you let me have a few weeks to get all of that in order?" I'd asked.

All four of them looked unimpressed at the prospect, but me getting the unit would be a win-win situation, of that I was certain. After all, I was Carter Emerson Royce IV, and a name that carried the weight of that much generational legacy wasn't something to walk away from. For as much as I wanted the penthouse, having my name on the deed would do wonders for the rent they would charge the rest of their prospective tenants.

In the end, they'd conceded seven days.

Which felt like not enough time at all to track down a man I hadn't talked to since college, who probably didn't even remember I existed.

No.

That was wrong.

Dalton remembered me, even if he didn't remember marrying me, which…

The wedding wasn't why I quit drinking gin. I didn't even remember the wedding.

But sitting back in my apartment with the shitty photocopy of a marriage license in my hand, pops and sparks of the last night

Dalton and I spent together began to trickle back into my mind. It was almost like my subconscious—fueled by liquor—had put up a wall to keep the memories out, and the wall had held up. Time, as she often does, had started to erode the block, though, and…

Apparently, Dalton and I got married.

I wondered if that had come before or after I'd sucked his cock into the back of my throat. Either way, we were different people now with separate lives, and I wasn't going to let a flimsy piece of paper stand in the way of my next big win. I was going to get approved for that penthouse, and there was no discussion to be had about it. Unfortunately, marriage law had never been my specialty, so I called up a friend of a friend from college, Sarah Walters, who owed me a favor.

After swearing her to secrecy, I gave her as much as I could recall about my two days in Vegas with Dalton, which amounted to the hotel we stayed at and his full legal name. I didn't remember what company I chartered the jet through, but that it was probably my father's, and I didn't remember the name of the chapel either. I didn't remember the chapel at all.

It didn't take long for her to track him down, less than a day, and she filled out everything required and hired a process server to pass off the filing. She'd gone above and beyond, which was unexpected and unnecessary, sending me a surprisingly detailed packet of information about Dalton Fox and the name he'd spent the last two decades building for himself.

And that was how I found myself on a Friday night at home, drinking gin, tracing my fingertip over the scrawl of his signature on the marriage license. Beneath that sat the mini-biography, which I was ashamed to admit I'd read through no less than five times since it landed in my inbox earlier in the day.

Without thinking, I reached up and scratched my head, mussing my hair and causing another pebble in the emotional block wall to break free and fall. The memory with that one was Dalton's hand in my hair, not quite pulling at me, but not being soft either, my name lodged somewhere in the back of his throat as he struggled to catch his breath.

"Shit," I cursed under my breath and shoved the marriage license to the bottom of the pile.

Dalton's smiling face shone up from the next page, and it was a wonder that it had taken drinking both our weights in alcohol to get up the courage to make a move on him. It had been ill-timed, for about a thousand different reasons, the least of them being Genevieve, but the gin had softened up both of our inhibitions and one thing had led to another, and then…

He'd seemed receptive at the time, though I did have a strong recollection of him telling me over and over that he wasn't into guys, that he'd never looked at a man with lust before, that he wasn't gay, he wasn't even bi. I'd asked if he wanted me to stop and he'd shaken his head no.

Dalton was very into men, we both found out. Or he was at least into me.

Or maybe it had just been the gin after all.

The rest of our trip was a blur, but I'd woken up alone. Dalton was gone, his things along with him. He'd scrawled a goodbye note on the hotel notepad by the phone and he'd left. I had no idea how he'd gotten back to campus, and when I managed my way back to California, I couldn't track him down. He ignored my calls and avoided me like the plague. It wasn't as if I could call him out for it. We were both so deeply in the closet back then, and it was too risky for both of us if I'd dragged our dirty laundry out in public like that.

I knew he graduated. I knew he passed the bar. I knew he stayed in California and got promoted at the firm he'd been working at since his first year of college. I did two of those things myself, but chose to walk away from the offers I'd had on the table in favor of returning to New York.

The paperwork from Sarah proved that staying in California had done well for him. Dalton was a partner at his firm, dealing mainly with high-profile clients in commercial real estate and contracts. He'd always had an eye for detail, which I figured was just part of being a good lawyer.

My phone vibrated against the coffee table, and my best friend Kale's face flashed up on the screen. It was my favorite picture of him, one he absolutely hated because it made him look like the tree-hugging hippie I knew him to be at heart. All love for him aside, I had no interest in moving from my spot, so I stretched my toe out and dragged it across the screen to answer the call, then I fumbled my way to the speaker button.

"What do you want?" I asked in lieu of offering him a hello.

"Beamer." He laughed at me, using the least favorite of my nicknames followed by a robust sound that vibrated from the center of his chest. "I want to know how your interview with the board went yesterday."

"Bit of a delay," I said.

"That doesn't sound good."

"Just some paperwork I need to track down for them." It wasn't a lie, but I wasn't about to confess that I was quickly approaching my fifteenth wedding anniversary, if it hadn't already passed.

"They already have five years of tax returns," Kale reminded me. "What else could they want?"

"My first-born child." I ignored the actual intent of his question, hoping he wouldn't pick up on my evasiveness. "What are you up to tonight?"

"Ford wants to go to The Black Door. I told him I would call and see if you wanted to join us. I was hoping we could celebrate your pending move to the Upper East Side."

Celebrating a win at our favorite kink club would have been a great way to spend the evening, but blowing off some steam with a willing partner wouldn't be a bad way to manage the delay either. I briefly wondered if I could find someone who would get off on being with a married man, the idea making me laugh so hard I hurt myself.

"What's going on with you?" Kale asked, after I'd finally quieted down.

"Nothing," I lied. "This entire process is just more stressful than I anticipated."

"You? Stressed?" He sounded like he didn't believe it was a possibility, and historically that wouldn't have been far from the truth.

I'd been raised a certain way, and ever since I was young, I'd always understood what was expected from me. Managing the unexpected was one of the many responsibilities I'd had growing up. Holding my own with my father's business partners was another, and I'd learned at a very young age what it meant to be Carter Emerson Royce IV.

Whether I liked it or not.

The one thing that I'd never admitted to myself was how much that two-day trip to Vegas with Dalton had changed my life. It was the first time I could be honest about things that had happened to me, honest about the things I wanted for myself. Much like many of our other friends and brothers, he also carried the curse of a generations-long familial legacy. He understood what it was like to be desperate to have something for yourself that didn't belong to anyone else.

I flipped to the second page of the printout from Sarah, finding Dalton standing with a group of men who looked like the same kind of men we'd both grown up to be. He stood a little closer to one than the rest, his arm looped casually around the man's shoulders. It looked intimate, and I wondered…

I wondered…

"Beamer? You there?"

"You know I hate when you call me that," I grumbled, shoving the papers onto the floor with another muttered curse.

"Then don't drive one, *Royce*."

The joke had been a long-standing one, the never-ending amusement from my closest friends that our family name aligned with a very expensive car that I'd not once bothered to own. It felt a bit on the nose to be a Royce driving a Rolls-Royce, and I'd happily owned nothing except BMWs for my entire adult life.

"Sorry, what was the question?"

Kale made a disgruntled noise on the other end of the line. "Are you sure you're okay?"

"I'm fine. I'm fine." I kicked the papers farther away so I didn't have to see Dalton's face. "I just didn't hear what you asked."

"I said Ford wants to go to The Black Door tonight. Do you want to come?"

I didn't want to get up and get dressed, and I definitely didn't want to leave my apartment, but if I stayed home, I would drink more gin and spend more time reading about Dalton Fox, and neither of those would be good for my mental health.

"Sure," I agreed, scrubbing a hand down my face and preemptively hating myself for all of the bad decisions I was about to make. "What do I have to lose?"

CHAPTER 3
DALTON

After making sure Barclay wasn't having a heart attack, I threw him out of my car and re-opened the divorce paperwork. Royce lived in New York apparently, and it looked like he'd been there for years. Alone in the parking lot, I let myself wonder what his life had been like after our fateful Vegas trip.

As for me, I'd caught a commercial flight home, thrown myself back into my books, and waited for graduation. I knew the bar was only a handful of months away and I needed to get Genevieve and Royce out of my head so I could focus on the theory of law, all of my upcoming study prep, and putting the both of them in my rearview for good.

It had proved to be partly impossible, the specter of my relationship with Genevieve hanging over me for years, and the memories of Royce's mouth and his hands lingering far longer than I would have ever dreamed. Eventually, I learned to deal with the fallout from Gen, but Royce...the memory of him had proven to be more persistent.

Before...him...

I'd never really thought about what it would be like to be with another man. It wasn't that I was against the idea. I wasn't homophobic or anything like that. I knew my parents would frown upon it, with the reliance on legacy and the family name always around my neck like an anvil. But thankfully for me, my older brother had married young and he'd married well, and I already had a herd of nieces and nephews to carry on the Fox name. On the flip side, though, my brother had never possessed the same sense for business as I did, and that part of the family tradition had landed squarely on my shoulders.

A fair split, he'd told me once.

A knock against the passenger side window startled me, and I threw the papers up in the air with an embarrassing and surprised shout.

"Shit. Fuck." I looked over, recognizing Archie's lithe form standing outside my car.

I swear to fuck, Barclay better not have said a word to him about any of it.

Unrolling the window a crack, I leaned toward the passenger seat and looked up at him out the window. "What's up, Arch?"

"You good?" he asked.

"I'm good."

The papers landed face down and mostly on my side of the car, so that wasn't even a lie.

"Barclay wouldn't tell us what happened," Archie said.

"Good."

"But you're okay?" His brow furrowed, making his worry clear, and I exhaled loudly, a small piece of the fight going out of me.

This man was my friend—all of them were—and they deserved the truth. It wasn't like I'd been willingly hiding a secret husband from all of them, but if I told them the truth about Royce, then they'd want to know about Gen, and there were just some things I wasn't quite ready to share with them. I didn't think I'd ever want to talk to them about her, or anyone for that matter, which was precisely why I'd gone to Royce.

"Just a blast from the past," I said, gathering the papers and shoving them back into the envelope. "I'll tell you guys about it another night. I promise."

"With less company?"

"Yeah, probably."

Archie let loose an old man groan and leaned down to stare at me through the window. "I've just never seen you so out of sorts," he said, frowning.

"Arch, I'm good. I promise. I just have to get home and make some phone calls."

And drown myself in a bottle of gin.

"You know where to find us if you need us," he said.

"I know. The group chat is the bane of my existence."

"I meant Rob's house, but that works too."

Archie slapped the hood of my car like it was a piece of shit Honda, then turned on his heel and headed back into Cunning-ham's. I tossed the paperwork onto my passenger seat and stabbed the ignition button a little harder than might have been necessary. My hands were still sweaty, I realized, seeing the slick reflection of my fingerprint against the button as the car roared to life.

I took the long way home, cruising through the streets before turning down Wilshire. Another twenty minutes and I was home, changed out of my work clothes, and into a pair of black nylon basketball shorts. I cracked open a fresh bottle of Hendrick's and mixed it with some tonic water and lime juice, then took the drink and my laptop into my living room.

I'd thought about Royce about a million times over the years, but I'd never gathered the courage to actually look him up. Well, I'd done it once, shortly after I passed the bar. I wanted to know how he'd fared with his own test. That was how I found out he'd gone back to New York, and something about having a continent between us tore open a chasm in my chest.

There was still so much for us to say to each other, not even about Vegas, but the rest of it, and…

Well, I'd ruined it.

By waking up hungover and disoriented, and running away from the one person on the planet I could most easily relate to. I saw him around campus and I saw him at graduation, but every time we connected eyes, I looked away. It wasn't that I was ashamed of what he and I had done together. I mean, I hardly even remembered it, save for the feel of my hands in his hair, his tongue in my mouth, the hard heat of his body against mine…

What I had no recollection at all was of a wedding ceremony.

Did we have vows?

What the hell would we have even said to each other back then?

With a healthy swallow of my drink, I typed his name into Google. The results populated on the screen before I could even situate my computer on my lap, his face and a little biography box popping up in the right hand corner of the results page.

Fuck, he was a good-looking man.

Royce had always had that traditional all-American look about him, with a square jaw, broad shoulders, and golden hair. He was the opposite of me in every way except for one. Or two, depending on how his sexuality had turned out over the years. After our night together, I had the impression I wasn't the first man he'd taken to bed, but I also knew I'd never even suspected he might be more toward the middle of the Kinsey scale than most.

The website yielded me his full name, which I already knew, his birthday, which I'd never bothered to ask about, and his height, which I'd never be able to forget. Royce clocked in at six-foot-three, and judging by the way his shoulders tested the seams of the suit he wore in his default picture, he weighed well over two hundred pounds.

God, he was big.

God, I loved a fucking big man.

According to Google, he was also very single.

Or is he?

"Stop it," I muttered, clicking the first website that came up on the results page.

It was his law firm, I realized. The one he'd started at after passing the bar. He'd been there for so long he'd made partner. The bio page listed some of the cases he'd won, some of his existing client load, and then down at the bottom, his contact information.

An email and a phone number.

Sending him an email felt impersonal, considering he was my husband. Considering he'd gone to enough effort to somehow find out we were married and serve me with divorce papers from 2,400 miles away. No, he deserved a phone call.

It was late for me, and it would be early for him, but he could have the voicemail as a treat for when he got into the office again. I didn't know what I wanted to say to him, but I just knew that I had to call him.

Before I could talk myself out of it, I tapped his number into my phone, then set it on speaker and dropped it on the arm of the couch. It rang four times and then…

"Hello?"

My breath caught. How could he sound so much the same and so different all at the once? I closed my eyes and groaned, stabbing my fingertips against my eyelids until I saw stars.

"Hello?" he asked again. "This is Carter Royce. How can I help you?"

It had to be at least two in the morning in New York. Did the man ever sleep?

I cleared my throat, watching numbly as the call log blinked up, adding one second after another after another.

"Hello?" he said again, one more time, the finality was clear in his tone and I knew I should let him hang up.

There was no love lost between us, and there wasn't even anything to say. We'd been dumb, stressed-out kids back then, making dumb, stressed-out kid decisions. The right thing to do was just sign the papers and send them back to his lawyer. They were straightforward enough, no demands for spousal support, no interest in my business and no offering of his. Just a clean slice through a legality I hadn't even known existed.

And still…

"Ivey."

It was less a nickname than it was an endearment, something I'd come up with sometime around our sixth round of drinks our first night in Vegas. His name was Royce, rather, everyone called him Royce because while he was many things, Carter wasn't one of them.

Carter Emerson Royce IV.

And while there'd been a handful of hours where he'd been Ivey to me, our circumstances had once again made him Royce.

The sharp intake of breath on the other end of the call confirmed he'd heard me, heard and recognized the name, but other than that, he offered me silence.

"You're up late," I said, hating the way my voice trembled.

"Just walked in the door," he said. "I take it you've...you..." He stumbled around, searching for a word that was nicer than the reality he'd given me.

"I've been served," I told him.

The sharp breath turned into a relieved exhale.

"How long have you known we were married?" I asked.

"I found out two days ago."

I scoffed, dropping my head against the back of the couch with a soft thump. "You work quickly."

"It's problematic," he said.

"Isn't it just."

He groaned, and I found it hard for me to picture his reaction. What was he wearing? Where was he sitting? Or was he maybe already in bed? Was he alone?

"I didn't mean it that way," he offered, tone sounding something very near an apology.

"Are you getting married for real?" I asked. "Is that why it's a problem?"

"I'm not getting married. It came up in an interview for a penthouse."

"An interview," I repeated.

Fucking shit, New York sounded like a hellscape.

"They think I lied about my marital status. I'm trying to right the wrong."

"Marrying me was wrong?" I laughed at the thought and just how very true it was. Nothing we did on that trip had been right.

"Obviously. But I meant the lie by omission to the co-op board."

"Right."

He didn't know what to say to that and neither did I, so the call lapsed into an uncomfortable experiment in silence until he cleared his throat on the other end of the call.

"How have you been, Dalton?" he asked.

"I've been…good." It was the truth. I had a good life, all things considered. It was stressful and anxiety-inducing a lot of the time, and while the Xanax and my friends helped, my long-running affinity for ropes and knots did most of the heavy lifting when it came to my mental health. "What about you?"

"Good," he answered quickly. "The same."

"I'm glad to hear it." I swallowed, unsure of where to go from there. "Uhm, I…"

He spoke at the same time, "It's good to hear from you."

I finished off the rest of my gin, letting the ice clank around in the tumbler when I set it down on the glass-topped side table next to the arm of the couch.

"I owe you an apology," I said.

"You left one on the notepad."

Shit.

My heart was banging around so frenetically, I had no idea how I could even hear his voice over the insistent battering of my pulse in my ears. "Did I?"

Royce chuckled, a warm and familiar sound I didn't even realize I'd missed until I heard it again.

"You did," he confirmed.

"Can I offer you another one?" I asked. "A sincere one that I'll have a memory of?"

"Is the apology for me or for you, Fox?"

Fuck, it had been so long since anyone had called me that. Hearing him call me by my last name was like being back in college all over again. A flashback I wasn't ready for and didn't even want. My heart skipped in the familiar way it did before I began the slide into a panic attack, and I hated my stupid brain for being so incapable of dealing with the smallest slights.

"Both of us, I think," I managed, voice still trembling.

I reached for my drink and sucked down the drops of water that had resulted from the melting ice and residual lime juice in the bottom of the glass.

"I'm listening," he said.

"Not like this. Not over the phone."

"What are you proposing?"

I made an amused sound, wondering again between the two of us which one had come up with the harebrained idea to go get married in the first place.

"Come to L.A.," I suggested. "We'll get drinks, dinner, and I'll apologize face to face."

"And the divorce?"

I didn't even have to think about the answer. "I'll have the papers signed before you even land at LAX."

"Alright," he agreed. "It's a date. Dinner and divorce, Fox. Just tell me when."

BOARDING A PLANE TO LOS ANGELES TWO DAYS AFTER TALKING WITH Dalton for the first time in fifteen years, I still had rope mark-shaped bruises around my left wrist from my most recent outing to The Black Door. I rubbed at them mindlessly, trying to focus on how grounded it had helped me feel to be splayed open and tied down, my mind racing a million miles a minute until…

Until it wasn't.

I wished it was possible to bottle the feeling that came with a good play scene and carry it with me across the country, but science in the twenty-first century was woefully lacking in that department, so pressing down on fading bruises would have to suffice. I promised myself everything would be okay. It was a handful of days in California, only a spattering of hours with Dalton, and then I'd be on my way back home with divorce papers in hand.

It didn't matter that talking to him, hearing his voice, had churned up feelings I was confident I'd long since buried. And I wasn't only talking about a simmering attraction I'd harbored for him. Genevieve was there again, back in the front of my mind in the same little crevice she'd hollowed out years before. I hated myself for letting her back in, and I shifted the touch of my own hand until my fingernail dug into the knobby bone of my wrist hard enough to leave another mark.

Dalton had offered to pick me up from the airport, but I'd politely—and insistently—declined until he'd gotten the hint. I had no issue taking a car from the airport in Burbank to Chateau Marmont. The drive time through the valley did little to calm me down, and I was shocked to find myself feeling something very close to stress for the first time in as long as I could remember.

It was Dalton's fault.

It was that stupid marriage license, that stupid forty-eight hours in Vegas that I didn't even have a proper recollection of. But for every day that passed when I knew I was married to Dalton, the memories and, worse than that, the feelings began to trickle back in.

I hadn't been in California since I'd left, which was very shortly after passing the bar. My father told me there was no point in taking the bar in California if I wasn't going to stay, but at the time, I didn't know I'd never be back. I took it anyway, then went to New York and had to do it all over again. Most people would have cracked under the pressure of it, but not me. I studied and I passed, I got a job, and the rest was history.

Staring out the window as the buildings on Sunset Blvd. whipped past, I called Kale, hoping he'd be able to settle me down with something topical.

"I don't want to talk to you," he said when he answered my call.

I thumped my head against the tinted back window of the town car. "Why not?"

"Because you're not being yourself and I don't like it."

"It's just this thing," I protested. "It's fine."

"It's fine," he mocked, and I smiled, picturing the sassy tilt of his lips when he parroted my own comment back at me. "It's so fine that when we went out night before last, you disappeared and didn't answer anyone's calls or texts until six the next morning."

"I was in a scene."

"With who?"

I'd actually been in two scenes. One with our friend Alex and one with a stranger. I didn't know which of them the bruises were from, but my money would have been on the stranger. I'd never bothered to ask his name. All I knew of him were the marks he left on me. The way he had stretched me out like a starfish, ropes tight around my ankles and wrists, then shoved a thick and round plug up my ass. I had told him I wanted to forget my own name and he'd gotten as close to making that dream come true for me as anyone ever had. The impact play was fine, if not a little lighter than I would have liked, but the bondage had been top tier. The man knew his way around some fancy knotwork, and it had almost been enough to send me over the edge I'd been walking for years. I didn't want to tell Kale any of that, though. My entire group of friends was entirely too protective of me, and the last thing I wanted was for any of them to go looking for a man who'd done exactly what I asked him to. They'd given Alex more than enough of a hard time when we'd started doing scenes together.

I loved hard play, rough scenes. I loved to be restrained, and I liked to fight because, in some way, that gave me the control I was so desperate for. But more than that, it gave me *the choice* to be there, the choice to submit. Being with dominant partners had always gotten me hard, but it had also gotten me into trouble on more than one occasion. As a result, I'd had to be far more selective about the people I played with, male or female, which drastically reduced the scenarios and scenes available for me. It was self-preservation at best, but it was also boring and predictable.

I didn't think that kinky sex was meant to be mundane.

"It doesn't matter," I told him instead of explaining the whole story. "It's not like there's anyone in that club who hasn't been fully vetted before they even get the address."

The club we frequented, The Black Door, was beyond exclusive, and that was saying something for New York City. The Black Door's rules and regulations made every other club I'd ever been to look like a backyard barbeque compared to how selective they were with the people they let in. Only the top of the top in the city even knew the name of the club, and only a few of that group were fortunate enough to receive invitations to *apply* for membership. I was lucky that Kale's brother owned the place, otherwise I might not have made the cut. But like all things in life, it came down to not just who you were, but also who you knew.

"It's irresponsible, Beamer, and you are not irresponsible."

I didn't do irresponsible, but I wanted to…

Sometimes.

Controlled irresponsibility, maybe. Was that even a thing?

"Don't take that tone with me." I pried my eyes open in time to watch the car pull up the drive at the Chateau, already lost in a daydream about a life that would never be mine. "You're not *my* Dom."

"Thank God for that," he muttered under his breath.

"We're such good friends because you've never tried," I reminded him.

"I've never even thought to try with you. You've never acted like you needed one, no matter what Alex thinks."

"Are you done, Kale?"

The car rolled to a stop and I checked my pockets, cradling the phone against the side of my face while I waited for the driver to come around and open the door.

"I'm done, Beamer."

He all but sneered the nickname at me, the two syllables laced with all the condescension a Dom—who wasn't *my* Dom—could muster, I imagined.

"I'm sorry that I didn't let someone know where I was before I took off," I conceded. "It's against the rules and it was out of character for me."

Our group had rules because even in light of our dedication to being risk aware and obtaining consent, we were sometimes reckless. In responsible ways, of course. But we'd always agreed to text or call or tell someone *somehow* if one of us was taking off from the group. There were too many things that could go wrong, even with the most seasoned of play partners.

"I'm worried about whatever is going on with you," he said.

The driver pulled open the back door and I swung my legs out, immediately finding myself far too warm for comfort.

"I thought L.A. had perfect weather," I muttered.

"Perfect for shorts, sir," the driver said with a crooked smile. "Can I get your bags?"

"There's just one. You can leave it with the bellhop."

I'd already arranged to tip him through the car service app, so I headed inside to finish my call with Kale and then get checked in. Dalton and I had made plans to get dinner later that evening, and I needed to freshen up beforehand. Not like I was trying to impress him or anything, because that couldn't have been further from the truth. In our line of work, our lifestyles, appearances were everything. And just because my mind was slipping, it didn't mean I'd let myself go completely.

"I assure you that by the time I return to New York, I'll be back to normal," I promised my closest friend.

"And once you're normal again, will you tell us what's going on?"

"Once I'm normal, it won't be going on anymore."

"You're insufferable." He groaned. "How does anyone put up with you?"

"You tell me." I inhaled a deep breath, striding toward the front desk. "Let me check in and get this trip over with, and then I'll think about spilling my secrets."

"There isn't anything mysterious about you," he said.

I laughed. Up until a week ago, I would have agreed with him. But having a secret husband of fifteen years definitely felt like something mysterious to me.

"I'm glad we agree," I told him. "I'll talk with you later."

"Bye, Beamer."

I disconnected the call and slid my phone back into my pocket, ignoring Dalton's name in the notification bar. Whatever he had to say to me could wait until I was in the bungalow, washed, dressed, and ready to face him.

As it turned out, all of that only took me an hour, and I found myself dressed in a pair of tan shorts, a white, short-sleeved, button-up, sitting on my private garden patio with my cell phone in hand, Dalton's message still unread in my notifications.

"Stop being scared of a stranger," I told myself, swiping the screen to see what he had to say.

Dalton was a stranger.

He'd always been a stranger to me.

Even in college, our fraternities were in constant competition so there was no love lost between us on that front. And while I never suspected Gen cheated on me with him, the fact that he was her rebound was another mark decidedly *not* in his favor. Dalton Fox had never been a name on the very short list of people that I'd wanted to be friends with at school, but when he showed up at the house the night things with him and Gen had gone south…

It was that night when I realized Dalton and I knew each other without speaking, in a way most people would never understand.

As it turned out, Dalton had texted me twice. Once while I was in the air and once while I was in the car on the way to the hotel.

Dalton Fox: I made us reservations at seven.
Dalton Fox: Hope that's not too late, since you're on Eastern Time.

Something tightened in the middle of my chest, taking up room that my lungs needed in order to fill. That had to be why I couldn't breathe. The thought and the consideration…

I didn't want it.

I wanted Dalton to stay a stranger because I didn't want to dredge up the history that had brought us together. I wasn't interested in reliving the past. All I wanted was his signature on a stupid piece of paper and the keys to my dream penthouse. That was it. He wanted to apologize for ghosting me and that was no sweat off my back.

Me: Seven is fine. What's the address?

He answered quickly

Dalton Fox: I can pick you up.
Me: Address is fine.

I turned the phone face down on my leg and it buzzed against my palm, no doubt with the address for dinner. I flipped it over to check the time, equal parts annoyed and relieved to see that I had at least two hours before the reservation. That was an hour and forty-five minutes too long to be alone with my thoughts, so I texted Dalton back.

Me: Did you want to meet early for drinks?
Dalton Fox: I can meet at 6.
Me: Alright. See you then.

An hour was still too much time, but like everything else in my life, I'd find a way to endure it.

CHAPTER 5
DALTON

I HADN'T KNOWN UNTIL I SAW HIM AGAIN, BUT I WOULD HAVE recognized Royce anywhere. As soon as I walked into Cunningham's, there he was. The broad swell of his shoulders, the close crop of his blond hair against the back of his neck. The mere idea that I'd ever forgotten him...in that moment felt even more outlandish than the fact we were married.

That was my husband at the bar.

And even though our union was a mistake, a technicality that neither of us knew anything about until days before...

He was my husband.

And I'd never wanted a husband before. Even after watching my friends find so much happiness with other people, it hadn't felt like a thing that was meant for me. I wasn't like Flynn, no. I hadn't ruled out the idea, but I had never expected or even searched for that kind of thing to land in my lap.

But there he was.

And for the first time in a long time, I didn't hate the idea of having a partner.

Commitment, trust, and respect were already such an important part of the relationships in my life, a husband didn't feel like that far of a reach. I already gave so much of myself to other people, whether in bed or at work. Wouldn't it be nice to get something in return? To have someone steady to come home to and rely on? I knew that man wasn't Royce, but the idea had taken root, digging into my brain like a vise grip that tightened down and refused to let go.

Even from across the room, he looked nervous, which wasn't anything like the man I remembered him being. Royce had always been unflappable, stoic, and contained. The only time I'd ever seen him let loose was with me in Vegas, and even then...

It had been circumstantial.

But there at the bar, his leg bounced up and down, foot resting on the rung of the dark wood and leather-bound stool. He had a tumbler of something amber in his hand, and I assumed it was whiskey or scotch. His drink of choice was the least surprising thing about him. I knew he'd done well.

I knew he was like me.

"Royce." I slid onto the stool beside him, and he startled, turning to face me so quickly some of his drink sloshed over on his fingers. He didn't bother to shake the wetness of. He didn't even look down. He looked straight at me, those unforgettable green eyes of his bright as bottles.

He pulled his lips between his teeth, brows knitted together while he studied me. I swallowed back the urge to ask him what he saw when he looked at me because, even though I wanted to know, it didn't matter. Royce and I weren't anything to each other anymore. We never really had been.

"You scared me, Fox," he said, finally realizing his hand was covered in liquor. Without looking, he swiped his hand dry on the leg of his pants and I knew then he either had less money than me or far more, because I wouldn't ever reduce my wool-blend slacks to the status of *napkin*.

"Did you forget I was coming?"

Flagging down the bartender, I ordered a gin for myself. The restaurant was next door, which was part of my design. When I booked the reservation, I hadn't planned on getting drinks beforehand, but I had counted on getting absolutely plastered afterwards.

With or without him.

"I just didn't…" He trailed off, clearing his throat and studying me again through a quick series of rapid-fire blinks.

"Didn't what?"

"Nothing." Royce reached out and clapped me on the back a couple of times, an awkward, finance bro move that I'd never been a fan of. "It's good to see you again."

"Is it?" I arched a brow.

"I know the circumstances aren't ideal."

A laugh bubbled out of the back of my throat, unepected and uncomfortable in a way that hadn't been familiar to me in years.

"They never are with us," I said.

"Right."

We lapsed into a silence that stretched through the rest of both of our drinks. He ordered us both a second round, or at least a second round for me. Who knew what it was for him?

I would have paid a decent percentage out of my checking account to buy a ticket into his brain during those moments. I found myself beyond curious to know what he was thinking, being with me, being in L.A., being married. It was somehow comfortable, but terrifying to be back in the same city with him, the same room.

I'd spent many years trying to bury the past, the memory of him along with it. Not by any fault of his own. It was more of a guilt-by-association kind of thing, and I figured it was the same for him when it came to memories of me. I would never fault him for it.

"I wanted to apologize," I finally said.

At some point during our drinking, he'd moved so both his forearms rested against the bar and he slid his drink back and forth between his waiting hands. The ice clinked around in the glass as it bounced off the edges and melted and resettled in the bottom.

"You don't owe me an apology," he said, not looking up.

"Then why are you here?"

The muscles in Royce's throat flexed as he swallowed, but he didn't speak. I figured he didn't have an answer, and I hadn't expected him to.

"I don't know why I asked that," I said, another apology.

"It's a valid question."

"I also…" I inhaled sharply, hoping the air would fill my lungs and kick off some scientific or biologic process I'd never understand that would turn the jumbled mess in my head into words that would make sense to either of us.

Things hadn't ever made sense between us, though.

Thankfully, I'd also never needed words. Royce had known what I'd needed just by looking at me.

And again, he turned to face me, taking the last drink of what I'd learned was scotch. The liquor shined against his mouth, a dark golden contrast to the otherwise pink paleness of his face. He looked the same as he had in college, just a little harder in some places and softer in others. His hair was cut in the same style, his face still clean-shaven.

Another memory flashed through my periphery.

The two of us lying together in a hotel bed, the bright lights of the strip glaring in through the window we'd left open. He was naked and asleep, the scruff on his chin growing in a darker shade of brown than I'd expected considering the blond on his head, the curling trail down toward his cock.

"Does your beard still grow in brown?" I asked, cutting myself off from the other thing I'd almost dared to say.

I wasn't ready for that.

And neither was he.

But if his reaction was anything to go off, he wasn't ready for what I'd actually said either. He raised his hand to his face, fingertips tracing along the sharp angle of his jaw. He was checking for stubble—I knew without asking. While he walked his fingers down his cheek toward his chin, he dragged his stare across my face with the same feather-light touch.

I didn't have to graze my hand over my jaw to know I hadn't shaved. I hated shaving, hated how young I looked without some semblance of a beard. I always had hair on my face. Nothing unruly, but enough to hide the flush I felt building under the tenderness of his appraisal.

"Yes," he answered, letting his hand fall back to the bar.

He looked away and then everything was loud. It was so fucking loud, like the string between us had snapped and whatever silent bubble had enclosed us popped. Without warning, I abruptly became aware of the fact we were in public. We were at a bar. We were at a bar I often frequented with my closest friends.

We were together.

"I'm sorry." I cleared my throat and pushed the stool back, standing and hoping that the weight of his stare had only impacted the state of my cheeks, not my cock. "Did you want to go eat? It's just about time."

Royce glanced down at his wrist, at a Patek Philippe that glinted like a diamond under the dim ambient lighting of the bar.

He definitely had more money than me.

Not that it mattered.

None of it mattered.

He cleared his throat and nodded. "Dinner. Right."

"It's just next door," I told him.

He gave me another curt nod, and I turned away from him quickly, not watching to focus on the way he was still so much taller than me and how that made me feel. It was a curious thing, I thought, as we headed toward the front door. In college, I'd been jealous of him, I'd hated him on principle, but I'd never stopped to wonder if I was attracted to him.

Even when we'd been naked in bed together, his lips wrapped around my cock, I hadn't cared about whether I found him attractive or not. Royce offered me something so much more important than physical attraction. He offered me safety.

But I was attracted to him. I knew that now.

"Lead the way." He stepped closer to me and I took a long

stride, putting space between us so I could breathe. He was wearing Chanel, I could smell it on him, and I couldn't get out of Cunningham's fast enough.

I hoped it wasn't obvious that I sucked in a huge breath of air as soon as my shoes hit the sidewalk, but it was impossible to get the smell of him out of my nose. I didn't want to do something stupid, say something stupid. As I listened to the sound of his shoes on the concrete behind me as I turned toward the restaurant, I cursed myself quietly, wondering what the hell I'd been thinking asking him to come out here.

I could have apologized over the phone, over a video call if seeing him had been so important to me. Could have signed the papers in the parking lot behind the bar and had them in his hand the next day. The divorce didn't need a phone call or a conversation. The past was best left behind us, and here we both were, dredging it up into the present.

"Asshole," I swore at myself, biting back any other insult that had settled on my tongue when I felt the heat of Royce's chest at my back. He stretched one of his long arms past me and grabbed the door handle to open it for me. I had to step back into him to make room, but we moved together fluidly, just avoiding contact.

"Let me get that for you," he said softly.

I gave him a jerky nod and a hoarse thanks. The door closed behind us and, in the tight nook of the host station, I could smell him again. Even stronger than the smell of pasta and pesto and garlic, I could smell Royce. But he'd been Ivey to me back then, when my memory had locked the feel of him and the smell of him together in my mind, bits and pieces forever twisted together.

"Table for two," I managed to tell the host. "Fox."

"Of course, Mr. Fox." The hostess stacked two menus in her hands. "If you and your guest will follow me."

"After you," Royce murmured, mouth hovering somewhere above my ear, even though my body would have sworn his lips were much nearer my cock.

This wasn't what I'd expected to happen after seeing him

again. It wasn't what I'd planned and far from what I wanted. As we followed the hostess to the small table tucked under a window in the quietest corner of the restaurant, I reminded myself there was no good to come from being attracted to the husband I didn't know I had, who was only in town to get a divorce.

No good at all.

CHAPTER 6
IVEY

Dalton looked like he wanted to crawl out of his skin and I didn't blame him. There wasn't enough alcohol in the world to ease the ache between us, and I wondered just how much we'd managed to put back in Vegas to quiet all of that noise.

"So," I said, glancing down at the menu. I knew there were words on the paper, words that combined together to detail ingredients and cooking methods, but all I could see were letters, and half of them didn't even look like English. "How's life been, Dalton?"

He snorted, dropping his menu on the table and tipping back his head to stare up at the ceiling. He swallowed, the strong corded muscles of his throat working as his Adam's apple bobbed up and down.

I clenched my jaw and looked away.

"It hasn't been bad," he said, daring a glance at me.

This was ridiculous. The two of us, men as we were, so skittish and nervous around each other because of the unspoken elephant in the room that didn't have anything to do with the fact we were married.

"Can we talk about—" I said at the same time as he said,

"I want to thank you."

To me, judging by the tight knit of his brow and the frown that looked like it was so engrained around his mouth it would never leave, it looked like whatever he had to say was more important than what I'd tried to open with.

"For what?" I asked.

There were two water glasses on the table, but water wouldn't do shit for the desert that had sprouted up in the back of my mouth from the first moment I'd seen him again.

"For…Vegas," he said.

"For getting so drunk that I forgot we got married, Fox?" I laughed. "I don't think you owe me anything for that."

"I don't remember it either," he reminded, *finally* looking me in the eye. "But, no. I meant for…"

I knew what he was trying to say, even if the words weren't coming for him. It was the elephant, after all, the same thing I'd been about to bring up.

"We don't have to talk about her," I said.

"Don't we?"

Licking my lips, I leaned back in my chair, suddenly unsure of what to do with my hands, where to look, how to breathe. Across the table, Dalton didn't look like he was faring much better. Sweat had begun to bead at his temple, and he reached up with a nervous hand to pop open the button on his crisp, collared shirt.

Always buttoned up.

Always put together.

I remembered that about him.

"You look like you're going to be sick," I murmured.

He scoffed, rubbing at his throat. His shoulders lifted with every breath, and the grimace on his face convinced me that every inhale was a struggle.

"Are you having a panic attack over this?" I asked.

Another derisive noise in the back of his throat, but he didn't deny it. That just wouldn't do.

"Come on." I stood up and stepped toward him, grabbing his bicep and hauling him to his feet.

Beyond the perfunctory slap on the back I'd given him upon

his arrival, it was the first time we'd touched in fifteen years, and I did everything possible to ignore the electricity that sparked against my palm when I felt the solid topography of his muscles beneath my hand.

"Where are we going?"

"Not Vegas," I assured him.

That earned me a laugh, and I guided him through the restaurant until I found the bathrooms and the back door that they'd tried to hide behind a rich purple velvet curtain. Swatting it out of the way, I used my hip to push the door open, then I pressed Dalton against the wall and bent him over at the waist.

"Breathe," I urged him, bracketing my hand around the back of his neck to keep him folded in half.

I leaned against the wall and looked up at the sky, focusing on the pale outline of the crescent moon above the power lines.

"Breathe," I told him again, loosening my hold around his neck and sliding my hand down his back. I traced the knobs of his spine up and down and up and down until I lost track of time in the quiet monotony of it.

When Dalton straightened, I let my hand fall to my side, the loss of contact cold and apparent.

"Slow," I warned. "You'll get dizzy."

"I'm already dizzy."

"So go *slow*," I said.

"I don't need you to tell me what to do, Ivey."

Dalton smacked his head against the back wall of the restaurant and covered his face with his hands. A quiet curse slipped out past his fingers, and we both pretended that he hadn't just called me Ivey again.

We stayed like that for a good ten minutes, backs against the wall and faces turned toward the sky. I crossed my legs at the ankle so my left leg didn't fall asleep, and slowly let my eyes close while I listened to the sound of Dalton's breaths as they evened out.

When I was confident he'd returned to normal, I asked, "Do

you have panic attacks often?"

"No, well…yes, but…" He dropped his hands away from his face. "I'm medicated."

"Enough?"

He snorted. "Clearly not, but I think finding out we're married hasn't helped my stress level much."

I tucked my thumb and forefinger under the cuff of my shirt, the bruises from the rope still yellow and purple beneath my skin.

"You need an outlet for your stress," I suggested.

"I have one."

"Do you use it?" I pushed my finger hard against the darkest and deepest bruise until it ached so badly I had to clench my jaws together.

"Not lately."

"Why not?" I asked.

"Not safe," he muttered. "It requires…too much attention."

"That doesn't sound relaxing at all."

He swiveled his head toward me, eyes fully back in focus and narrowed in on me with a tired kind of vitriol that I hadn't seen in years.

"You don't know anything about me, Royce," he snapped.

I hummed, shrugging my shoulders and locking my eyes onto his stare. "I liked it better when you called me Ivey."

"You're not helping," he ground out, fisting his hands. "Can we go back inside?"

"Did you want to?"

Dalton glanced past me toward the door, shoulders heaving. "Not really."

I scrubbed a hand down my face, doing my best to ignore all the ways this felt like college all over again. An uncertain kind of tension coiled around the base of my spine like the unspoken fear that came with *knowing* the things we knew.

"We don't have to talk about Genevieve," I promised. "You don't have to apologize, and you don't have to thank me. None of it even matters. We're different men than we were before."

"I don't feel all that different," he muttered, shoving his hands into his pockets.

"I know," I agreed. "Neither do I sometimes."

"Are you okay if we skip dinner?" Dalton pushed himself away from the wall, again not looking me in the eye. "I think drinks before weren't the best idea I've had all day."

"We can skip it."

"When are you back to New York?" he asked.

"Whenever I want to go," I said.

In actuality, I had a jet booked for the day after tomorrow, but it wouldn't take much money or time to change it one way or the other. On the heels of his panic attack, the last thing Dalton needed from me was pressure.

"I left the paperwork at home." He shrugged. "Just slipped my mind on the way out the door. I can get it to you tomorrow if that's okay. I know I said I'd have it signed already—"

I cut him off with the press of my fingers against the back of his arm. My touch sent a visible shiver up his spine, but instead of taking my hand away, I slid my fingers once again around the girth of his arm.

"I don't want it tomorrow," I said. "I mean, it doesn't matter *when* I get it. But I don't think you're in any condition for me to say goodnight and send you home."

"I didn't drive," he protested.

"That hardly matters."

"Iv…Royce." He took another step away from me, tone turning tight and exasperated. Dalton ran his fingers through his hair, messing the carefully styled strands into something that bordered on a disaster. "Respectfully, I don't need this from you."

I crossed my arms in front of me, shielding the jumble of feelings in my chest from his view. Not like he would even look at me to see them in the first place.

"I'm not trying to be your fucking Dom, Dalton. Calm down."

As soon as the word *Dom* left my mouth, he did turn toward me, jaw set and nostrils flaring.

I didn't know why the suggestion had set him off. I'd never even wanted to be a Dom, but being a submissive would never erase the fact that I was a natural caretaker. My life had made me accustomed to putting other people before myself, and the service aspects of submission had always been some of my favorite parts.

At least until I learned about how much of a masochist I was.

The pain and the aggressiveness spoke to a completely separate part of me, and for years I had struggled to reconcile the two of them. It took a lot of soul searching to understand how doing things for others could be perceived as dominant by some and submissive by others, and I'd learned it had to do with how people identified those own traits within themselves.

"I'm just trying to be your friend," I said.

"We're not friends."

Then it was his turn to cross his arms over his chest, and I found myself curious what he was hiding from me besides the obvious…all the baggage, and the wounds, and the memories.

And speaking from my own experience, the occasional nightmares.

"You're right. I'm sorry." I bit the tip of my tongue between my molars, trying to quickly decide how best to handle him in that moment. "I can go. I…I don't think I should have come. You can just email the papers back to my attorney."

I sealed my hand over my mouth, pulling my lips against the suction of my palm as I took a step back toward the door, putting more space between us. When Dalton was too close, I could smell the soap on him, which was different from before, and the gin, which was not.

Well, it was far more expensive than it had been before.

"Ivey, wait." He reached out for me, and I took another step back, the endearment catching me off-guard even though I'd already told him I preferred it from his mouth. "I'm sorry."

"For what now?" I asked.

"All of it."

"You can't just let it go, can you?"

His arm was still outstretched toward me, a silent plea. In answer to my question, he shook his head and let his arm drop against his leg.

"There's no one else I've ever told," he said. "Besides you."

"That's fine, Dalton."

"Well, and my therapist." His mouth twisted into the flash of a smile before falling flat again.

"That's fine too."

"With you here, it just feels very unsettled again."

"Fresh," I supplied.

He nodded and sucked in a breath, letting his shoulders rise and fall, taking the weight of his upper body with them. Another deep breath, and he dared another glance at me.

"Fresh," he confirmed.

"I have dreams about it sometimes," I admitted.

"About Vegas?" Dalton winged a brow toward his hairline.

Yes, I did have dreams about Vegas, more in the recent days than I would ever care to admit to him, but Vegas wasn't what I'd been talking about so I let it slide.

"About her," I said.

He scratched the scruff on his jaw and nodded his agreement.

"And you haven't told anyone?" I asked, wanting to be sure. "Just me?"

"Just you."

The only solution for the two of us was quickly taking shape in my head and I only saw one way out of this, whether we liked it or not.

"I know before we came outside I said we weren't going to Vegas..." I trailed off, and another smile ghosted across Dalton's face, bringing some color back to his cheeks.

"But?"

I inhaled, hoping I wasn't making a horrible decision for us both.

Again.

"But maybe we should."

CHAPTER 7
DALTON

I'D NEVER LIKED VEGAS, BUT FROM THE PENTHOUSE ROOM WE'D booked, I could—for once—see the appeal. Dropping my forehead against the floor-to-ceiling plate glass window, I squinted down at the street and tried to count the people herding their way around the street below. They were too small and there were too many of them. They moved too quick, just anonymous blurs passing through in the blink of an eye. What would my life have been like if I could have been as anonymous as any of those people down on the street?

"Have you been back to Vegas since the last time we…" I didn't have the fortitude to finish the question.

After we checked in, I'd gone straight to the window, staring out like a brooding child. The adrenaline from my panic attack had started to wear off after we started the descent into the desert, but the wary way Royce regarded me without a word was enough to keep that spark simmering somewhere low in my belly. In the room, he'd toed off his shoes from the couch and ordered room service, giving me time and space to settle in on my own.

But at my question, he was up and right beside me again, behind me. I could have sworn his fingertips dragged against the small of my back, but I didn't look. It could have been a ghost. Vegas was full of those.

"Once," he said. "But I don't like it here."

"Then why are we here?" I asked.

Down the street, the Bellagio fountains shot up into the night sky and the watching crowd squealed in delight.

"Felt like a good idea at the time," he said.

My wrist itched.

My fingers were surprisingly steady as I undid the button at my cuff so I could get in to get a good scratch around my wrist bone. After I'd sated the itch, I left the cuff undone, popping the other one open for good measure. The top two buttons were still undone from my earlier panic attack, my heavy breathing dusting against the swell of my chest with every exhale.

"And now?" I asked.

He was saved from answering by a knock on the door.

"That'll be room service," he said, stepping back. The air behind me turned cold, and if I'd been a betting man, I would have put down that he *had* been touching the small of my back. But then again, maybe it was the mere presence of him that weighed so heavily against me.

Behind me, Royce bustled around and made room for the delivery, and it was the smell of salmon that finally brought my attention around to the room. The penthouse was obscenely posh, and more spacious than either of us needed. It was as much a show of wealth as his slacks, which I realized were Prada while we were getting on the jet in L.A.

The door closed, and we were again alone, but this time with plenty of food and far too much alcohol.

"I can't believe you still drink gin," he said, reaching for the bottle of Hendrick's that had come up with the food. He mixed me a drink and set it on the table.

"My friends favor whiskey, and I drink it plenty." I went to the table, where he'd sat in one of the dining chairs, turned away with his legs stretched out in from of him. He looked comfortable, at ease. I remembered that about him from school. Remembered being jealous of how unaffected he always was. About everything.

He kicked the chair beside him out, making room for me to join him. The carpet in the hotel was surprisingly thick and soft, also surprisingly white. I collapsed into the chair and mirrored his pose, using my toes to work my socks off so I could dig them into the high pile beneath my feet.

Royce slid the gin and tonic in my direction, and I raised it to him in a toast before taking a drink. He'd also ordered champagne for himself in lieu of liquor, and he sipped cautiously at the rim of the flute, eyeing me with an indescribable look.

"What?" I asked.

"I'm just looking at you," he murmured. "Waiting for you to talk."

A judgmental sound exploded in the back of my throat, and I rolled my eyes, taking another swallow of the gin. "About what?"

"About why we're in Vegas again."

"Well." I chuckled, shrugging my shoulders. "Let's see. Two days ago I found out that, for the last fifteen years, I've been married to my ex-girlfriend's ex-boyfriend. And he showed up out of nowhere with divorce papers, dragging up all kinds of memories and feelings I thought I'd buried, but as it turns out... I was wrong."

Royce laughed and nodded, indicating the feeling was relatively mutual.

I went on. "And I wanted to thank him...thank you, apologize to you, which I could have done over the phone. Should have done over the phone. But instead I asked you out to dinner and now you're here and I only have one Xanax left in my pocket, which doesn't feel like it's going to be anywhere near enough to get me through this ordeal."

"We can get you a fresh prescription," he offered.

"I think I'd need a lobotomy."

He laughed again and took a drink of his champagne. I studied the way his throat worked while his muscles chased the overpriced and bubbly drink down into his stomach. Then I looked away.

"Can I ask you something?"

"You just did."

Royce snorted, reaching behind him to pluck a handful of French fries off one of the room service trays. He dragged them through a bowl of ranch dressing before stuffing them into his mouth. Much like I'd watched him swallow, I watched him chew, noting the way his tongue darted out to lick some stray dressing from the corner of his mouth.

My brain was gracious enough in that moment to supply me with another memory. This time, of Royce licking a very different white substance from the same spot. But instead of being in a chair, he'd been on his knees, and I…

I looked down at my hands, turning them palm up and spreading my fingers. I could still feel his hair if I tried hard enough.

"Something else," he said.

I cleared my throat, embarrassed that he'd flown me to Vegas to help me cope with all the feelings that I'd brought on myself from being an idiot who couldn't leave well enough alone. Even more embarrassed that I still found myself thinking about him sexually.

"Sure."

I flipped my hands back over and curled my fingers around my thighs, like if I pressed down hard enough, I could somehow keep myself rooted in these new moments and not the old ones. But being in Vegas with Royce was enough of a reminder that all the memories weren't bad ones. There'd been bits and pieces, little breaths and touches that had made the rest of it…

Well, not *okay*, but survivable.

"I have two things actually." He poured a little more champagne into his glass. "One is probably less appropriate than the other."

Something about the honesty of his assessment unwound some of the tightness in my chest. I pointed toward the plate of fries and he pushed it closer so I could get a few for myself. "I don't think there's much that's appropriate about any of this."

"Says who?"

I opened my mouth to reply, but I didn't have an answer.

"Okay." He ignored my gaping mouth and the subsequent sound that followed when I snapped it closed. "First. When we were back in the alley at the restaurant, you told me you didn't need a Dom. Is that because you have one?"

I couldn't stop the laugh that burst out of me, the idea of *me* having a Dom was so utterly preposterous. Pressing my hand against my chest to keep my ribs together, I laughed at the idea until my head ached and my throat scratched, then I polished off the gin left in my first drink and shoved the glass toward him for another.

Through my fit, he looked amused, the corner of his mouth just slightly quirked up in the corner, matching his raised eyebrow. But he made me another drink without protest or question while I tried to get my breathing back under control.

"No," I eventually managed to answer him. "I don't have a Dom. I *am* a Dom. Why do you ask, Ivey? Do *you* have a Dom?"

His pale cheeks turned a delectable color of pink at the question.

"I don't have a Dom," he whispered.

"Of course not," I agreed, taking the fresh drink from him. Our fingertips brushed against each other and there it was again, that fire, that heat… "Why would you?"

The quirked-up corner of his mouth fell, and he cocked his head to the side, regarding me thoughtfully. "Why *wouldn't* I?"

The implication was there, loud enough to make it through the gin-soaked haze of my brain.

"Why…" I didn't quite get the inflection I'd hoped for, because I hadn't meant to speak out loud. I was thinking to myself, sliding puzzle pieces around in my head until they made sense, but the liquor was like sludge.

Everything moved slower than I wanted. Closing my eyes, I pushed the drink away, thankful the room hadn't started to spin.

And there was another memory.

Ivey wrapped in my arms and both of us tumbling backward onto a hotel bed. My face buried in the crook of his neck, my knee lodged firmly between his legs, pressing up against…

I scrubbed both of my hands down my face, trying to wipe my brain, but instead it all came into sharper focus. The way his hands had fumbled between us until he'd gotten a hand around my cock. The thickness of his wrist in my own hand when I'd stopped him, when I'd said…

Let me drive, Ivey.

"I've never been one for taking the wheel," he said softly.

"Shit."

"Are you all right, Fox? Heading toward another panic attack?"

"No." I shook my head. "I mean, yes, I'm fine. No panic attacks yet."

"You look like you've seen a ghost." He took another sip of his champagne, chasing it down with three more French fries.

I couldn't help but notice all the food he'd called up. There was salmon, which I'd smelled on arrival, soup, and salad. There were two burgers, a heaping plate of fries, fried chicken, even a steak, steaming with a sprig of rosemary on top.

"Did you order the whole menu?" I asked.

His eyes went wide before he offered me a shy smile, glancing toward the food spread out on the table beside us. "Just about."

"How much liquor?" I asked.

"Less than last time."

I stretched my hand out, pushing the drink further away, almost out of reach. "What do you remember about the last time we were here?"

He made a thoughtful noise, lips pursed. "I don't think we're done with this initial line of questioning yet."

"Remind me?"

"We were talking about me having a Dom," he said.

"And I asked why wo—"

Oh.

Oh.

"You're not dominant," I managed.

He shook his head. "But you are."

It was an honest observation that felt very undeserved in the moment. I was a dominant, and I had been for years, but I hadn't been acting the part, especially not around him. If anything, I'd been playing the part of a helpless child, with him helping me through my panic attacks and my fumbling and mumbling. And he'd been the one to book the flight and the hotel, and order the food.

"Not yours, though," I murmured, thinking once again about what his hair had felt like in my hands, my cock in his throat. The hotel we'd stayed at the first time didn't have carpet anywhere this nice and I wondered if he'd gotten rug burn.

"No," he agreed, cheeks still flushed. "But not because of the reasons you're thinking."

"What are the reasons I'm thinking?"

He slid my drink back toward me, and I sighed, taking it in hand.

"You've handled all of this. Handled me."

"Well." He sucked in a loud breath, letting it out so long I wondered if he was going to melt into the chair. "I don't owe you any of the things I've done because, like you said, you're not *my* Dom, but that doesn't erase who I am."

I knew my voice was going to crack, but I asked the question anyway,

"Who are you, Ivey?"

CHAPTER 8
IVEY

I was a man who wanted to take Dalton Fox apart with my teeth.

Which was news to me, though probably not such a revelation if I were to step back and look at the writing on the wall.

"If you want the answer to that question, we have to talk about her."

The wrinkles around the edges of Dalton's eyes crinkled deeper, and he threw back half of his drink in one swallow. I appreciated the way he'd tried to cut himself off, but I also knew the things that existed between the two of us sometimes needed a little lubrication. My sincere hope had been that we could both be open and honest about the things that had happened before between us.

That marriage license might as well have been a knife slicing open a very old and very sore wound. And spilling the truth of it all, signing the divorce papers, that would have to be the final suture, sealing it back up. This would be painful, but necessary.

"I know," he agreed. "She was yours first. You start."

"She was never mine," I said, rubbing the bridge of my nose and forcing my mind back to college, back to Genevieve. "You know, things were great at first."

"They always are."

"Sometimes, I try to look back and see if there were things I could have done differently with her, said in a…gentler way."

Dalton shook his head. "You can't control that kind of person."

"Is that why you try to control everyone else now?" I asked.

He bit the inside of his cheek, hollowing it out as he sank his teeth into the sensitive flesh. "You were saying."

"It started with words," I admitted, swallowing down champagne-flavored bile. "Well, actually it started with my father. Our families have been close for years. I grew up with Gen. Well, as much as someone can grow up with another person when you're in two different boarding schools."

"Summers and holidays," he murmured.

"Barely that," I said. "I didn't even get to know her until college and my father was so pleased that she and I were getting along…I think he married us off in his head before I even asked her on our first date. But even back then, I should have known."

He hummed, rocking his drink side to side so the ice would settle. "What was her tell?"

"The waitress brought her club soda instead of tonic water." The memory was blaring and jagged in my mind, slashing through my sophomore year of college with little concern for anything else. "She threw it on her."

"Of course she did."

"But she chalked it up to the way we'd been raised. You know?"

Dalton studied me carefully, his expression almost unreadable. The three of us had all come from money, but I had no doubt the way I'd been raised in New York was very different from how he'd been brought up in California. Old money and less old money didn't operate the same way, and I'd never looked down on Dalton and his family. They were formidable in their own right, but it had been different then.

"She had expectations of the people around her," he said, which was the excuse she'd given me after dousing that poor girl with ice cold, lime-twisted club soda.

"Right. And for a while, her vitriol was always directed at other people. I told myself she was just spoiled. It was what her parents had taught her..." My whole body hurt with the recollections, every muscle tense like she was in the room again, ready to strike. "It started innocently enough."

Dalton scoffed, shaking his head like a protest.

I knew.

I *knew*.

"I don't even remember the first time. Back then I didn't think it was something worth committing to memory, you know? She got mad about something and shoved me against the wall. It should have been laughable because she was so much smaller than me, but..."

Dalton shifted his weight, stretching past me for the champagne. He took the empty glass out of my hand and replaced it with the half-full bottle.

The gesture said *it's okay, this is going to be a long night.*

This was what we should have done the first time. But instead we'd gotten married.

I still didn't know how that had happened.

"The first time she hit me was a slap," he said softly, rubbing his chest, right over his heart. "Right here, and here..."

He dragged his hand from side to side, eyes twisted shut like the memory pained him to recall. I imagined it did. His shoulders curved inward, back bowing while he hunched in around himself.

"She was so tempestuous," he said. "So unreasonably jealous."

"Not at first, though, right?"

"Not at first. It almost came out of nowhere, and the first time she hit me...I couldn't defend myself, you know?"

"I know."

The champagne bottle was cold and wet against my palm, and I pushed it aside, then wiped the moisture off on the leg of my slacks. A nervous habit that I'd developed years ago. Gen hated it and said it made me look small and nervous that I was always wiping my hands on my legs like an unsure child.

It was below my status, she had said.

"I wonder sometimes," I said, connecting some dots for the very first time. "How much of the way I am as an adult is because of her."

"How do you figure?"

"I was raised a certain way. Taught how to be and how to act, but...as far back as I can remember, I've always done well under pressure, but I don't really remember *needing* to... until her."

By the end of our relationship, Genevieve had become so volatile, I was always on eggshells around her, but I had to keep that all to myself, keep it all buttoned up. I couldn't talk to anyone about it, couldn't let on. Because if they knew what went on behind closed doors, what would that say about me?

I'd been raised to be hyper-aware of public perception, and what would it say about me if my family, my friends, my future colleagues found out that I was getting physically assaulted by my five-foot-six girlfriend? Would they look at me as being weak for allowing it? I could almost hear my father's voice in my head when she would go off on me, fists and words flying.

Don't show weakness, Carter.

People expect something of the Royce name, Carter.

Grow a pair, Carter.

"I don't understand how you could submit yourself to other people after her," he said, almost under his breath.

"I did it before her." The hair on the back of my neck stood up and I squared my shoulders, immediately on the defensive. "I didn't...I'm not this way *because* of her. I've always...Maybe that's how it happened—she saw an opening."

"Well, I'm *not* that way," he said, body the complete opposite from me. He was stretched out and casual, almost languid, but I imagined that was a result of all the gin.

God, how did he still drink that shit?

"I'm not that way," he said again, as if I could forget the way dominance had always leaked from his pores, even in his darkest and drunkest nights. "And she still..."

A small silence settled between us, and Dalton's eyes went hazy, like he was lost in a memory. I hated the two of us sitting there, dragging up memories that should have stayed buried, but it felt important. Like they needed to finally see the light so they could be buried for good.

"Why did you come to me?" I asked him. "After she…"

"Do you mean how did I know that I *could* come to you?"

I nodded.

"The whole way to the house I was so mad. I was going to ask you why you hadn't warned me about her. Why you'd watched me take her out, knowing what kind of person she was…" Dalton trailed off, not finishing the question, but I didn't have a good answer for him anyway.

I hadn't said anything to him about Gen because he and I weren't friends. We never had been. And giving him a heads-up about what had gone on between her and me would be airing the dirtiest of my laundry, and that just wasn't something the men of the Royce family did.

"And I got there," he went on. "And I banged on the door, and when you opened it and you saw me…"

"I knew."

Dalton had showed up on the porch of my frat house with a fingernail-sized scratch across his cheek, the blood already dry. Under the porch light, I could make out the telltale shadow of a bruise beneath his left eye. It would get darker in a few days.

At least, mine always had.

"And I didn't have anything to say," he whispered. "Not anymore."

He dragged his tongue across the front of his teeth. The light in the hotel was better than the light on the porch had been, and the unshed sheen of tears in his eyes was clear as day. He gave a small shake of his head, holding them at bay.

"I just needed to be with someone who understood," he admitted, voice barely louder than a whisper. "Someone who wouldn't judge me, and then…"

His face twisted, uncomfortable and nervous, but he looked up at me just the same. A tear leaked from the corner of his eye, racing down toward his chin with record speed. He swiped angrily at it, tracing his fingers over the place her nails had cut him.

He hadn't scarred.

At least, not physically.

"And then I don't know what happened," he said.

"What happened was we drank too much because the weight of what she did to us was just too much to carry, Fox."

"Did…did I take advantage of you that night?"

At the question, another tear fell down his face, then another and another. He didn't bother to wipe them, but the worry in his eyes made it crystal clear to me that he was more worried about how he'd treated me than the way she'd treated him.

"I don't remember a lot about that night, but I don't think so."

"Would you tell me if you did?"

"I wouldn't be here with you if you had," I promised.

That seemed to mollify him, and he took a steadying breath.

The silence settled between us again, feeling less daunting than before. There was no need for us to go into detail about the abuse we'd suffered at her hands, but back then, we hadn't talked about it at all. He hadn't said a word, never uttered her name. But I'd known what she'd done, and he'd somehow also known what she'd done to me, and that had been enough.

Dalton exhaled, using his whole body to release the breath, release the tension. His lips puffed out, making a ridiculously laughable sound as he emptied his lungs.

"And then we got married," he said, leaning back in his chair and dragging his hands down his face. When they fell into his lap, he almost looked like himself again. The tease of a cocksure smile ghosted across his lips, and he shook his head, laughing to himself.

"And then we got married."

He shoved himself up from the seat and went back to the window, looking out at the strip.

Dalton was a sight to behold. He always had been, though.

With his hands bracketed against his narrow waist, I gave myself the opportunity to appreciate him for the man he was, the man he'd always been. Dalton was handsome and cocky, almost arrogant, but it was all deserved. He was smart and talented, gifted, fucking rich, and dominant to boot. He would have been a catch for anyone, and maybe in a different life…

He shifted his weight from foot to foot, his arms falling loose at his sides.

"Did we…" He angled his head to the side, giving me the stoic profile of his face, backlit by the bright lights of Vegas behind him. He snapped his mouth closed before finishing his thought and turned back toward the window.

Ignoring the champagne and the way it made my head swim, I got up to join him. His breath might have skittered when I stepped into his space, but when I softly pressed my hand against the small of his back to steady him—to steady myself—he didn't tense.

He relaxed.

I closed my eyes and tried to narrow my drunk sense of focus down to the pads of my fingers and the way the rich weave of his shirt felt against my skin. Through the material, his skin was hot to the touch, and I wanted desperately to get burned.

How had it always been like this for us?

For me…with him?

Back then, maybe it had been some kind of trauma bonding, but even through the alcohol and the confessions, my attraction to Dalton was undeniable. Being around him again only served to remind me of just how much I wanted him, of how frequently I called back the scant memories I had of our weekend together.

"Ivey," he whispered my name, and I knew. I *knew* he felt it too.

I stood right behind him, chin hovering near his ear. I loved that he was shorter than me, smaller than me. I loved that he felt safe enough around me to let down his guard, but more than that, I loved that I could do the same. With Dalton, I didn't have to always be *on*, and it was possible to hate the circumstances that had brought around the safety, but…

Having it again, I didn't want to let it go.

"Fox." I turned my head toward him, just barely, and he did the same, and then my arms went around his back and his hands were on my face and our lips pressed together in a kiss I didn't realize I'd been waiting fifteen years to have.

The sound that left my mouth was embarrassing, and Dalton's smile tasted like gin. Our tongues tangled, sloppy and wet, and my cock was immediately hard between my legs. So fucking hard that my brain was in the process of telling me to get on my goddamn knees before Dalton changed his mind.

But I was too slow, too sluggish from the drinking and the talking.

"Ivey." Again he whispered my name into my mouth, breaking the kiss. He pressed our foreheads together, breathing heavily.

I could smell my champagne on his breath, and I dug my fingers into his hips, not willing to let this go.

"Ivey," he said again, shaking his head. "We can't. We're drunk."

I knew about consent, understood it better than most, but in that moment...I could not have cared less. My brain was bogged down with the past and my body had stepped up to ask for what it wanted.

"We did it before," I reminded, chasing after another kiss.

He gave me a chaste and resigned peck, no tongue.

"I don't want to repeat the past," he said quietly. "If we're together again, I want to remember it."

As soon as Ivey's lips touched mine, I was gone. He kissed me without fear, without prohibition, and for as loud as the voice in my head that wanted him was, the voice that told me why all of these things were happening was louder. We were both too drunk for the kind of trouble a kiss like that would lead to. A kiss like that was undoubtedly how we'd ended up married.

"If we're together again?" he asked, hands still firm around my hips, nails searching out my skin through the barrier of my shirt.

I groaned, closing my eyes and praying the floor didn't slide out from under me. "I'm too drunk for this, Ivey. And so are you."

"But…" He folded his lips together between his teeth, pale cheeks flushing violently.

"But what?"

"Nothing." He let go of me and stepped back, a rush of cold air snaking between our bodies. It was probably for the better, like a blast of cold water to bring us back to our senses.

"There's no *if*, if you're not forthcoming."

"Big word for all the gin you've put back today," he murmured, shoving his hands into his pockets.

The night played back in my mind like a highlights reel, and I was thankful we were already married because there was no other worst case scenario than that. There wasn't anything we could do in this damn city, in this massive but somehow still suffocating hotel room, that we hadn't already done.

Well, maybe a couple of things.

"I don't just play pretend about the way I am," I said, beckoning him closer. He didn't argue, just took another step toward me, but I stopped him at arm's reach with my fingers against the buttons of his shirt.

"That's good news," he said. "I mean, if there's an if for us."

I plucked at a button until it opened, then worked my way down the placket of his shirt until it fell open, revealing the broad expanse of his fit and toned chest. I tried to not touch him. I knew better than to touch him because we were both far too drunk for the things we both wanted. But he sighed softly and I helped him out of his shirt, letting my fingertips graze over his skin as the material slid down his arms.

He reached for me and paused, but I gave him a slow nod and he did the same to me, though his fingers wandered more than mine had. More than I should have allowed, but his touch was fire, and with my head swimming in champagne and gin, I was sure I'd developed a death wish.

With both our shirts off, he reached for my belt, and I cursed myself before stopping him again.

"Let's sleep this off," I said. It wasn't a question. I needed it to not be a question.

"Are you sure?" he asked, cocking his head to the side. "Maybe it's better if we don't remember it this time either."

"Am I so regrettable?"

Even through the drunken haze that masked his face, Ivey looked at me like I was insane. Like he had a thousand things to say to me that would prove just how delirious I was with the statement, but his brain was muddled. Much like mine. He opened his mouth, sucking in a breath before his lips sealed closed again.

"Let's sleep it off," I said again. "I wasn't asking the first time and I'm not asking now."

"Jesus, Fox." He let out a sound that came out half like a whine, half like a growl. "You can't just…"

"Bedroom, Ivey."

"If you want me to go to sleep, then you need to stop making me hard."

At his comment, both of our stares flickered down to the impressive bulge that tented the fly of his pants. Before I could say anything else, he furiously tore open the button and tugged down the zipper. Shoving his pants to his ankles, he managed to get out of them without falling, but before he stood back straight, he gave me his back and stalked toward the bedroom.

I took my own pants off with much less dramatics and followed, finding him angrily tearing back the layers of bedding.

"All that from a kiss?" I asked.

He glared at me, climbing into bed and yanking the duvet up to his stomach. The sheets and blankets were so voluminous, the erection in question was obscured.

"Not just a kiss," he muttered, flopping onto his side when I climbed into bed behind him.

Not just a kiss.

I lay on my back and folded one of my arms behind my head, staring up at the gaudy painting and molding that wrapped the edges of the ceiling. The suite was over the top, but Ivey had never done anything in halves… and when had he become Ivey again?

He was Carter, but he was Royce, and he'd been Ivey for me once.

For one night a very long time ago, and even if my brain couldn't call up the visuals, my body remembered how he'd responded to the endearment. Even now, he lit up when I used it, but I hadn't meant to wield it like a weapon. For me, the nickname was more like a comfort blanket. It was a reminder there were parts of him that were just for me, and parts of me that belonged only to him. But more than that, they were the ugliest parts, the pieces we were most ashamed and embarrassed of, yet neither of us judged the other for them.

And he was Ivey.

My Ivey.

Even though…

He wasn't mine at all. I knew that. I really understood that being married was a mistake and a technicality, and I had no claim on him, no right to call him anything special.

"I can't sleep it off if you keep thinking that loud," he grumbled, tugging the blankets.

"I never pinned you as a brat, Royce."

"Fuck you, Fox."

I chuckled, dropping one leg out of bed to see if it would slow the rotation of the room.

"Good night," I whispered, fisting the long edges of the pillowcase in my hand.

"Good night."

He gave another jerk and twist of the blankets, pulling them off the left side of my body entirely. I fell asleep smiling, listening to the sound of Ivey's soft snores, which started as soon as I closed my eyes.

Morning came too soon or not soon enough, depending on which one of us you asked. The bed was burning like a fucking furnace under the sheets. But I didn't have any of the sheets, I realized. He'd stolen them all, but to make up for the slight, he'd covered me with his body instead.

At some point in the night, I'd rolled onto my side, facing away from him, and he'd chased after me. Ivey had slung one leg over my waist, and an arm over my chest. His soft breathing puffed against my neck and his cock speared the back of my thigh, hot and hard.

I didn't have to reach between my own legs to confirm that my cock matched his, and slowly prying my eyes open confirmed we were still in Las Vegas. Still married. And far more sober than we'd been the night before. There was a dull ache behind my left eye, but I knew some water and breakfast would clear it up. If I was able to get out of bed without jostling Ivey, at least.

"You're thinking too loud," he whispered, lips ghosting across the back of my neck. He was so warm and so close, all wrapped around me like we'd done this a thousand times and not just once.

Or twice.

I didn't know for certain.

"I'm trying to understand how you and I always end up like this," I said.

"I'd hardly consider twice always." His lips against my neck again, but definitely a kiss and not just a whisper.

"We have a 100% incidence rate."

"Need a broader sample study." Another kiss, and his hand slid down my ribs toward the waistband of my boxer briefs.

Closing my eyes, I grabbed his fingers seconds before the slid beneath the elastic. He groaned, hard cock jerking against the back of my leg in response to the denial. I tried to ignore it.

I *tried*.

"This feels like a bad idea," I murmured.

He flexed his fingers against the palm of my hand.

"You implied that last night, but I'm sober now. You're sober. And…" He wiggled his fingers out of my grasp, but instead of reaching for my cock like I half-expected, he pressed his fingers against the straining cotton of my underwear, pushed the material that had pulled away from my body back against my skin, as if demonstrating my arousal without going too far. "You want it."

I didn't want *it*.

I wanted *him*.

And wanting him felt problematic, even if I was too hazy and lust-drunk to articulate all the reasons that giving into that want was a bad idea.

"Ivey…"

"If you don't want me, then you're going to have to stop calling me that."

"I do want you, but I…"

"No buts." Ivey kissed the back of my neck again, his tongue messy and wet against the bottom of my hairline, and I sighed, tipping my chin toward my chest so he could get his mouth around me better.

Jesus, he was a persuasive son of a bitch.

"Take control, Fox." He licked his way around the back of my neck to the curve of my shoulder. "Tell me how you want me."

The problem was I wanted him every way, all ways.

The blurred memories of our first night together overlaid the sharp focus of the present moment, and I wanted to fill in all of the blanks for myself. For the both of us. There had never been any denying that Ivey was a gorgeous specimen of a man, classically handsome, tall, and strong. He was smart and he was rich, and was always the exact perfect amount of put-together.

But things with him had always been complicated, and being married and living across the country from each other…there was no future or plan in any of this. If he could stop touching me for two seconds so I could get my brain right, so I could remind myself this was a one-and-done kind of situation. It was just me getting to act on an attraction that was most likely borne from a really dark and messy place, but it was still an attraction.

And I had never been one to deny myself the things I wanted.

That was how I'd gotten into this spot in the first place.

"You're still thinking," he murmured, tapping his fingers against my hip bone.

"I'm just trying to be responsible."

"I have condoms in my toiletry bag," he said, huffing a laugh against my shoulder.

"I didn't mean with your body."

"I mean…I'm negative, you know."

"Jesus, Ivey." I groaned and untangled myself from his touch, climbing out of bed to get space from him so I could get my head straight.

The heat of his stare as I pressed my back against the far wall of the bedroom was enough confirmation that even though I'd undoubtedly wanted everything that had ever happened between us, he'd been the instigator.

"That's not what I meant," I said, reaching down and tucking my cock beneath the waistband of my underwear, trying to make my erection less obvious.

And failing.

My dick was achingly hard, leaking precum, and I'd brought my arousal into focus because the tip of my dick poked out and smeared its proof against my stomach. Ivey licked his lips, moving onto all fours like he was ready to pounce off the bed and slam me into the wall.

Devour me.

"What did you mean?"

"I meant…" I swirled my hand near my temple like the gesture would answer where the words couldn't. "I meant this isn't anything, right? It's just…"

"It's nothing." He rose off his hands and leaned back with his ass against his heels. The wet spot against the white cotton of his underwear was dark and quickly spreading.

I groaned, running through a quick mental checklist of reasons why I should and shouldn't fuck my husband for the first and last time.

The pro list was considerably longer than the con list, and I screwed my eyes closed, wishing I could get out of my head for an hour or three. It wasn't like I'd never fucked someone for fun before. It had been years since I'd had a boyfriend, but not nearly as long since I'd had a hookup. If Ivey had been anyone else, I would have already been balls deep inside of them, their underwear shoved so deep into their mouth they would have been worrying about choking to death.

"There you go," he whispered.

The thoughts must have been clear on my face as I talked myself around to giving into the positively feral urge that had taken up residence in my bones.

"I want this. I know you want this."

He's an adult.

I'm an adult.

I repeated the list to myself, wondering what I'd blow on a breathalyzer. I wasn't drunk, but was I really sober? Did it even matter anymore?

I listened to Ivey climb off the bed, bracing myself for the heat of him again, but his footsteps grew quieter as he walked out of the room. I wanted to open my eyes and look, I wanted to go after him.

I just *wanted*.

And then he was back, the sheets rustling as he rearranged himself on the bed. I had no idea here he went, but when I opened my eyes and found lube and a condom beside him, the answer was confirmed.

"Turn that brain of yours off," he said, and I took a breath, opening my eyes.

It was a small and quick death when he came into focus.

Ivey was on his back, naked. He'd bent his legs at the knee and planted his feet on the edge of the mattress. I took a little longer than was necessary to take in the view of him, and he caught my stare and nodded, waiting until I nodded back at him.

Yes.

Yes.

Yes, I want this. I want you. I want you. I fucking need you.

His fingers were slick with lube, and he lifted his balls and teased his way around his hole, not quite giving himself the touch that I knew he was desperate for.

"It's nothing," he said again, spreading himself open. "It's just chemistry, Fox. Right?"

The tip of his middle finger disappeared inside of him and the last shred of my control snapped.

GROWING UP IN A FAMILY LIKE MINE HAD ITS PERKS, ONE OF WHICH being I knew how to get what I wanted.

And I wanted Dalton inside of me.

He was on me before I could blink, my wrists secured in one of his hands and my back flat against the mattress. The length of his dick pressed against my hole and I sighed, sinking down and appreciating the weight of him on top of me.

"We've never done this before," I whispered, angling my head toward the other corner of the bed. Dalton buried his face in the crook of my neck, peppering frantic and messy kisses up the line of my neck and higher toward my ear. I moaned, finishing the thought, "I'd remember."

"Fuck."

Dalton bit my earlobe, humping against me. I spread my legs wider, ready for him.

I would have happily taken him the night before, drunk or not. I was human, and he was a gorgeous man. He always had been. I knew about consent and being risk aware. I knew about making good decisions, and I'd wanted Dalton since before I started drinking. Even with the past between us, my attraction to him hadn't dimmed, and there was no amount of liquor that would make me do anything with him that I wouldn't do sober.

Maybe talking about some of the history that had brought us together came easier with some alcoholic lubrication, but none of it had been revolutionary. The things we shared last night were truths that were known, even if they'd been unspoken.

Above me, he shifted, pinning my wrists against the sheets.

"Don't move," he said, pulling his hand away.

Without taking his eyes off of me, he reached for the lube and the condom, his fingers working on that task while his eyes took stock of my body, hard and bare before him. His eyes were as soft against my skin has his mouth had been, a sharp contrast from the rough force of his hands.

"Who did that?" he asked, stare lingering on the rope bruises around my wrist.

"Not you. Don't pretend it matters."

"You're my husband," he murmured, tearing open the condom wrapper, eyes still fixed on my wrists, crossed obediently above my head.

"Are you jealous, Fox?"

He cleared his throat and looked me dead in the eye. "I don't know what I am when you're around."

The confession felt just as heavy, if not more so, than the things we'd spilled out the night before. I wanted to offer him some concession or some understanding, but he wasn't the only one. We were married on a technicality, and that was going to fix itself as soon as my lawyer got his signature on that divorce paperwork. And the shared past aside…it didn't change the fact that Dalton was a catch of a man.

So was I, for that matter.

And I'd spent my time with him trying to reconcile the people we used to be with the people we were now. If Dalton and I were anyone besides who we were, there wouldn't be a problem with what we were about to do. But the attraction felt heavier, more serious, with the history between us. Even though it had been fifteen years, was this reaction still just a trauma response?

Or was it more?

His answer made me feel like it was more, and I didn't know whether or not I wanted that to be true.

"You can leave me your own marks if it would make you feel better," I promised.

His nostrils flared, and he rolled the condom down the impressive length of his erection.

"Don't say things you don't mean." Dalton reached for the lube and poured a dollop on his cock, then a decent amount on his fingers.

I spread my legs wider, making more room for him between my thighs. My hands were still above my head and he was braced on his forearm, fingers brushing against my hair, our noses too close, mouths almost touching.

"I mean it," I whispered, the rest of the words dying in my throat as he pushed two fingers into me. Once he'd looked back at my eyes, he hadn't turned away, and the intensity of his focus was almost overwhelming. The attention burned like a pile of hot coals at the base of my spine, and my lashes fluttered when his knuckles breached my rim.

"Don't close your eyes," he said, twisting his wrist and pulling out, easing back in, then out, then in…

My heart slammed against my sternum, desperate to crack my ribs and escape my body. Even though I was bigger than him in almost every way, his weight was solid above me, the demand in his eyes even more so.

"Watch, Ivey."

"I'm trying."

My breath caught in my throat.

"Try harder."

I managed a rough nod as another of his fingers tried to enter me. He nodded back at me, much like he had earlier, then he pushed the third finger all the way. It wasn't a lot to have inside of me. In fact, I knew his cock would hurt more, but I'd always found something so intimate about fingering. The positioning, the movements… I couldn't pinpoint why, but with our hard cocks and his arm between us…

"You're still thinking too hard," I said after his hand stilled and his brow furrowed together over the bridge of his nose. "I'm trying to enjoy this."

"Are you not?" He leaned back enough for the cold morning air of the hotel to ghost over my slick and hard cock.

"You know what I mean."

"I don't know you at all," I murmured.

He pulled his fingers out, mouth angled into half of a frown.

That might have been the wrong thing to say, but it was the truth. I didn't know much about Dalton's personality or what he liked on his pizza, his favorite movie. But all of that aside, I did *know* him in ways no one else ever would. And he knew me in the same ways, and that…

It was a little daunting. Even on a good day, which we were not in.

"Now you're just trying to rile me up," he said, calling me out on the half-lie. He lined up the head of his cock with my hole.

"Is it working?" I grinned up at him, but the sharp snap of his hips took not only the smug smile off my face but also the breath out of my lungs. "Shit."

Dalton's eyes did a little roll toward the back of his head and he dropped his forehead against mine, the breath leaving his lungs in a rush.

"Is it working?" I asked after my words returned.

"Shut up, Ivey."

He licked his lips, re-adjusting himself above me, inside of me. I shivered, the stretch of his cock almost uncomfortable. But among other things, I was a masochist, and the burn only made my own dick leak even more against my stomach.

"I don't think I want to," I said, gritting my teeth as I tried to fight back the crest of my orgasm.

I wanted to rile him up, I wanted to see him lose control, but I didn't want to come.

At least, not yet.

"Can we talk more about how you're jealous that I'm wearing another man's marks?" I asked.

He pulled back so far his entire cock left my body. My hole gaped and contracted, needy to get filled again. But instead of pushing back inside, he held himself like that, inches away from me, so close to what we were both mad for wanting.

"I'm not jealous."

"I meant it when I said you could mark me too." The tip of his cock teased against my hole without going in. "It'll be like a souvenir."

One thrust and he slammed inside of me again with so much force he almost folded me in half. A laugh left my throat at the same time as my breath, and his face was back in the crook of my neck, teeth buried in the muscle and skin.

The bite of his teeth was shocking, even though I'd asked for it, and I whimpered, body fighting against him on reflex. But he was all the way back inside of me, all of his weight on top of me, and then his hand was back around the bruise on my wrist, pinning me down.

Dalton sucked so hard at my neck I knew it would immediately mark. He alternated between tongue and teeth, all the while his hips setting a torturously slow pace. His cock pulled and dragged, two inches out and one inch in, six out, six in. I couldn't predict how he was going to move next, and his lips worked their way down my shoulder, leaving a trail of bite marks and bruises in his wake.

In my ear, he growled, seating himself fully and raising back onto his knees with a gasping breath. His chest had begun to sweat, the spread of his pecs glistening as daylight dared to filter in through the window on the other side of the room. Dalton looked down at me like whatever he was about to say was going to send us both straight to hell.

As if we hadn't been there since college.

"I want more from you," he murmured, reaching down and giving one of my nipples a sharp twist.

"Take it," I pleaded.

I was beyond being a brat to get my way, beyond taunting and teasing. I wanted to be consumed, and I wanted it to scar so when all was said and done and we'd parted ways, I'd at least have something to remind me of him.

For a few more days.

"I want to make you cry."

"I don't think you could," I admitted, lifting my hips off the bed, chasing after any friction or movement from him. The holding pattern was going to drive me up the wall. "I'm a bit of a masochist."

"That sounds like a challenge."

"Sounds like we don't have the time or the tools."

Dalton chewed his lower lip between his teeth, then grabbed the pillow from the head of the bed. I had the fleeting though that he was going to smother me to death for being contrary, but he fisted the pillowcase in his hand and jerked his arm behind him until the pillow landed against the carpet with a soft thump.

So no smothering, but suffocation was on the table, I thought, as he whipped the pillowcase until it had spun itself into a makeshift rope.

A gag, maybe?

Had I finally talked myself against a wall with him? Figuratively, of course, since I was very clearly on a bed, but the logistics of Dalton trying to take me against a wall were enough to send a bolt of heat right through my balls.

"Can I tie your arms?"

"Not if you ask."

He rolled his eyes, but not in the sexy, losing control way from before. In the maybe-this-pillowcase-would-be-better-as-a-garotte kind of way.

"We're not at a point where I can just…"

Oh, God. There he was, balls deep inside of me and about to retreat back into that gorgeous, hard head of his.

"You can tie my arms," I said. "If I want you to stop, I'll say stop."

As Dalton wound the first edge of the pillowcase around my wrist, I realized I should have asked about his stance on orgasm denial, but I was already so close I probably didn't even need a hand to get there anyway.

He made quick work of looping the material around my wrists, leaving six inches of it gathered between my hands. There was a tail of fabric loose on either side of my wrists, and he wrapped the ends around his fist with such a fierce look of control on his face I had to think about going home to New York without him to stop myself from coming.

"Pinch your nipples," he said, voice lower and rougher than I'd ever heard him before.

"I'll come," I warned.

"I don't care."

I shivered. "God, you're so fucking hot when you're mean."

Dalton tipped his head back and swallowed, jaw clenched. With his other hand, he grabbed my face, cheeks smashed together between his fingers until my mouth puckered like a fish.

"You haven't even seen me get mean," he whispered, digging his fingers into the hollows of my cheeks until he worked my jaw apart. Gooseflesh broke out and raced up my legs, down my arms. The tight grip of his hand hurt, and my cock leaked in approval. My hole constricted around him and he grunted, mouth twitching up in the top corner.

He wanted me more than once. I could see it all over his face.

Dalton was a loud thinker, and his eyes were telegraphing every thought and idea that crossed his mind, and he mourned the fact that there was a country between us. And so did I because, even though he'd been right earlier—I didn't know him—I had the sneaking suspicion that Dalton may very well be the kind of Dom I'd been looking for.

Irony of ironies.

"Now pinch your nipples," he said again, releasing my face with a shove.

I wanted to push him more, to test my theory, but I also wanted to see what he'd come up with on his own, so I took my nipples gingerly between my fingers and waited for further instruction.

At first, he didn't do anything, but he started to move again.

A small grace considering how strung he'd made me. With every pump of his hips, the head of his cock dragged over my prostate, wreaking havoc on my ability to formulate thoughts or sentences. He started up again with that unpredictable pace that had me less than five seconds away from bucking him off of me and throwing him onto the floor. I didn't just want to come; I needed it.

I needed *him* to make me come.

"Whatever you do next, Ivey…" He tightened his grip on the pillowcase. "Don't let go of your nipples."

I didn't know what to expect, but I twisted down with my nails, grabbing my nipples in as much of a grip as I could manage, and then he tugged the pillowcase up, trying to get me to break my hold. I pinched them tighter and he lifted higher, until the heat that had pooled at the base of my spine collapsed in on itself like a black hole imploding.

Dalton didn't make me cry, but he was definitely about to make me come.

With a rough yank and twist of the pillowcase, he tried to get me to rip my nipples off my chest, but I hadn't been lying when I said I wanted him to make me cry. The pain was like a sunrise, an awakening, like it always was. And my cock erupted, hands free, spouting jet after jet of cum against my stomach, my chest, my hands.

"Fuck yes, Ivey. Just like that. Oh, my God."

With his hand still pulling mine away from my body, he went still. His thick erection pulsed as he came, spilling into a condom with so much intensity, I swore I could still feel the heat of his cum inside of me. His hips twitched and spasmed, almost involuntarily, and my vision went dark around the edges, the pain in my chest coming into a sharp and agonizing focus as the initial wave of my orgasm fell away.

Dalton gave one more rough tug of the pillowcase and I let out a very unflattering whimper. It was nowhere near my normal pain tolerance, but with him…it was different.

It always had been different with him.

Finally, Dalton let the pillowcase go, and my wrists landed against my chest, fingers still tight on my nipples. He fell forward, wrapping himself around me in a way that felt possessive and welcome all at once. With his hand curled around my throat, his face once again pressed against my neck that he'd left a trail of bruises on earlier, he kissed the shell of my ear.

"Let go of them, Ivey," he whispered, cock still twitching inside of me.

"It'll hurt," I protested.

"That's the point."

Grumbling, but still fuzzy and compliant in the ways a good orgasm made me, I forced myself to release the vise grip I had on my nipples. As expected, blood flow returned and the pain went from borderline unenjoyable to absolute agony. But I was stubborn and I didn't want him to know how affected I was.

Even though my body was a traitor, the muscles in my channel convulsing around him and milking the rest of the cum from his balls, I kept my jaw clenched. And under my breath, I cursed Dalton Fox and all of the things he had no right to make me feel.

"What the fuck is that?" Ivey grumbled against my chest, stretching his legs while keeping his chest as close to mine as he could manage.

After we fucked, we both must have dozed off, but the incessant and insanely loud vibrating sound had roused us both at the same time.

"I don't know."

"Is it your phone?" he asked, rolling onto his back.

I rubbed at my eyes, unsure of what day it even was, let alone what time. Whatever the vibration was, it wasn't constant, but it hadn't stopped and I had a sneaking suspicion it was, in fact, my phone.

"Probably."

Flinging my legs out of bed, I shuffled into the dining room to find the offending device. It was on the table next to the cold and soggy plate of French fries, screen bright with incoming text messages.

"Yeah," I called over my shoulder toward the bedroom. "It's me."

My legs were somehow still shaky from the sex, so I collapsed into one of the six chairs that were scattered around the table. The clock on my home screen let me know it was Sunday afternoon, almost four. At least I hadn't lost a day like the last time Ivey and I had went to Vegas. The messages were from my friends, and my heart sank. I didn't think Barclay would have offered up my secrets, but for a fleeting moment, I wasn't sure.

There were too many text messages to count. Fuck, I really hated that stupid group chat sometimes.

Rob: Last minute Rapture outing??
Archie: That sounds like Grayson talking, not you.
Rob: His request.
Archie: His fingers????
Rob: This again? Doesn't it get old?
Flynn: There's Rob.
Flynn: I'm down. Rose is working.
Archie: I have to ask Owen.
Archie: What about you, Barclay?
Flynn: He's probably asleep.
Barclay: I'm not asleep.
Barclay: I can meet you there.
Rob: Is Val coming?
Barclay: I don't know.
Archie: That sounds sus.
Barclay: Sounds like you don't know what you're talking about.
Flynn: Where is Dalton?
Rob: He probably blocked the chat.
Barclay: I would have been the first.
Archie: LOL he would never.
Flynn: He's probably with Drake. I'm sure he'll come around. What time?
Rob: Ten?
Archie: So late.

The text messages went quiet, then resumed around three.

Archie: I'm honestly impressed if Dalton is still with Drake.

I hadn't even thought about Drake since I'd gotten served with divorce papers. The thing between him and me had always just been casual sex, but I probably owed him an explanation. He hadn't been trying to chase me down in my absence, though, which kind of made me feel like whatever was going on between us had always primarily been because of convenience. There weren't any feelings there; it was purely physical.

I'd just talk to him when I got home.

Wait.

What?

I'd talk to him about *what*, exactly?

Ivey was a one time—or two time—thing, and as soon as we wrapped up our ill-advised trip to the desert, he was going back to New York with signed and sealed divorce papers. There wasn't anything between us to tell Drake about. Ivey would leave, and I could go back to sleeping with him…

Why did *that* feel like cheating, though?

"Everything okay?" Ivey shouted from the bedroom, yawning audibly.

"It's fine," I said. "Just my friends."

"Are they giving you a hard time about being married?"

He shuffled out into the dining room, naked as the day he was born. He settled into the chair opposite me with a tired groan. He surveyed the soggy and room temperature food on the table in front of us with a frown.

"Are you hungry?" he asked.

"Not for any of this."

"Now answer the other question." He swiped across the screen on his phone, stare flickering between it and my face.

"They aren't," I said.

"How did they take it?"

"I didn't tell them."

That earned his full attention, eyes going wide before settling back into what I would have called a generically vague expression that didn't betray anything going on in his head. But because I was me and he was him, I could read it. He was surprised and a little bit hurt.

"What about your friends?" I asked. "I assume you have them."

"Quite a few," he murmured, finishing up on his phone before tossing it onto the table. "And I didn't quite tell them either."

The hurt in his face suddenly felt a lot more complicated.

"I mean, no reason to. Right?" I asked.

"Right." He cleared his throat. "I ordered us some more food, so I should put some pants on."

"Shame that," I murmured.

Ivey's cheeks flushed, and he went back into the bedroom, giving me an impeccable view of his backside. It was the first time I'd really gotten to see him like that, and…

To call the man breathtaking was an understatement.

He was the quintessential Ivy League kind of man, with a chiseled jaw and defined features that looked like they'd been carved from marble. His ass and thighs were no exception to the rule, and I found myself wanting to bend him over, spread his legs, and bury my face between those cheeks of his.

I had a few hours left—at best—to do anything and everything I could get his consent for, and instead I was sitting at the dining room with day-old food, reading text messages from my asshole friends. When had I started making such shitty life choices?

There were a recent influx of messages on the screen, most likely the ones that had woken us up from our post-sex/hangover nap.

Flynn: Dalton isn't with Drake. Wasn't last night either.
Rob: Should we be worried? Does this disappearance have to do with the mystery lawsuit?

Flynn: I'm sure he's fine.
Barclay: If I were you, I'd have minimal worry.
Archie: Minimal is more than zero.
Flynn: Don't you have some spray cheese to eat?
Archie: I'm out and my main supplier is MISSING.
Rob: I thought you only ate it when you were being emo. Everything okay with Owen?
Archie: Is emo a word you learned from Grayson? Can you define it for me?
Flynn: I called Dalton twice. He hasn't answered.
Archie: VEGAS?!
Rob: I'm still in bed. I have no plans to go to Nevada.
Archie: No.
Archie: NO, I MEAN DALTON IS IN VEGAS.
Flynn: How do you know that??
Barclay: I really think he's fine. He's an adult.

God bless Barclay for trying to defuse the situation with the limited social skills that he had, but I could tell there was no getting out of this one.

Me: How do you know I'm in Vegas?
Archie: YOU'RE ALIVE.
Me: You're unnecessarily dramatic. Now answer the question.

Ivey appeared in the doorway again, unfortunately wearing pants, but they weren't done up at the fly. The white material of his underwear was visible between the split of the dark fabric. He went to the front door of the room and pulled it open, making conversation with an employee. Considering I was only in my underwear, I shuffled into the bedroom and pulled the door closed behind me to finish the conversation with my friends.

Archie: I have all of you on friend finder.

Rob: You WHAT?
Flynn: WHAT?!

I sighed, sitting on the edge of the bed.

Archie: You're all flight risks.
Archie: CLEARLY PROVEN RIGHT, since Dalton is literally in Las Vegas right now.
Flynn: Are you getting married?
Me: I'm not getting married.

In fact, I was getting divorced.

Me: I'll be home later today. We can talk about it on Monday.
Rob: Today is Sunday.
Me: I said what I said. Now I'm putting all of you on mute.

I put the entire phone on silent and threw it on the bed, waiting until I heard the hotel room door close before heading back out after Ivey. He'd ordered another smorgasbord of food, but what caught my eye was the tray with the steaming, silver carafe and two white mugs beside it.

"Coffee?" I asked, sliding toward it like it was magnetized.

He poured us both a mug and cocked his head to the side, studying me with a curious look on his face that I was still too tired to make complete sense of.

"How are your friends?" he asked.

"Annoyed they can't meddle from another state."

"Did you tell them where we were?" Ivey added a little cream into his coffee, stirring it with the tip of his pinky before sucking the drops of light brown liquid into his mouth with a wet *pop*.

"They know where I am."

"The differentiation stings a bit, Fox."

"Your friends know about me?" I sat down and took a drink of the coffee, which scalded my tongue. How had he stuck his finger in his? He must really be a masochist, through and through.

"No," he admitted, as if I needed the confirmation.

"I'm going to have to tell them about you when I get home," I said. "But it'll be what it is. I accidentally got married when I was in college, and now we're getting divorced."

"That doesn't quite explain why we're in Vegas now," he murmured.

"Do I have to explain it?"

He leaned back in the seat, stretching his legs and crossing his arms in front of his chest with a long sigh that caused him to sink down into the overstuffed chair a few more inches.

No, I knew the answer. I didn't have to explain it, but they weren't going to let me *not* explain it.

"One last hurrah?" Ivey suggested.

"I don't know how to tell them about you without telling them about her."

He made a thoughtful sound. "The history is a bit complicated, isn't it?"

"I don't have any issue talking about you. I think they'd expect you of me, if we're being honest."

Ivey licked his lips, a slow drag of his tongue from one side to the other. If I didn't know better, I would think he was trying to distract me from the conversation. Which…maybe.

"Expect me how?" He took another drink of his coffee, then another lick of his lips.

"You're not the kind of man I normally go for—"

He cut me off with a grin. "Tell me more."

"But I think if they knew you, it would make sense."

"Too bad they won't ever know me."

I cleared my throat, scratching the side of my nose at his observation. There was no lie in it, but the truth of it lodged itself into my ribs like a jagged piece of sheet metal, scraping and tearing and cutting its way through my lungs when I tried to breathe.

"What about your friends?" I asked, changing the subject.

"I'll tell them I was righting a wrong."

I clenched my jaw at the explanation, then shoved up out of my seat. "Right. Well, we should get on with that, then."

"Come on, Fox. You know what I meant."

"I know exactly what you meant."

I did, and what he'd said was the truth, but I still hated it and I didn't know why I hated it. It was this piece of him that had been inside me for the past fifteen years, this salve he'd offered me when I needed it. I didn't realize how tightly I'd held onto his kindness, his silent presence when I hadn't been able to give voice to the trauma. And even with years of therapy, this...*this* was something that hadn't been addressed.

This thing with Ivey wasn't just a trauma bond. There was an attraction there, and there always had been. With so much time between then and now, we were practically new people and the attraction was still there, not just simmering either. The sex we'd just had was incendiary, and because of a wedding neither of us even remembered, we were both just going to blindly walk away from it.

Back in the bedroom, I made quick enough work of getting dressed in my clothes from the night before. Neither of us had bothered to pack a bag. The toiletry case had been pure luck, tucked inside a leather messenger bag that Ivey had brought with him when we got onto the plane. Luck or not, if he'd traveled without it, I wondered how far things would have gone between us.

If one hypothetical version of events would have been better than another.

"Leaving so soon?" he asked when I came back to the dining room.

He was still sitting at the table, pants undone and coffee mug in hand. He looked disappointed, but far from surprised. This was my MO, after all. Especially when it came to Vegas hotels and him.

"It's for the best, I think," I said.

"Is it?"

I dragged my tongue across the front of my teeth and looked around the room, focusing on the dark wallpaper and the big windows, anything to avoid focusing on him. I didn't even need to look at him, though. I could see the broad swell of his shoulders when I closed my eyes. I could hear the needy whimpers he made when he came. Ivey was as much a part of my DNA as my parents were, and leaving him alone in a hotel room wasn't going to change any of that.

I let Dalton go.

Not like I could have stopped him without starting a fight, and I didn't want to fight. The conversation and the sex had left me feeling exposed enough, and the lingering ache in my ass when I sat down too long didn't help matters.

I gave him three hours to get a flight back to L.A., and only then did I bother scheduling my own flight back. After a quick trip and a cab ride to the hotel, I was back on board and headed east.

Headed home.

His friends had been incessant in their attempts to reach him, and mine had acted much the same. Unlike him, I ignored them until I was back in the city. I would have ignored them longer, but when I go home, Kale was leaning against the front door of my apartment, his arms crossed over his chest and a bored look on his face.

"How long have you been here?" I asked, pushing him aside so I could get to the keypad on the door.

"If I told you I've been here for two days, would you feel bad?" he asked.

"I'd ask why."

Shoving the door open, I stepped into the apartment, which hopefully wouldn't be home for much longer. The penthouse was so close, I could taste it. All I had to do was send the signed papers to Sarah…

Shit.

Fuck.

FUCK.

Dalton hadn't given me the signed filing.

Scrubbing a hand down my face, I dropped my bag onto the floor and shuffled further inside and flung myself face down on the couch with a muffled scream into the cushions. Kale closed the door and came to the couch, moving my legs out of the way so he could sit down. He dropped my calves back onto his lap and patted the backs of my knees.

"Did you forget that I have access to your flight tracker?" he asked. "I know you went to L.A. for twelve hours, then Vegas for a little longer, then back to L.A., and now you're here. If I didn't know better, I would think you went to meet an internet pen pal, got yourself married, and then fled the state in regret."

Oh, if only he knew how close that story was to the truth.

I rolled onto my back and scooted so my shoulders were jammed against the arm of the couch. Kale adjusted my legs on his lap, kicking my feet out beyond his thigh so I didn't smash his balls.

"I did not go to Vegas to get married," I said carefully.

Kale arched a brow at me.

I was a hypocrite. Thinking back to the argument—or whatever that was—that Dalton and I had gotten into over coffee at the hotel…the jealousy he'd expressed about whether our friends knew the truth, the possessive streak that had shown like a lightning bolt when he saw the bruises on my wrist, the easy concession when I'd given him the right to mark me in return. I rubbed my neck, the bruises from his mouth burning my palm through my shirt. He'd decorated my neck and shoulder like laying a wreath around my bones.

Kale watched me rub my clavicle, stare unwavering.

"Fuck, alright. But there's more to this story and I'm not interested in sharing all of it with you right now, okay?"

"That's fine, Beamer. I just want to make sure you're fine."

"I am fine," I promised, even though it tasted a little bit like a lie. Maybe I wasn't fine in that moment, horny and reeling from whatever had happened with Dalton, but I would be fine. I always had been and that wasn't going to suddenly change.

"Tell me what happened. Or, at least, tell me what you can."

There was no shortcut for the confession, and I knew the best way out was through.

"I didn't get married in Vegas," I said, rubbing my closed eyes with the tips of my fingers until my vision sparked like fireworks. "This time."

Kale laughed, a deep sound that didn't make it out of the back of his throat.

"I went to Vegas with someone from college right before we graduated. We had too much to drink, and we got married."

"I can't believe you never told me that," Kale said, mouth twisted in an amused, if not somewhat hurt, half-smile.

"I didn't know until it came up with the co-op board." I dropped my hands into my lap with a tired groan.

"Ohhhh. That makes a lot more sense." Kale gave my knees a gentle rub, trailing his fingers down my calves.

"Sarah tracked him down and served him—"

He interrupted, "Him?"

"Him."

That earned me a look that gave every indication he planned to circle back to that tidbit of information at a later date.

"Anyway. Tracked him down and he called me up, wanting to get together and talk."

"Re-live some old times?" Kale chuckled.

"We didn't have old times. It wasn't like that for us."

"That's the part you don't want to talk about?" he hedged.

I nodded.

"You don't have to," he said.

"I know. So...I went out to L.A. We had to talk about some of the things I don't want to talk to you about, and we ended up in Vegas."

"Good thing you were already married, it sounds like."

He didn't know how true that was, because things could have gone very differently between Dalton and me if we hadn't been. But everything before us felt messy and impossible to untangle. I didn't think a divorce would fix any of it, but at least it would sever the knot of whatever chaos followed behind us. Maybe we could both finally leave it all behind.

"Dalton and I have history, that's true. And it's hard to get away from. We tried and failed."

"And now you're back home," he concluded.

"Now I'm home and once he sends Sarah the filing, I can stop looking in the rearview."

"And the penthouse is yours."

I swung my legs off his lap, folding myself in half and bracing my forearms against the tops of my thighs. "I hope so."

If I had done all of this to not end up with the penthouse, I didn't think I'd be able to find the value in any of it. Digging up the past for nothing would have been a cruel joke for the both of us.

"You look like there's more," he said, scooting closer and stretching his arm around my shoulder. I leaned against him with a tired groan, letting my eyes close.

Even though Dalton and I had fallen into an hours-long sex coma after we hooked up, I hadn't gotten a good night's sleep since I'd found out about the marriage. I was an insomniac on the best of nights, and the concern about the penthouse and the interview process hadn't helped at all. Still, I was nothing like Dalton.

The memory of his restaurant panic attack was fresh in my mind, and the way his back heaved against my hand as he struggled for breath in the alley as clear in my head as Kale beside me on the couch.

"It's just complicated," I said.

"Do you like him?" He scoffed, giving me a shove onto his lap and tucking a throw pillow beneath my head.

I grunted, tucking into his lap and curling my legs so I fit beside him on the couch.

"Doesn't matter," I said. "We're getting divorced."

"So you said.

I craned my neck to stretch it, and Kale huffed, reaching around the front of me and popping open the buttons on my shirt.

"I'm fine like this," I told him with a yawn.

"I bet you are." He tugged the collar of my shirt down and I didn't have to open my eyes to know he's caught sight of the trail of hickeys Dalton had left on me. "Are you also fourteen?"

"Shut up." I yanked my shirt out of his hand, but didn't bother trying to cover myself back up.

"You can't hide those from Ford and the rest of them," he said gently.

"I know."

"They're going to ask questions."

I flipped onto my back and glared up at him. "They can ask all they want, but they're not entitled to answers about my private life."

"Our lives have never been personal, Beamer."

Wasn't that the fucking truth.

"Kale, I'm tired." I forced myself off the couch, leaving the pillow on his lap.

"I was trying to let you sleep."

"You were fishing."

He rolled his eyes and flung the pillow onto the couch, standing up and smoothing out the wrinkles on the front of his slacks. "I fish because I care."

"You fish because you're nosy." I dismissed him with a flick of my wrist.

"You're no fun when you're a brat," he grumbled, reluctantly turning and heading toward the door. His comment made me think of Dalton, as if he wasn't already taking up enough space in my mind.

"I'll talk to you tomorrow," I said. Then I gave him the finger and left him to see himself out.

Even though I knew he would leave, I closed my bedroom door behind me, resting against the sturdy wood until it didn't feel like my heart was going to skitter out of my chest. I'd left my bag in the living room so I didn't have my laptop, my phone, or anything remotely entertaining. That was probably for the better, because the more access I had to Dalton, the more likely I was to do or say something more regrettable than I already had.

Stripping out of my clothes, I tossed them all into the hamper and went into the bathroom.

For as excited I was about the prospect of relocating to the penthouse, I loved the bathroom in my current apartment. It was huge and white, sleek slabs of marble and brushed gold finishings with black accents. The shower had sprays coming out of the walls and a massive soaking tub flanked the back wall behind a glass divider so I could go from spray to submerged without tracking water all over the floor.

The space was a little sanctuary that I'd curated over my years there, but bigger was better and I'd get a chance to make the penthouse mine over time as well. And that bathroom had a view of Central Park that my present place hadn't ever dared to dream about.

The future would be better than the past, better than the present.

Or that was the hope I repeated to myself in the mirror, tracing my finger over the outline of Dalton's mouth and teeth as I recalled his journey from my neck to my shoulder and the over the swell of my pec. His lips had burned; his tongue drove me mad. The possession in every nip and lick had spoken of things he had no right to give voice to, so maybe that was why he hadn't. He used his body to say things we should never say out loud.

And that had probably been worse because there was nothing

to get lost in translation when we talked that way. The chemistry between us was undeniable, and that had nothing to do with Gen and even less to do with Vegas. Dalton was a handsome and accomplished man, but more than that, he was a dominant man. I was some of those things, but not all, and the way it was so fucking easy to serve him…

I ordered him food. I made him his coffee. I offered my body to him when I had nothing left to give, and when it had been too much for him, I took it all back without complaint.

That was my life, though.

Carter Royce IV, the ever-obedient servant of everyone I'd ever met, save for myself. And that was the crux of it, I thought. Dalton saw *me*. He saw through to the core of me, and without any fault or judgement, he saw me and he knew me. But in the wake of that exposure, I'd finally realized what a fucking curse it was to be known.

WHEN I STUMBLED BACK INTO MY HOUSE, THE FIRST THING I SAW WAS the stupid divorce papers sitting on the kitchen island. Ivey was probably long gone—and good riddance for that—but I owed him the papers either way. But it was Sunday and it was late, and I would deal with scanning them to his attorney first thing Monday.

The second thing I saw was a can of spray cheese sitting on my coffee table next to a bottle of Nolet gin.

Archie had been here, and I tried to remember when he'd gotten such unrestricted access to all of our lives. He'd probably had it for years, and it just never bothered me until I had something to hide. Hell, we'd shown up at his house unannounced during his split with Owen, and I lost count of the times we'd all stumbled into Rob's back yard to drink and swim without asking permission.

It was the way of our friendship, and even if it felt like a curse in that moment, I knew it was a gift. I had people in my corner always. People who cared about me and wanted the best for me, even if they went about it in unusual ways sometimes. We'd never been cut from the same cloth as everyone else. The way we loved each other shouldn't be an exception to that very exceptional rule.

That didn't change the fact that I had confessions to make, whether I wanted to or not. I knew whatever had just happened with Ivey wasn't something I could shake off and get past before tomorrow, when they'd all be banging my door down for answers. It didn't have anything to do with being married to Ivey or whatever feelings he'd churned up inside of me back in college. No, it had everything to do with the way he made me feel *now*.

It had to do with the way he catered to me when we were together, the way he soothed me through a panic attack and tried to fix it. It had to do with the way his mouth felt against mine, like soft velvet, and the way it felt to be inside of him, absolute heaven. Those minutes I'd been inside of him, the night I'd spent wrapped around him, those were some of the best moments that I could remember. The way my brain quieted down and my heart listened to everything he had to say, even when words weren't spoken. Being with Ivey was like being recognized, but not just because of my face or my name. Ivey knew me down to my soul, and that was equal parts terrifying and exhilarating.

Ivey wasn't a dream I could wake up from, but he wasn't within reach either.

The worst part was, I knew I'd acted poorly after we had sex. The rope marks around his wrist *had* made me jealous, even when I had no right to have those specific feelings. It wasn't like he and I had met up with the plan to hook up and we definitely weren't dating each other. The sex never should have happened because it meant nothing and everything all at the same time.

How would I have even been able to articulate any of that for him? He lived on the opposite end of the country and that wasn't even remotely beneficial for me if we agreed to keep hooking up. I knew we both had obscene amounts of money, but flying from coast to coast for dick was beyond the realm of acceptability, even for me.

So what was the point of telling him I had some kind of feelings for him? I didn't even know what they were, but I knew no good would come from them. Leaving him again was the best choice I could have made for the both of us. He'd believe that sooner or later…

And so would I.

That didn't change the fact that I already missed the annoying way he poked and teased me to get what he wanted, the way he called me Fox when he felt like I wasn't listening or when he wanted to prove a point. It didn't change the fact he'd always be Ivey to me now. Even if we never talked or saw each other again.

There was no point in stewing over it.

Or hiding it.

But before I could make sense of which way was up, I was asleep, twisted against the arm of the couch like a pretzel.

I woke with a start a few hours later, the sun glaring through the windows and indicating it was yet another day. Tired and disoriented, I fished my phone out of my pocket to check the time. It was nearly six, which meant my friends would be up, getting ready for work. Most likely drinking coffee, reading the paper, all mundane things that felt foreign to me in that moment.

Swiping across my screen, I didn't even bother reading the text messages that had come through after I put my phone on silent the day before. I searched out Archie's contact and he answered on the second ring.

"You must be home," he said, voice tinted with amusement. I suspected he'd been behind the cheese spray, and I was right.

"I'm home," I confirmed, the can of spray cheese the only thing standing between me and the edge of another panic attack. Something about the ridiculousness of it kept my breathing at a reasonable pace.

"It's just barely Monday. I didn't expect to hear from you until closer to midnight."

"I just woke up." I leaned forward and grabbed the gin, twisting off the cap as I settled back into a more comfortable position on the couch. I knew six a.m. wasn't an acceptable time to drink gin, but it was Nolet and the coffee wasn't within reach.

"Are you calling because you want to talk?" he asked.

"I don't want to. But if you and Barclay come over, I probably will anyway, " I said, taking a swig straight out of the bottle. It was probably the best I'd ever had, all saffron and citrus as it washed around my mouth. "Also, this is ridiculously good gin."

"I'll ignore the fact you're drinking gin before lunch and instead tell you that it better be for seven hundred dollars a bottle."

I choked, almost spitting what I would have estimated to be eighty-four dollars' worth of gin all over my lap.

"Jesus, Archie. That feels extreme."

"Desperate times and all that," he said dismissively.

"Was I that obvious?" I asked.

"More than."

I set the bottle of gin on the table and let my stare wander back to the papers on the kitchen island. "So, are you coming?"

"Just me and Barclay?" he asked.

I wasn't trying to draw lines or keep any more secrets, but I didn't think I could handle spilling the truth to all four of them at once.

"For now," I said.

Archie made a curious sound, but agreed. "I'll round him up. We'll be there shortly."

"Alright. I'll see you then."

After ending the call, I threw the phone onto the couch and groaned up at the ceiling as if it would help.

I didn't know what to say to the two of them, let alone the rest. Even though I'd managed a lot of my feelings in therapy, sharing the truth of what had gone down between Gen and me wasn't something I'd ever felt comfortable doing. With Ivey, I never had to because it had happened to him too. He understood without words what I'd been going through, and even though we'd just talked about it...

It had all been vague half-sentences, and I supposed...

I supposed that should be enough for Archie and Barclay too.

"Fuck it." I shoved myself up from the couch and went into my bedroom. I'd take a shower, wash Vegas off of me, and start it all with a clean slate.

But as I rustled up the fabric of my shirt to deal with the buttons, I was assaulted by whiffs of Ivey's cologne, the smell of his skin. I knew it would be the last of him and there was no point in holding onto it. No point in asking for more.

Shaking it off, I balled the shirt up, but fell short of throwing it into the hamper. I tossed it across the foot of my bed, along with my slacks. With some semblance of decency, I got my underwear and socks into the hamper, then locked myself in the bathroom in a shower so hot it should have scalded off every part of my skin that Ivey had touched.

I knew when I got out, Barclay and Archie would be waiting for me. I knew I'd left the divorce papers on the counter, so if they hadn't seen them the first time, they'd find them now.

"It's okay," I promised myself.

There wasn't anything to be ashamed of. Genevieve was something that had happened to me, not something I'd done to myself. I repeated the mantras my first therapist had offered me until I believed them. Then when I had the slightest grasp on the truth, I turned off the spray.

I took my time drying off, lingering in front of the mirror, whispering to my reflection about the things I allowed myself and the things I deserved. And when I was as dry as I'd ever been, I stepped into a pair of black lounge pants, then went in search of Archie and Barclay.

"Are you enjoying my gin?" I asked, finding them both on my couch, half-drank glasses of clear liquid in hand. "Thought it was too early for all that."

"Have I ever told you about Rob's kitchen whiskey?" Archie asked, raising his glass in what I assumed was meant to be a greeting. He continued before I could answer, "It's quieter, he says, but I think it's more expensive."

"Of course it is," Barclay agreed.

"I like it better than the hooch in his library."

"The hooch," I mused, wondering how Rob would react

hearing his precious five-hundred dollar whiskey being talked about with such little concern.

"Rob's kitchen whiskey, your coffee table gin," he said.

"It's on the table because you put it there." I grabbed my phone and the bottle before he could move to refill his glass. "Let's call it patio gin."

The air in L.A. wasn't nearly as stifling as the heat of Las Vegas, and sitting on my back patio, I took what felt like the first full breath of air I'd had in days. Archie and Barclay followed close behind, and Barclay dropped the divorce paperwork onto my lap before sitting across from me.

"Morning gin," he murmured.

"Well. Let me get to it, I guess." I cleared my throat. There was only one easy way to admit the truth, and it was a lot like the way I preferred to fuck, fast and hard. "In college, I was in an abusive relationship and when that ended, I went to Vegas with a friend of mine and we accidentally got married. And now we need to get divorced. So, that's what I've been dealing with the past few days."

Archie spit a hundred dollars of gin all over his shoes.

Barclay just sighed. "I'd hardly call Royce a friend," he finally said.

"I appreciate that was your takeaway from the whole confession." I dared a glance to my right, only to find him studying me with a deep groove of concern knit together between his eyebrows.

"What, uhm..." Archie set his glass down and toed off his shoes, kicking them toward the house. "What part of that do you consider to be the most offensive?"

"None of its offensive," Barclay was quick to correct.

I held up a hand to wave him off. I appreciated the unwavering way he came to my defense, but I understood the intent of Archie's question.

"It's fine," I assured him, turning toward Archie and holding up the paperwork. "I didn't know I was married until the night I got served."

He held his hand out and I passed the papers off to him.

"So, I wasn't terribly embarrassed about that. I don't think I'd be the first person to get too drunk to remember getting married in Vegas."

"Far from it," Barclay said.

His expression had softened, turning reassuring in its tenderness. I was so thankful for him and his kindness.

"I'm sorry I didn't tell you before," I said.

He shook his head. "You're allowed your secrets."

"I was ashamed." I dragged my tongue across the front of my teeth while Archie scanned the papers. "Because she was a woman, you know. And not only had I chased after her for so long, but…"

"No one talks about men who are abused," Archie said. He tossed the paperwork back onto the table and picked up his gin again. "It makes sense you wouldn't want people to know that part."

"You didn't know what she was like," Barclay reminded me. "And it wasn't like you and Royce were friends before…"

"Who is Royce?" Archie asked, looking between us.

I frowned, already hating him being anything besides Ivey.

"Her name was Genevieve, and before she…" I cleared my throat, grabbing Barclay's glass and taking a hearty swallow of gin. "Before she abused me, she abused him. When it happened, or… when it got bad, I didn't know where else to go. I didn't know who would understand."

"Except for him," Barclay said softly.

"I didn't even have to explain it. He just knew." Without thinking, I pressed my fingers against the spot on my cheek where her hit had cut my face open. There wasn't a scar, at least not a physical one. "Took me out of town, drinking to forget and all that. We weren't even friends. I'd never even thought about him sexually before. Or any man for that matter."

"You don't have to do this," Archie interrupted, but I frowned, shaking my head.

"Yes, I do."

He leaned back in his seat, waiting.

"We obviously drank too much," I said.

Barclay chuckled, breaking some of the tension, which I was thankful for. My palms were sweaty from my nerves and I rubbed them dry on my thighs, thinking about Ivey and the casual way he smeared his spilled whiskey over that expensive wool.

"Drank too much, hooked up, got married." I chewed the inside of my cheek, stare landing once again on the divorce papers. "I didn't know we'd gotten married, though. And the next day I woke up and freaked out. Not about him, but about the fact he knew about her. And what that meant for me. So I wrote him a shitty apology, went back to school, and never talked to him again."

"Until." Archie tapped his fingers on the cover page.

"Until. And then I wanted to apologize for all that shit, and we talked and he came out here."

"And you went to Vegas again," Archie said.

"Got drunk again. Hooked up again."

"Good thing you were already married," Barclay said with a low laugh. "You're worth more money now. Getting married at this age would be a horrible decision."

"Right, well." I shrugged. "Do either of you have a pen?"

Archie reached into his pocket and produced a Montblanc that we'd gotten him two years before on his birthday. I looked at it and he looked at it, then his cheeks flushed.

"You sentimental shit," I teased.

Pulling the papers toward me, I flipped to the last page, trying to not look at the looping scrawl of Ivey's signature dissolving the union we never even knew we'd had.

"The past is the past," I said. "I'll tell Rob and Flynn about it, but I don't want to talk about it anymore. It's not a part of who I am anymore. Okay?"

"Whatever you need," Barclay said. "We'll support you."

I uncapped Archie's pen and lifted my hand to sign, but Ivey's name flashing across my screen stopped me in my tracks.

Archie and Barclay both craned their necks to check the caller ID, but I knew neither of them would recognize the secret endearment.

"Who is calling this early?" Archie asked.

"His husband," Barclay answered before I could.

"Carter Royce?"

"The fourth," he said. "IV…Ivey."

"Oh, you asshole." Archie reached over and smacked me across my forehead. "Now who's the sentimental bastard?"

With a loud exhale, I answered the call, cradling the phone against my face.

"I know I owe you my signature," I said, not bothering with niceties. "I was about to sign it and send it back to Sarah before I went to work."

"Right." Ivey sounded as tired as I felt, and maybe a little nervous too, which wasn't like him at all. "Uhm, about that…can you…maybe not do that yet?"

I WAS LEGITIMATELY CONCERNED ABOUT WEARING A HOLE IN MY FLOOR, but after pacing for six hours, the tile didn't show any signs of wavering under my weight.

A sharp knock on the door startled me, even though I'd been expecting it, and I practically ran to get it open before Dalton could change his mind and catch a flight back home.

"Thank you," I said, yanking the door open.

His shoulders heaved with a deep breath, and he gave me a jerky nod. No hello, no you're welcome.

Not that I deserved one.

I'd asked something of him I had no right asking.

"You can call it my last apology," he muttered, heading inside with a black leather garment bag slung over his shoulder and a very tired look on his face. His shoulders heaved toward his ears as he breathed, and I worried he was coming up on another panic attack.

"You smell like gin." I closed the door behind him.

"Considering I was telling two of my closest friends about the chain of events that led to our wedding, I think that's allowed." He pursed his lips, tense. I realized panic was not the emotion he'd been battling.

"Well." I took a step toward him, holding out my hand. "Do you want me to take your bag?"

"I'm not sure I'm staying." Dalton shifted his weight, looking around my apartment. I would love to have been a fly on the wall inside his head, if not in that moment, at least for a minute on the flight to New York or when I'd called him earlier in the day. Before the goddamn sunrise had even reached California. "Tell me again what you said on the phone."

"Did you want to at least sit?" I asked, gesturing toward the couch.

He frowned at the couch. "Not yet."

"That's fair." I raked my fingers through my hair, suddenly aware of the fact Dalton wasn't just in New York, but he was in the middle of my apartment. And so soon after we'd…after he'd…

"Tell me again, Ivey."

I relayed the series of events in my own head, still in a state of shock over how quickly they'd taken a turn.

"I found out about our marriage because I had applied to a co-op board for a penthouse on the Upper East Side—"

He cut me off. "I remember that part."

"God, you're in a mood."

"I'm tired," he snapped.

"I offered you a place to sit." I gestured again at the couch, annoyed that he was making this into more of a problem than it needed to be. I would sooner walk away from the penthouse of my dreams than deal with him treating me like shit for weeks.

"Not that kind of tired," he said under his breath, the tension leaking out of him as his shoulders sagged.

"The short version of the story," I said, "is that we can't get divorced until I sign the deal on the penthouse. I need you to pretend to be my husband."

The update had come as much of a shock to me as it had to him, I was sure. After splitting up in Vegas, I'd fallen asleep at home only to be woken abruptly Monday morning by a call from the co-op board. My delirious exhaustion and jetlag had stopped me from promising them the marriage was on the verge of being annulled before they'd been able to drop their own bomb on me.

"It's just customary for us to also meet with your partner," they told me. "It's a huge bonus for your application that you're married. When can we set up an interview with the both of you?"

I'd stammered through a lie that my husband traveled for work and that was why I'd been handling all of the paperwork and the application. As far as I could tell, they bought the story, but I owed them a call back with a time and date where they could sit down at meet my husband.

Dalton Fox.

I repeated it all back to him, feeling incredibly small under the weight of his weary scrutiny.

He blinked slowly, rubbing his cheek with the edge of his middle finger. Then as if he'd talked himself into staying, his other arm slid down and he extended the garment bag in my direction. I snatched it before he could take it back, clutching it to my chest like a security blanket.

"Are there rules?" he asked.

"I'll make sure you know everything you need to know before you talk to the board," I promised.

Dalton licked his lips, eyes flickering toward the ceiling on a long exhale.

"I meant between us," he rasped, that dark stare of his landing back on my face. The exhaustion he'd been wearing like a suit of armor fell away, revealing the man who'd very recently taken me apart and put me back together, one thrust of his hips at a time.

"How so?" I croaked.

"Are we sleeping together again?"

"Well." I rubbed my chest, eye squinting as I angled my face toward the short hallway to my right. "Technically, yes. There's only one bed."

"I didn't mean technically, but that would have been useful information to have before I agreed to this idea of yours."

"Would it have changed your answer?" I asked. "I can sleep on the couch if it's such a problem."

"It doesn't matter." Dalton shook his head and groaned, mouth twisting into a deep frown.

Again.

"Will you please let me show you the place? Then you can shower and lie down awhile. We can talk about this tomorrow or later. Whenever."

"Fine."

Every one of Dalton's footsteps that grew louder and closer behind me as we went toward the bedroom sounded like a small victory that I'd never be able to properly celebrate. I hung his garment bag in the closet, then flipped on the lights for the en suite.

"Towels are under the sink," I said. "The nozzles are pretty self-explanatory. The buttons have pictures."

Dalton gave my bedroom as much of a onceover as he'd given my living room, then he sat down on the edge of the bed. I expected him to toe off his shoes, but he just inhaled another long breath and braced himself on his hands, looking up at the ceiling. His eyelashes were so long I could see them flutter every time he blinked.

The urge to get on my knees for him was greater than it ever had been, and that couldn't have come at a worse time. Dalton was doing me a huge favor and if he wanted to pretend it was something he owed me for leaving Vegas on a different flight, then I wasn't about to tell him otherwise. But I also didn't need to tell him that it was somewhat probable, if not very likely, that I'd started to develop feelings for him beyond the ones in our shared history.

"Can I..." I stopped, biting my tongue before another word made its way out of my mouth.

"Can you what?" he asked without looking down.

I wanted to climb onto his lap and lick his throat.

"Nothing," I muttered, staring at his feet.

"Can you what, Ivey?" he asked again, the question now punctuated with a demanding inflection that didn't offer a man like me room do anything other than comply.

But even with that in my head, I knew I couldn't say the words…at least, not in the way they'd formed in my head. That kind of ask came after a conversation and an agreement…an understanding, of which Dalton and I didn't have. It wasn't even really my place to initiate or drive, though that was more out of my own personal preference than any social expectation.

Submissive males were not meek and mild.

Dalton dropped his chin against his chest, eyeing me carefully as I tried to overthink my way to an answer that wouldn't send him back to L.A. on the first flight he could charter.

"I was going to ask if there was anything I could to do help you."

His response came achingly quick. "No, you weren't."

"I was," I half-lied, taking a step back so I could use the wall for support.

"You can start the shower for me," Dalton said.

A sharp flare of arousal sparked in my belly, and I covered my stomach with my hand, like he would somehow be able to see it. Whatever was happening between us…it was new. Though, I supposed everything between us was technically new, this was a different kind of new. This was uncharted, but not entirely unwelcome.

If not ill-advised.

"Okay," I rasped, slinking into the bathroom.

I was afraid if I lifted my shoulder from the wall that I would fall over on the spot, or worse, go straight to my knees and say something *really* embarrassing. The weight of Dalton's stare was a tangible thing, pressing hard against my spine, right between my shoulders, until I was past the wall and out of his line of sight.

Gasping for breath, I turned on the shower with one hand and pressed the heel of my other palm against the base of my cock.

Sometimes I wondered if there was something truly wrong

with me, and not in an un-therapized PTSD kind of way. Sexual arousal over being told what to do couldn't be a normal thing. Getting hard from being handled like a toy…that…

Surely, that had to fall outside of the realm of acceptability.

I'd simply gotten lucky and stumbled into a friend group of people who had the same kind of trauma response as me, or something. That would have to explain it because what else was there?

I waited in the bathroom for him to join me, but the corner had already started to steam and there was no sign of Dalton. With a final press against the base of my shaft, I forced myself back into the bedroom, finding him where I'd left him, sprawled across the edge of my bed like it was his.

There was that heavy stare again, that scrutiny laced with…

Something different.

"Did you get out a towel?" he asked.

"They're under the sink," I said. I know I'd already told him that. He must have heard me.

"So you said." Dalton sat up a little straighter, shoulders lifting with a silent breath. "That wasn't what I asked."

I shifted my weight, bringing my hands together in front of me. My fingers, without thought, tangled together, twisting nervously against my palms. I knew what was happening, but I didn't know why it was happening. Or I maybe it was what I wanted to be happening, and I was making something out of nothing. I had a habit of doing that sometimes…making something out of nothing.

This didn't feel like nothing.

After I didn't respond, Dalton asked me, very softly, "Do you want me to stop, Ivey?"

I shook my head, the movement barely perceptible.

"If I was married, there are things I would expect from my husband," he said. "Just like there are things you'd expect from yours, right?"

"Right," I whispered.

"And if you want your housing board to buy into this act, we should make sure we're convincing. Right? That we're really playing the part."

My body wasn't reacting like this was a game, but what was a scene if not a game? The rules were the same. It was all pretend whether it was here or at the club or with someone else. Nobody lived like this all the time, even though sometimes I dreamed about that kind of life. I knew it wasn't a real thing for me to work for. Even friends of mine who were in long-term kinky relationships, the lines of their roles bled over time and they settled into domesticity and companionship.

It all just became a game. The roles were natural, but everything was temporary.

"Right?" he repeated.

I must have taken too long to answer.

My balls *ached*.

"Right," I agreed. "Yes."

"So, did you get out a towel for me? Or did you need more time?"

I fought against my eyes, both of them desperate to roll back in my head for how aroused the line of questioning was making me.

"More time," I croaked.

Dalton watched me expectantly until I realized what he'd meant for me to do. Cursing under my breath, I went back into the bathroom and pulled a towel out from the cabinet under the sink. It was soft and white, and I hung it carefully on the wall rack by the showerhead. I smoothed my hands down the rich terrycloth like it could wrinkle if I wasn't careful with it.

"You're an idiot," I whispered to myself, aroused and angry all at the same time.

But my feet carried me back to the bedroom anyway, back to Dalton.

"I hung a towel out for you..." I trailed off, because the honorific was on the tip of my tongue and we both knew it.

He didn't prompt me for it, and I didn't know if that was a courtesy to me or to him. This had to be doing something for him too, right? There wasn't a man who would make these demands if it didn't also make him hard. He'd told me he expected things of his husband. These had to be the things. This had to be it.

"Good…" He also trailed off, tapping his toes against the floor until I dragged my stare from his face to his feet. "Help me with my shoes."

The ask was designed to humiliate, but going to my knees had always come as easily as breathing. Closing the space between us was the hard part, but Dalton was like a magnetic pole and before my brain had even thought to take a step, I was on my knees at his feet. When I landed, he sucked in a sharp breath and I looked up at him, my own lungs unable to get themselves full.

Dalton's nostrils flared, and he curled his hands around the edge of the mattress, almost like he was holding himself back. I didn't want him to hold back. Men who held back were the problem. Men who held back were the ones who made sure this couldn't ever be more than a temporary game of pretend.

He tapped his toes again and I cleared my throat, remembering I had a task to complete. I plucked at the laces of his sneakers, both of which were pristinely clean like they'd never been worn before. Not that it would have mattered if they had been. It was the act. It was all in the act of service, and I pulled one of his feet free and then the other.

"Socks also?" I asked, not able to look up at him.

"Yes."

Peeling Dalton's white socks off, I tucked them into his now empty shoes, then rocked back onto my heels and waited for the next instruction.

"I wish you could see yourself."

It took every ounce of control I possessed to not throw myself on top of Ivey and take him down to the ground. The way I wanted to rut against him, tear him apart with my hands and my teeth, fuck him until he cried and begged for more and less and all of it at the same time.

Never in my life, never in my fucking life had I met a man who submitted as naturally as Ivey, and… fuck.

Fuck.

Because there was no future in anything for us and this wasn't just temporary, it was also pretend. But the erection that had taken root between his legs was very real, as were my own urges to bury my cock so deep inside of him that I'd never be able to get out. He kept his eyes downcast and I stood up, the bulge between my legs coming level with his face. If only he would look up. If only he could see.

"Ivey."

He looked up, chest almost going concave with the way the air rushed out of his lungs. His chin quivered, a shiver that ran down his shoulders and his arms. His fingers were splayed against his thighs, trembling and grasping. My heart beat in my eyes, interrupting the flow of my breath, my thought.

"Now the rest," I said, praying for restraint, for control.

Those shaking hands of his came to my belt. His wrists brushed against my erection, and I ground my molars together to swallow back the groan his touch deserved. I needed to keep my shit together, at least until I got into the shower. This penthouse thing was important to him and playing this part for him felt like some kind of penance.

Ivey had been there for me when I needed someone the most, and I hadn't treated him fairly. And when he'd come back into my life, I'd still treated him less than he deserved. Coming to New York for a few weeks and getting him through this interview process so he could have the life he wanted most…it was an easy thing. It was the least of what he deserved from me. But this…this wasn't part of that ruse, and it could ruin everything if we let it. Because control and choice were dangerous things. We both knew that far too well.

The crisp crack of my leather belt pulling from the loops on my pants brought me back to the present, back to Ivey's bedroom. He was still at my feet, my belt now in hand. We both stared down at it, knowing and wanting. The bruises around his wrist were fading and the way I wanted to give him new ones, all over his body. Lasting marks so anyone after me would know I'd been there.

"Take off your shirt," I rasped, that familiar tangle of confused possession flaring up again.

Ivey dropped my belt and reached behind him, rucking up his shirt before pulling it over his head and off. The chain of bruises I'd sucked into his neck and shoulder were still there, darker than they had been the night before and I wanted to bite each and every one of them. I wanted them to darken and hurt, so *he* would also remember.

"What are you doing to me?" I asked, more to myself than him.

"I don't want to stop."

Of course he didn't. Neither did I.

"My pants, then," I said. "Underwear too."

Ivey made quick work of my fly, and I used his shoulder for

balance to step out of my pants after they'd fallen down my legs. When I was there in my underwear, his posture wavered like he was dizzy with arousal. His body swayed forward, and somehow I just knew what he wanted.

"You can do it," I whispered. "You won't get in trouble."

God, the thought of Ivey being in trouble, though. The promise of him deserving a punishment?

He let loose a quiet whimper and then buried his face into my groin, shoving his nose as close to my balls as my underwear would allow. With his hands still against his thighs and his face burning hot against me, Ivey breathed me in. Over and over, his body rocking forward. With every breath, more of his weight leaned into me, and I threaded my fingers into his blond hair to steady him.

This was why I'd left Vegas early, because not only did he stoke the flames of unbridled arousal that I'd never felt for anyone who *wasn't* him, he also drew out the darkest and most controlling parts of my dominance. Ivey made me nearly feral, and I knew enough about myself to know how dangerous that could be. My life, after Gen at least, had been built around moderation and control. Sure, I dabbled and played. I dated. I even had serious relationships, but it wasn't ever as entwined as this.

I didn't know how something that was just pretend could feel so very fucking real.

"That's enough." I tugged his head back and he blinked up at me, dark pupils obscuring the gorgeous blue of his eyes. His cheeks were red, his lips moist and parted, silently asking for more.

Asking for me.

"Get on with it, Ivey."

He blinked quickly, like he'd forgotten himself.

So had I.

He curled his fingers around the waistband of my underwear and gently pulled them down, careful to not snap or tug against my dick. Then they were discarded alongside my pants, and I took my own shirt off because the idea of him getting up off his knees felt like the worst thing that could happen to either of us in that moment.

"You look like you have something to say."

He licked his lips, almost shaking his head no before he stopped himself. My fingers were still in his hair, and I softened my hold. I wanted him to know I saw the redirect and I approved of it. But as the strands of his hair slipped out of my grip, he whimpered like it had been a loss.

"I want to suck you," he whispered, imploring me through the fan of his lashes. "Please, let me suck you."

"I'm really tired, Ivey. I wanted to shower and take a nap before dinner."

It was a partial truth. I was *very* tired, but I was also more aroused than I'd ever been and short of an act of God zapping us both up to the heavens, there was no way that my cock was not going to end up in his mouth.

"I'll be quick," he promised.

"You better be—"

I didn't remember if I had more to say, but his mouth was around me so fast that any other words and thoughts were raptured right out of me.

Ivey's mouth was hot and wet, and he sucked me slowly. God, he sucked me slow like he was savoring every inch of skin that dragged across his tongue. He made noises of approval when he choked around the thickest parts of my shaft, and I held on to his hair for dear life. I didn't want to direct him, at least not yet. It was something like an honor to give him the space to treat my cock in the way he wanted, without my direction or suggestion. Because Ivey sucked me like my cum was a thousand dollar dessert that he wanted to enjoy for the rest of the night.

More sounds, hums in the back of his throat that shot straight up my spine, sending me cross-eyed. I lost my feet, falling back onto the edge of the bed. Ivey chased after me, keeping as much of my dick in his mouth as he could manage and then swallowing the rest back down once I settled. He bobbed up and down my length with hollowed cheeks and tear-filled eyes.

"Stop." I did give a soft pull to his hair, with half my shaft in his mouth.

He went still, lips spread wide and spit trailing down his chin. My dick shined under the light of his bedroom. He'd made me so hard and so wet. I traced my thumb back and forth across his cheekbone, just below his lashes. His eyes were filled to the brim with unshed tears, and I wanted them.

Lifting my hips, I pushed another inch of my cock toward the back of his throat. He groaned, almost gagging but not quite. So I gave him another inch and he spasmed around me, blinking quickly until the dam broke. Tears slicked down his cheeks and I caught them against the pad of my thumb, smearing them into his skin before bringing my hand to my mouth. He watched every move, and I sucked my thumb into my mouth, relishing the taste of his tears against my tongue.

"Okay," I managed to tell him. "As you were."

His eyes rolled back in his head and he took the last few inches of my dick into his mouth. Ivey sucked and sucked, using the flat of his tongue against the underside of my shaft, around the sensitive and swollen flared tip. He muttered something that I couldn't quite hear, but didn't stop.

I knew I'd told him to be quick, but he felt so fucking amazing. He sucked my cock like he'd been born knowing how to do it, like his mouth had been made for my dick. I realized that I'd never stood a chance against him. He hadn't been this good when we were in college, but it wasn't all skill. It was just...*him*.

And that was what finally brought around my orgasm.

It was Ivey with my cock in his mouth again, and Ivey on his knees for me. It was the desperate and pleased sounds that left the back of his throat when he choked around me and the way he pushed his head against my hand if I wasn't holding his hair tight enough. It was this powerful and rich and sometimes cocky man doing what he was told, waiting and asking before taking.

"Can I come in your mouth?" I asked.

I was gone for him, but not for courtesy. There were a lot of things we hadn't talked about and there was definitely a conversation to be had. But first…

He nodded and swallowed me down to the hilt, using his throat and his tongue to coax my release into his mouth. The orgasm shattered me, slamming into me with as much force as it had in Vegas, and I crumpled forward, bending in half over him as my cock spurted cum onto the back of his tongue.

Ivey whined and wiggled, sucking and licking until I pulled him off. Trails of spit connected his mouth to my cock and he looked like he was already so far off into subspace that he'd never return. Staring at him, I realized how heavy I was breathing. The rise and fall of my chest, the loud gasps of my own breath. In the blink of an eye, I was back in the present, back in my body. Everything closed in around me, bright lights and sharp noises—and it wasn't a panic attack.

It was just reality.

Unable to look at him another second, I closed my eyes, holding his head at what surely was a miserable angle. But I needed to catch my breath. I needed to get back to earth.

To him.

"Thank you," he whispered, like I'd done him a favor.

It was those two words that told me how deep his submission ran. Those two words that let me know how much trouble I was already in because wasn't that what I'd always wanted? Wasn't he the kind of man I'd spent my whole adult life chasing after? Through the whole ordeal, he'd never even touched himself. He hadn't touched me because I hadn't told him he could.

He was simply there on his knees, between my legs, still dressed. With swollen lips and hooded eyes, and a cock that I knew had to be hurting.

"Your shower is ready," he murmured, and I remembered how this whole thing had started. "It won't run cold. Don't worry."

I pried my fingers out of his hair, smoothing the soft waves flat.

His eyes closed and he leaned into my hand like he was a cat being pet.

"Do you want to come?" I asked.

"To the shower?"

"No." I pressed my foot between his legs, the heat of his cock and balls scalding, even through two layers of fabric. "Do you want to *come*?"

He blinked slowly, licking his lips like the thought hadn't even occurred to him. Then we both looked down at the bulge between his legs, at my toes against his ball sac.

"I want you to get your shower," he rasped, shoulders sagging. His words were barely louder than a whisper. "And your nap."

"That wasn't what I asked."

"Yes." Ivey gave a weak nod. "I'd like to come."

I used the ball of my foot to apply pressure to his balls, drawing a sharp gasp from the back of his throat. "Make yourself come then."

He had his pants open faster than he'd gotten through mine, and Ivey beat his dick so fast and hard, I couldn't even make out the outline of his fingers. It took less than two minutes for him to come, white jets of cum spouting across his fingers. He cried out, dropping his forehead against my knee as his body was overtaken with violent spasms.

His arm finally slowed, his breathing returned to normal, and he rocked back on his heels, giving me a slow and thankful nod. He didn't have to say it. I could see it in his face, in the shape of his muscles and the way he held himself before me. I chewed the inside of my cheek between my molars, a stab of pain to remind me that this was only temporary.

It didn't matter everything about *him* was perfect.

Because everything about *us* was so fucked.

DALTON WAS A FURNACE, WITH ONE OF HIS ARMS FLUNG PROTECTIVELY across my chest and our ankle bones brushing together at the other end of the bed. His breath came at a slow and steady pace, but I knew my alarm was less than two minutes away from going off and the peace was about to be shattered.

The night before, after…

Well, after whatever that was, he took a shower and I ordered some food, and then we ate together like we were friends and not estranged husbands on the road to divorce. I found out we liked some of the same shows, so we watched a documentary about street food in Asia and he fell asleep halfway through with his head resting against my shoulder.

I'd finished the rest of the show, appreciating how exhausting the past few days of emotion and travel must have been for him, then gently woke him up before eleven to get him into bed. He stripped down to his boxers with his eyes closed and climbed under the sheets, holding them up for me to join him.

Like he was inviting me to my own bed.

I wanted to ignore that, but my brain decided to keep me up thinking about it until two in the morning. Unfortunately, by the time I finally fell asleep, I wasn't anywhere closer to making sense of him or whatever was happening between us. Sure, we were pretending to be married, even though we were, because it would help me get the penthouse. We had to be convincing to the board or there was no point in all of it and this was just us getting comfortable with each other.

The sex…

That was just…

Just another part of it.

Or something.

My alarm clicked on, a slow and melodic wind chime that slowly grew louder. It was at the max volume by the time I scooted to the edge of the bed to grab my phone from the nightstand, Dalton's arm over me like a fucking anvil against my chest. He grumbled, rolling onto his side and hauling my back against his front.

"Not a morning person?" I asked with a quiet laugh.

"What time is it?"

"It's six."

"It's three," he muttered, burying his face against the back of my neck.

For someone who had been so upset about my apartment only having one bedroom—and one bed—he didn't seem to be too unhappy with the outcome now.

"Six for me and my boss is in this time zone."

I wiggled out from beneath him and padded softly into the bathroom, closing the door all the way before I turned on the light. Having a bright, white bathroom was really great unless you didn't want to look at yourself, and I wasn't sure if I wanted to spend as much quality time with my reflection as my bathroom allowed that morning. The bruises on my neck from Dalton's kisses were still dark, some of them going soft and fuzzy around the edges, but for the most part, their intensity remained.

I turned off the light before I showered, then I got dressed in the closet in the dark. Dalton hadn't moved from where I'd left him. The worry in my brain wanted to check if he'd set an alarm, to ask if he needed anything to get his day going, but I bit all of that back. Standing in the doorway, I watched him sleep for another minute, then forced myself away.

Time for coffee, time for work.

I left him a note next to the coffee pot, then grabbed my bag and locked the apartment on my way out. I'd have to get him a spare key while he was here. The last thing I wanted was for him to feel trapped inside or tied to me, but Ford and Kale had my spare keys and neither of them liked this whole pretend game of house I was playing.

It was a twenty minute walk to my office, and when the lobby elevator doors slid open, my friend Ford was already inside. He had his shoulders pressed against the back wall, leather satchel hanging in his hand. When he saw me, his mouth cracked open into a wide, mischievous grin.

"There you are," he greeted, sliding toward the corner.

"Have you…" I stepped into the car, a dozen people squishing in behind me and shoving me right against his chest. "Have you been riding this elevator up and down just waiting for me to get here?"

"That's a silly idea."

"That's not a no," I said.

He bit his tongue between his teeth and chuckled at me.

"Did Kale put you up to this?" I asked, trying to arrange myself so we weren't chest to chest. There were so many people in this goddamned elevator, this entire fucking city.

"Kale said you had an out-of-town guest," he said. "That's all."

"Your face says otherwise."

The elevator stopped and three people exited. The doors closed, and the car went one more floor before stopping and opening again.

"I know more than you'd like me to know, but less than I want," he said.

I pulled my phone out of my pocket and swiped open my calendar to check my meetings for the day. I had one at eight, and I cursed my past self under my breath for being so ambitious with the scheduling.

"Do you want to talk about this at lunch?" I asked him.

We were two floors below my office.

"I want to talk about it now," he countered.

"I have an eight-o-clock."

"I know." Another evil grin. "It's me."

The doors slid open on the sixty-fourth floor, and Ford gave me a shove into the lobby of my firm. He set a box of pastries in front of my secretary, then winked at her as he gave me another push toward my office at the other end of the floor.

"Did you bribe Amanda?" I asked, shaking my head.

I opened my office, and Ford made himself at home on the low-slung leather couch that faced my desk. He dropped his own bag on the floor and stretched his legs out, crossing them at the ankle.

"I'm not above bribery," came his answer.

"What did they tell you?" I asked, sitting behind my desk. I could ignore Ford as much as my brain would allow, so I checked my email and confirmed that he wasn't lying about being my eight-o-clock.

Amanda tapped her nails against the door frame, two coffees in hand.

"For you and Mr. McKinley," she said.

I waved her in, taking the coffee and rolling my eyes at the way Ford flirted with her when she tried to hand his off.

"Stop sexually harassing my staff," I warned after she had left, closing the door behind her.

"Stop making me sound like a monster."

I sighed, debating the merits of pouring the coffee all over my face to get out of this conversation. If I closed my eyes, I was back in my bedroom, back at Dalton's feet. It was nicer there, quieter, and everything made sense. When I was in the moment with him, I didn't question, I didn't doubt. It was when the afterglow faded and reality settled back in that I debated my sanity.

"I assume Kale told Alex I was married, so I imagine you also know that I'm married," I said.

Ford dramatically splayed his fingers across the center of his chest, eyes going wide. "That's shocking news, Beamer."

His tone indicated it was not, in fact, shocking news.

"It was a youthful indiscretion. A college thing," I went on.

"I'm so glad I never joined a fraternity."

I arched a brow at his assertion. "You make it sound like it was your choice."

Ford had definitely tried to join Greek life, going through rush but not getting a bid. It had been a shitty time for all of us, trying to celebrate the lot of us who had without rubbing it in his face, but Ford had been a late bloomer. All knobby joints and thick Coke bottle glasses with ill-fitting clothes because he'd been that kind of prep school kid. The rejections had been a kick in the ass for him, though, and before any of us knew it, he was broader and more handsome than the rest of us.

A fact he never let us live down.

"Who knows how I would have turned out if they'd let me in," he said. "But, anyway, you're married."

"Right, to Dalton Fox."

Ford smirked, a chuckle bursting out of the corner of his mouth. He raised his coffee to toast me like it was a drink.

"I can't imagine a better way to get back at your ex than marrying her boyfriend," Ford teased.

"They were broken up before Dalton and I..."

"Tied the knot," he supplied.

I nodded, taking a drink of my coffee which was far from hot enough to cause me traumatic bodily harm. Damn Amanda for knowing that I hated to wait to drink it. She had probably pre-poured it at quarter to eight, anticipating my arrival.

"Neither of us remember it happening," I said with what I hoped was a casual shrug. "We had too much to drink and it was right before graduation. We didn't talk after we got back to school."

I knew I was leaving out a very important part of the story, but it was too early to air my dirty laundry. And I had a group of friends who deserved to know the truth, but I had no intention of telling them one by one, so it could wait. It wasn't important to the current state of affairs, which revolved around the fact I was married and would remain that way for the foreseeable future.

"Apparently," I went on, "the co-op prefers that I'm married so the discovery wasn't as horrible as I first thought it would be. Dalton is in town for a bit."

"Pretending to be your husband."

"He *is* my husband," I corrected. "We're pretending to be married."

"I think that's the same thing."

"It's not."

"If you say so." Ford's head sort of bobbled from side to side and the look on his face said it was very much the same thing.

"It doesn't matter. Once I get the penthouse, we're divorcing and he'll be going back to L.A."

"Okay."

I narrowed my eyes. "What do you mean, okay?"

"I was just agreeing with you."

"Your tone isn't one of agreement," I told him.

"This isn't court, Beamer. Don't try to analyze my answers or I'll start to pick apart yours, and we both know I'm a better lawyer than you."

I scoffed, angling my chair toward my computer screen and away from him. "Don't you have somewhere to be?"

"Right here," he said, making a show of spreading himself out over my couch. "At least, until eight-thirty."

"You know how slow the elevators are here," I said, turning my attention to my inbox, which had a shameful amount of things that needed my attention.

"Good point." He groaned as he stood, rolling his neck to the side to crack it. "But we can revisit this later. And you have other people to tell."

"Hasn't Kale already done the honors?" I glanced up at him, keeping my face trained on my computer screen.

"Not in such glorious detail." Ford grabbed his bag and slid it up over his shoulder. "By the way, I can't wait to meet your husband."

"You're not meeting him," I snapped.

"You're not going to hermit yourself into your apartment until you get that penthouse," he countered.

"Watch me."

"We have keys," he said.

"I'll change the locks."

"Come on." He laughed and pulled open my office door. "We just want to meet the man who has your heart."

I snatched a pen out of the cup on my desk and flung it at him. He dodged it, using the door as a shield. It bounced off the wood and landed on the floor at his feet.

"I know what you want," I warned, pointing a judgmental finger at him. "And you can't fuck him, he's off-limits."

Ford smirked at that, another playful tilt of his head. "Why not, Beamer? I thought things with the two of you were just pretend."

I tried to swallow, but my spit had lodged in my throat, making it impossible. He had a point…a point I didn't want to look at.

But if Ford thought he was going to call my bluff like that, if he thought I was going to choke in front of him, he had another thing coming. I stared at him, holding my breath until he finally gave me a slow—if not knowing—smile.

"See you and your husband around," he said, stepping out and closing the door behind him.

I waited until the door lock latched into place, then I slammed my hand onto my desk, sputtering and coughing until I could breathe again.

CHAPTER 17
DALTON

The scent of Ivey's soap was still heavy in the air by the time I woke up for real. The memory of his body against mine was enough to ensure my cock was hard enough to cut glass, and I groaned, rolling onto my back and pushing the sheets down to my thighs.

"Ivey?" I called out for him, but didn't get a reply.

I knew waking up in a different city, a different apartment, a different bed, it all should have been disorienting, but it wasn't. I waited for the panic to set in, for the trembling and the cold sweats, but they never came. Waking up in Ivey's bed felt just like waking up in my own.

"Fuck," I cursed myself then pulled my phone off the night-stand, leaving the charge cord connected.

It was just shy of eight, which meant my body thought it was five and was in desperate need of coffee. I had cancelled all of my meetings for the day, pushing back what I could to later in the week. Jetlag wasn't something I'd ever struggled with, but the back and forth of the past couple days had definitely taken more of a toll than normal on my energy levels.

I had some messages from my friends in the group chat that I had no interest in reading. Barclay and Archie had both been there Monday morning when I'd gotten the call from Ivey, and while I was apparently good at keeping secrets, my face wasn't. There was no way for me to have the conversation with him about our marital status without the two of them knowing every detail.

I would never ask them to lie for me, but I did ask them to run interference.

After I'd gotten off the phone with Ivey, the three of us had come up with a tolerable explanation, that I had to go to New York for work. Which was more of a lie than I would have wanted, but felt livable.

For a while.

Or so I'd thought.

I'd been betrayed. The group chat sat ignored, but I had messages from Flynn.

Privately.

Flynn: Archie told Owen about your little secret. And Owen told Rose, and Rose told me.
Me: What did he say?
Flynn: That you're shacking up with a college friend in the city.

I didn't realize I'd stopped breathing, but I sucked in a loud breath when I realized he didn't know the whole story. But still, fucking Archie and his mouth.

Me: Old friend. Needed a favor.

That wasn't a lie.

Flynn: Anything you need help with?
Me: No. I have it all under control.

That *was* a lie.

Me: Thanks, though.

I pulled the charge cord out of my phone and tossed it onto Ivey's pillow. I didn't know how long he'd been gone for, but I hoped he didn't mind me making myself at home in his apartment because, without him around, I didn't have much choice. All he'd managed to show me the night before was his gorgeous bathroom and his prettier cock.

Fuck.

I didn't know what had gotten into me, besides Ivey.

It was impossible to be around him without wanting to be inside of him, and we desperately needed to have a talk about just how committed we were to this pretend husbands bit because I knew myself enough to know it would be a short slide to getting in over my head with him. He ticked so many of my boxes, and I didn't just mean the way he looked or the things he liked it bed. Though, the latter was definitely a bonus.

It also could have been a curse.

I grabbed my phone again and pulled up Ivey's name, sending him a quick text.

Me: Can we have dinner tonight? I think we need to talk.

His response came almost immediately.

Ivey: Last time you suggested we have dinner, we ended up in Vegas.
Me: I assure you I'm not ready to fly back across the country again.
Ivey: Dinner is fine. But you could have just said yes.

I reeled back, not sure of what his comment implied because if there was any track record for our relationship, it was that both of us said yes at least one time too many. I dropped my phone back onto the pillow and climbed out of bed. My cock was still hard and my joints were just as stiff, but as soon as I made it into the bathroom, my mind was back in the previous day. Thinking about Ivey drawing my shower, Ivey taking off my clothes.

I scrubbed a hand down my face, trying to clear the visual.

A quick wank in the shower gave me enough of a fresh slate to start the day. I ignored the way it tightened my chest to see our clothes beside each other in his walk-in closet. I needed to get my head on straight. This wasn't anything…this was just a charade to get him an apartment that would end with both of us getting a divorce.

The last thing I needed to do was catch feelings for him.

Dressed and almost ready to face the day, I found a note in the kitchen next to the coffee pot, penned in Ivey's unique and scrawling cursive.

Let's get dinner tonight. We should talk. – IV

Well, that explained what he'd meant with his text message. But great minds, I supposed, or something like that.

I made myself a coffee and sat down at the counter with my laptop. Focusing was not going to happen, so I decided to snoop. There were things I'd have to know about him if he wanted me to be convincing at the interview, so I didn't really see the harm in it.

Save for the bathroom, which held a modest amount of character, most of Ivey's apartment reminded me of Flynn's place. Or rather, Flynn's place before he started dating Rose. There wasn't much color and it looked like the decorations had been picked out by someone who'd been paid to have taste. There was a small sideboard underneath the TV, and that seemed to be the only place that held anything that wasn't generic.

There were a handful of framed photos, Ivey at various ages with an array of people. There was a photo of his parents from our graduation ceremony. He looked the same, but somehow less himself. His eyes in the shot looked hollow, and even though he was clean-shaven and smiling, I could tell he was miserable. That had only been a handful of days after our trip to Vegas, and I didn't know how it made me feel to see how affected he'd been by the whole ordeal.

Was he upset that we'd gone? Mad that something had happened between us? I remembered coming home and being ashamed of how things had gone with Gen. My avoidance of Ivey had only revolved around my own selfish concerns. I'd never once thought of him back then as anything besides a comfort for me, and now, well past thirty, I wanted to go back in time and slap the younger version of myself for being so self-absorbed.

I picked the photo up from the table and traced the tip of my finger across the bags under his eyes, studying his face and the faces of his parents, his older brother and younger sister, trying to pinpoint all the resemblances between them. He had his father's nose and jaw, his mother's full pout. He was tall like his father and brother, broader than either of them. But all five of them had the same pale skin, the same golden hair, and blue eyes.

Trading out that photo for another one, I found myself faced with an older version of Ivey at a bar or lounge that reminded me very much of Cunningham's. He was with four other men, one that I remembered from school even though I couldn't place his name. Apparently Ivey wasn't the only one who'd made it back to New York after graduation and I took some small comfort in knowing he hadn't come back here alone.

The men all looked to be close to his age, and judging by the way they held themselves, I assumed the same income level as well.

"Trophy Doms," I muttered, thinking about my own friends, thinking about what Ivey would learn about me if he'd been left alone to dig through my house without my supervision or oversight.

My own living room was as sparse as his because I preferred to spend most of my time in my office, which was where I'd gathered all of my favorite things. I'd painted the walls black, which my designer hated, but went along with because people did all kinds of things for money. Massive bookshelves lined the walls, stacked with books on law and real estate, trinkets I'd collected on trips, and framed photos of my own.

I returned the picture of Ivey and his friends to its spot in favor of another shot of the same group. This one looked like it had been taken on New Year's Eve, the group of them all dressed in varying stages of formal wear. One of his friends had a noisemaker hanging out the corner of his mouth, a glass of whiskey raised like he was toasting whoever was taking the photo. Another one of them had on a crooked cone party hat, decorated with gold and black tinsel.

The one common denominator between all of the photos, I realized, was that Ivey was always in the middle. Even the photos with his family, he was flanked. The mood was different—where his parents oozed detached connection, the pictures with his friends reeked of ownership and propriety. I had the fleeting vision of him sleeping with all of them, one of them, *some* of them, and jealousy curdled in the pit of my stomach at the thought. Why else would they crowd around him the way they always did? Possessive hands on his arms, the back of his neck, like they had any right to touch him that way.

"Get it together, you fucking psychopath."

I set the photo down and turned my back on the wall, needing to get a breath of air that wasn't laced with fantasies of him taking four dicks at once. Raising the mug to my mouth, I took a drink of coffee, hoping the caffeine jolt would be enough to snap me out of whatever embarrassing and unwarranted spiral I'd just sent myself into. It was a start, but not enough. I had to put physical space between my body and the pictures, pacing across the room to look out the window.

Honestly, why did anyone like living in New York? Ivey's view was right into someone else's apartment, which felt voyeuristic and not in a sexy way. I took another drink of the coffee and decided the best course of action was to mind my own business.

Back at the counter, I tried to organize my thoughts for work, but the prospect of dinner floated right outside of my periphery and I found myself constantly distracted by the conversation we were going to be having later that day. And if I wasn't thinking about that, I was thinking about the day before and how pretty he looked on his knees with my dick in his mouth.

On the marble counter, my phone gave a quick buzz and I flipped it over, finding Archie's name on my screen. A simmering anger bubbled at the sight of his name, and I swiped open the text message, very ready to rip him a new asshole, but his message stopped me in my tracks.

Archie: I thought about things after you left and there was no way your lie was going to work, so I made you a new one.

Half the fight went out of me.

Me: You told them I was here as a favor for a friend.
Archie: You're awake.
Me: Of course I am. It's three hours later here.
Archie: Oh. LOL

He knew this. There was no way he didn't know about the time change or which way it went because his boyfriend was from the East Coast, but Archie was almost always playing at something, even if he didn't know what it was.

Archie: Please don't hate me, but honestly it's more believable this way.
Me: I wish you would have told me first. Or asked.
Archie: I tried. Scroll up.

Sure enough, I had a quick flurry of messages from him the night before. Messages that I'd missed because I was busy playing dangerous games in Ivey's bedroom.

Me: I missed those.
Archie: Yeah. I bet you did.

I didn't need to hear his voice to know the tone. He knew exactly what I was doing out here, even if I didn't.

DALTON HAD TEXTED ME A COUPLE OF TIMES THROUGHOUT THE COURSE of the day, but he'd been quiet for the most part, which had my heart residing in my throat for the entirety of my walk home. We were both in agreement that we needed to talk, and I hoped that we'd be able to manage that with some kind of civility, and I hoped we'd be able to stay fully dressed for it too.

It wasn't my fault.

There had always been something about Dalton that disarmed me and having him all up in my space wasn't making it any easier for me to be around him. He made me want all kinds of things I had no place hoping for. I used to imagine a future with a faceless man who could own me in all the ways I wanted, but now…

Now I imagined him.

Which was futile because we were just pretending to be together since he felt like an asshole for walking out on me twice and felt like it was some kind of penance for his sins. I wouldn't argue the point with him because I wanted the penthouse, but I had to actively remind myself when all was said and done, he would be going back to L.A. and we would be divorced.

Not like our marriage had ever meant anything real in the first place, but still…

The last message I'd sent to Dalton had been when I was

packing up for the day, so arriving home to find a buffet of Lebanese food spread out across my kitchen counter was shocking, to say the least. Dalton was in the kitchen, one hip cocked and resting against the counter, his phone cradled in the palms of his hands. He glared down at the screen, brow furrowed, and when he looked up…

When he looked up at me, his entire expression changed.

His features softened, then turned nervous. He set his phone down on the counter, and that was when I realized he was still in pajamas which amounted to nothing more than a pair of sinfully soft sleep pants that hung dangerously low on his hips. They had a drawstring that I wagered was just for show and I imagined the waistband was being held up by my own willpower alone. Because we needed to have that conversation and we needed to do it dressed.

"Can you put a shirt on?" I blurted, scrubbing a hand down my face and turning away from him.

Dalton made a noise in the back of his throat, and I glanced over my shoulder in time to see him smooth a hand down the muscular planes of his chest, right toward that drawstring that couldn't have rested more than an inch above the base of his cock.

"Sorry," he mumbled. "I lost track of time."

"You ordered dinner, but forgot I was coming home to eat it?" I asked.

He gestured vaguely at his phone. "Work."

I dropped my chin to my chest, head nodding slowly.

How quickly I'd forgotten that Dalton wasn't here on vacation. He was here for me and he was working, and he was also three hours behind me. It was still the middle of the afternoon in California and I imagined he'd be working well into the night.

"Sorry," I apologized, clearing my throat. "Do…"

I bit back the question, swallowing it with a groan.

"What?"

"I was going to ask if you wanted me to get you a shirt," I admitted.

Apparently it was impossible for me to suppress the absolutely primal urge that had taken up residence in my bones to serve him. At the question, his nostrils flared. He opened his mouth and snapped it closed, pursing his lips and letting out a long breath through his nose.

"I do," he said softly. "But we should eat and talk first."

"Right."

Dalton took a step toward me, gently resting his hand against the small of my back and giving me a gentle push toward the hallway.

"Come on," he said. "Let's get comfortable for this."

Comfortable would have been me naked on my knees, holding a plate for him while he ate and then fed me as he pleased, but I didn't think that was what he had in mind.

He led me through my own house, flicking undone the top button of my shirt, then the second one. Instead of going for the third, he reached past me for an undershirt, one of mine, I noticed. He knew what drawer in the closet to open, and some unexplained kind of feeling surged up my legs, making my knees tremble. He'd been in my place all day alone. He'd gone through my things. He'd made himself at home. It was so perfect and…wrong and right, all at the same time.

Without asking if it was okay, he put my shirt on himself, then took a step backward.

"I'll let you take care of yourself this time," he said, almost under his breath. The threat and the promise clear in his voice.

Dalton left me alone in the closet, cool air brushing against the exposed V of my chest. I'd spent the whole walk home, the whole day, trying to convince myself that this was just a game, a small ruse, but it suddenly felt very real.

And worse than that, it felt attainable.

The only thing left to decide was whether I wanted it for myself or if I was content to let this be a thing that ended when Dalton went back home. Still not convinced one way or the other, I changed into basketball shorts and an old t-shirt I'd stolen from

Kale, then joined Dalton in the kitchen. He sat at one of the barstools, an empty plate and a bottle of beer gathering condensation in front of him.

"I figured you liked this place," he said, drumming his fingers against the edge of the counter. "The menu was stuck up against the side of your fridge."

"It's one of my favorites."

"I didn't know what you liked, but when I called, they seemed to know what you ordered."

He looked at the food spread out across the counter, clearly more than enough for one person because I ordered Lebanese most often after we'd stumble back from a night out at The Black Door.

"My best friends and I eat it a lot," I told him. "Do you remember Kale Wallace?"

"He was in your frat?" Dalton asked, finally shaking himself clear of whatever feelings had paralyzed him. He scooped some kibbeh onto his plate, then a huge spoonful of tabbouleh.

"Yeah."

"I remember the name, but I couldn't place him in a lineup. I'm glad the two of you stayed close."

I dug out some spinach pie from the foil tin and dropped a piece onto the other clean plate Dalton had set out.

"We're *friends*," I stressed the platonic nature of my relationship with Kale, because even though we'd snuggled naked together on more than one occasion, Kale was and would only ever be my friend.

"You have your whole life, Ivey." Dalton gave the beer bottle a little spin, but didn't lift it for a drink. "You don't have to explain yourself."

"Are you jealous?" I asked.

His head snapped to the side, mouth still pulled into a tight and uncomfortable line. He hadn't shaved, dark scruff peppering his jaw and neck. I could see the sharp line across his cheek from where he normally kept it trim, sporting a five o'clock shadow as a daily look, but not a full grown-in face. But even the dark hair against his tanned complexion wasn't enough to hide the flush that crept up his cheeks.

"What if I was?" he countered.

I dragged my tongue across the front of my teeth, the confirmation feeling like a victory, even if it was a confusing one. "I think that's what we're here to talk about," I reminded him.

He leaned back from the counter, tapping both his palms against the marble top. He still hadn't taken a single drink of his beer, and I wondered if any of the food was going to get eaten or if it would all go to waste because we were two stupid men who couldn't talk about their feelings.

"I'm not jealous of your friends," he said slowly, carefully. Each word was chosen with thought. I could tell by the fine wrinkles that deepened around his eyes with each syllable.

"That's good."

He made a thoughtful noise, then raked his fingers through his hair.

"I haven't been able to stop thinking about last night," he finally said. "Haven't been able to get the sight of you on your knees…the way you undressed me…"

"Did you like it?" I rasped.

Dalton scoffed and grabbed the base of his cock through the thin material of his pajamas. He was hard and thick, already tenting the fabric, even without the assistance of his hand. "Did I like it?" he parroted, mocking me. "I more than liked it."

"Did you want to do it some more?"

"I want to do it a lot more," he said quickly. "But…"

"But?" I prompted, when the silence had stretched so long I couldn't breathe.

"But it's…" He almost grimaced, top lip twitching into a frown before his expression fell completely. "It's…you're…you're something special, Ivey."

Dalton looked at me with defeat splashed across his face, from the tired set of his mouth and the inevitable loss already dark in his eyes. He gave a halfhearted shrug. "I don't think I can do this with you in a half-measure."

"I'm going to have to ask you to elaborate on that a little."

The spinach pie was going to have to go into the oven to crisp back up, I thought.

"I've waited so long for a man like you, Ivey." Unexpectedly, Dalton reached out and grabbed my hand. He raised it to his mouth and kissed each of my fingertips, holding my stare the entire time. The defeat had turned into something else entirely, and it sucked the air right out of my lungs. Dalton's thumbs kneaded into my palm and he left my fingers to rest against his mouth for the next part. "I can't do this with you and then walk away."

My brain spouted off before I could stop the words from tumbling out of my mouth. "You always walk away."

He licked his lips and looked down, my fingers still against his mouth. His palms wrapped the sides of my hands, clammy but steady.

"I'm sorry," I mumbled. "That wasn't fair."

"It was true," he said, leaving another burst of kisses against my hand. "But I haven't been able to stop thinking about you, thinking about the way you make me feel, the things you do—"

I cut him off. "The whole package, then?"

He huffed, shaking his head and letting my hand fall away from his mouth, but he didn't let go. He kept my hand tucked between his own, and we both looked down at the way our fingers tangled together in the air between us.

"Last night was a taste of something I didn't think was real." He glanced up at me, looking every ounce the dominant man I knew him to be.

Dalton was confident and competent, but he was careful, and he was tender when he needed to be. I wondered how much of it came from being a lawyer, learning how to read people and negotiate to get the best deal, and how much of it came naturally. Then I figured it probably didn't have anything to do with it, because I was a lawyer and I didn't have a dominant bone in my body unless someone else put it there.

My submission came with a thoughtful kind of service, and all I wanted in return was to care for someone who cared for me so naturally they didn't even have to think about it. And Dalton was right here, with my favorite food on the counter and my shirt on his back, looking like he could be at home with me. Looking like he could be all those things if I let him.

The problem with Dalton was he looked at me like I was going to disappear, which…if someone looked at the history between us, that had always been more his speed than mine. But I couldn't make these decisions for him. That wouldn't be fair for either of us, and it wasn't the kind of person I was. Those weren't the roles.

He wasn't being skittish about me. He simply didn't want to get hurt, and considering the history between us, that felt fair. I'd always prided myself on being a good communicator, in and out of the courtroom. That was something I needed to carry through to this moment, to this man. Submission required honesty and transparency, and Dalton deserved that from me.

He deserved that and more.

So, I offered him the truth. "I don't want that with you, Dalton."

CHAPTER 19
DALTON

At Ivey's confession, I bit the inside of my cheek so hard that I drew blood. I tried to take my hands back, but he dropped his other hand into the mix and held on for dear life, even against my slippery palms.

"Last night was a game," he said. "It was pretend."

"I wasn't pretending," I choked out.

He shook his head. "Neither was I. But the premise, Dalton…"

He was right. We'd gone into that under the idea that we had to be convincing for his co-op, that it was to get familiar with each other so people would believe we were married and committed to each other. And I'd gotten so lost in my head with him, I'd forgotten it wasn't real, that it wasn't mine.

"Right." I cleared my throat, turning his palms up in mine so I could stroke my thumbs along the length of his hands.

"That's how I am, how I want to be." Ivey's cheeks were as red as the tomatoes in the salad. "But it's not just…it's not just the submission. I like pain too, and I want pain."

"Why are you telling me all of this?"

"Because I want it with you!" He shook his hands out of my hold and stood up, pacing across the apartment to get away from me.

"I want it with you," he said again, still not looking at me. "I want it with you and I want what we did in Vegas, but I want more of that. A lot more."

I had to have heard him right. There was no way I'd misunderstood what Ivey was asking of me, which was nothing short of everything.

I wasn't lying when I told him I didn't think the things he and I had done together were something I'd ever be able to have. For years, as long as I'd been into the lifestyle, I'd had an idea of the kind of man I wanted to be with. And there'd been times after college where that fantasy had looked like Ivey, but only because there hadn't been anyone else to fill the role in my head. As time went on, and I watched my friends pair up and fall in love, I'd begun to worry there was no perfect match out there for me.

It wasn't that I was a particular man, but I wanted a lot.

And Ivey was right here, willing to give it all to me.

Ivey, in New York with his penthouse and me in Los Angeles with a life I'd fought hard to build for myself. What could come of that in the long term? He couldn't undress me and draw me a bath over a video call, and I sure as shit couldn't give him the pain he was so clearly after from two thousand miles away.

"How does that work?" I asked him, asked his back because he still hadn't turned around to face me. "With you here and me there?"

"I don't know." He shrugged. "But we've been back and forth across the country more times this week than I have in the past six months, so I'm sure it's doable with a little bit of work."

I'd opened a beer as soon as he'd texted he was on his way home, but I hadn't found the strength to drink it. Even though liquor made being honest with him easier, I knew the conversation we'd been heading for deserved sobriety. But all the same, I gave the drink a longing glance before I climbed off the stool and closed half the space between us.

"Is that what you want, Ivey? Is that the life you want?"

"Forever?" He turned halfway back toward me, his profile

coming into silhouette, tall and proud. God, the way I wanted to fucking tear him down. "I don't know, but I want it for now."

"For now feels a lot like the little game of pretend from last night," I said.

"That's not how I meant it."

"How then?"

"I don't want to hold myself to anything. I'm human. We are human, and feelings change, circumstances change." Ivey licked his lips, glancing at me but not looking at me head on. "But I want this to be real for us for as long as feels right."

The breath left my lungs because, while part of me had hoped that we would possibly end up here, I hadn't dared hope for it. And what did that say about me? That I was so desperate for the things I wanted, desperate for *him*, that I would take a promise of now over a promise of forever?

"The whole thing?" I asked, hoping he understood what I meant.

That must have been the right question because Ivey finally turned to face me full on, shoulders squared and his chin tipped up. He was already taller than me, and I watched while he studied me down the length of his nose, like he was sizing me up, determining if I was up for the challenge.

"All of it," he whispered.

"Then wipe that cockiness right out of your fucking posture, Ivey." I took a step toward him. "You know your place with me."

A shiver tore through him and his chin hit his chest as fast as his knees hit the floor. He sank down low, palms resting against his knees, stare downcast. I watched him from a distance, waiting for his breathing to level out. He was as nervous—as ready—as I was, and while I was many things, I wasn't a pushover. I wasn't going to let my own eagerness to once again have him on his knees get the better of me.

The moment, the concession, was special. And I wanted to savor it.

I wanted *him* to savor it.

"Tell me something." I took four steps and then I was right in front of him, my fingers tangled into his golden hair. I petted the top of his head, stroked him, but didn't draw his gaze away from my feet.

"What do you want to know?" he whispered.

"I want to know if you call your Doms Sir."

"Yes."

"Why?" I let my hand fall at my side. There couldn't have been more than an inch between us, electricity sparking in all the contact points where I wanted to touch him.

"Because they tell me to," he answered simply.

I hummed, flexing my hand into a fist and letting it loose again.

"Then I don't want you to call me Sir," I told him, "at least not until *you* want to."

Ivey made a small noise of protest but swallowed it back and answered me with a nod. He might want to because it was habit or reflex, but he was a smart man and he knew what I'd meant. I wanted him be aware of my ownership of him so strongly that he could feel it in the marrow of his bones before he let that honorific leave his mouth. Because it might have been selfish of me to fixate on for now versus forever, but I couldn't handle the loss of *everything* I'd ever wanted, only parts of it.

"Yes," he said softly. "Thank you."

I rewarded his concession with a soft pet against the top of his head. He practically purred, and my cock, which I'd been ignoring, jumped at the sound. Right in front of his face.

"Look at me."

Ivey angled his head back, gazing up at me with pupils so shot I couldn't even see the blue of his irises.

"You have toys here?" I asked.

"Yes."

"Rope?"

He shook his head. We'd have to remedy that one because my fingers itched to wrap him up in knots and have my way with him.

"I have cuffs," he said.

"Where?"

While Ivey was at work, I helped myself to going through his apartment and I hadn't found a single thing. The lack of revelation had been surprising, but I knew he'd have something stashed somewhere, even if I hadn't been able to find it. I also knew he wouldn't care that I looked because he wouldn't have left me alone if it had been a problem for him.

"In my gym bag. In the closet."

My snooping had only gone so far, and I'd seen the bag but incorrectly assumed it housed sweaty sneakers and a towel that probably needed a wash. I'd kicked it to the side, right against a box of Prada dress shoes.

"Why so hidden?" I asked.

"Not hidden, just easy to transport."

"You have to go out looking to get fucked the way you like, Ivey? Is that it?"

He huffed out an exhale that sounded like half humiliation, half arousal. But I wanted to be sure. I needed to be sure.

"Tell me to stop if I ever go too far," I demanded, trusting that he would.

He clenched his jaw and nodded.

He liked it.

"Yes, you understand or yes, you have to go out looking for dick?"

"Yes to both," he muttered.

"Go get the bag out of your closet, dump it all onto the bed, and wait for me."

Ivey let out a low whimper, and I helped him to his feet. As he stepped away from me, the scent of his arousal filled my nostrils, and I couldn't stop myself from smacking his ass as he turned to go. He moaned at that, and I knew the desperate little sounds he made at every touch and every word were going to be the absolute death of me.

He took no time at all, which...I'd hoped to have at least a minute to regain my composure before following after him. But I heard the closet, and then the zipper pull, and then whatever he had in the bag clattering around as it all landed on his bed. The bag landed on the floor, and then silence.

I found Ivey in the bedroom, facing the pile of toys he'd dumped out at my instruction. He was so fucking tall, so solid, so sure.

"Take off your clothes."

He startled at the sound of my voice, turning toward me. His cock was hard, tenting at the nylon basketball shorts he'd changed into after getting home. He stripped out of the weathered t-shirt and shorts, tossing them both onto the floor and facing me, thick erection pointing right at the ceiling.

I palmed my own length, almost in pain from how hard I was. "Dig out the cuffs," I told him.

Angling away from me, he rifled through the pile until he produced a pair of soft leather cuffs connected together with a clasp between their matching O-rings. I closed the space between us, pressing my clothed chest against his bare back. He shuffled forward, knees bumping into the edge of the mattress as I took the cuffs out of his hand. I didn't need to see his wrists to get him hooked up, one around each wrist, and I chained them back together in front of him.

I reached around him and fingered through the pile, finding nothing that really caught my eye. A standard issue pair of leather floggers, a wooden paddle, a handful of butt plugs in varying shapes and sizes, a ball gag. It was painfully vanilla.

"I thought you said you liked pain," I teased, picking up the flogger and examining the falls. I had to lift onto my toes to rest my chin on his shoulder, but he took the message and squatted low enough that it didn't strain my calves.

He really was the most perfect submissive.

"I do like it," he answered. "But that doesn't mean everyone gets to hurt me."

"Judging by the looks of this bag, *no one* gets to hurt you."

"I'm not a pain slut, Fox."

I dug my chin into his shoulder until he grunted, and then I pressed down harder until his knees buckled and he went to the floor.

"I'm not sure I believe you," I whispered.

"I'm not," he protested, rolling his neck and letting his head fall back against my thigh. "But I could be. I want to be."

"For me?" I asked, petting his hair.

He tipped his head back further, until I could see the sliver of his pupils as he tried to crane his attention back up at me.

"Maybe," he said.

"Tell me what you want." I shoved his head forward, pressing his forehead against the side of the bed. "Tell me the things you want that you've never dared ask for."

I went to my knees behind him and reached around his front, taking his cock into my hand. Hard.

Ivey gasped and leaned back against me, ever ready and always pliant.

"I want it to hurt," he whispered. "I want to be roughed up and fucked hard. I want to bleed and cry, and…"

I pinched the tip of his cock between my thumb and forefinger, cutting off the rest of his sentence.

"And what?" I prompted, even as I squeezed him hard enough that it almost made *me* see stars.

"I just want…I want to submit. I don't want to choose. I don't want to think. I don't want to worry about someone going too far and needing to safeword out." He sucked in a breath as I twisted my grip on the head of his dick.

"What else?"

He shook his head and I grabbed him around the back of his neck, fingers digging into the soft spots beneath the back of his skull. "What else?" I asked again.

"From you," he finally circled back to the question I most needed an answer to. "Please, I want that with you."

CHAPTER 20
IVEY

"WELL." DALTON CLEARED HIS THROAT BEHIND ME. "YOU MAKE IT incredibly difficult to give you what you want. With a toy bag like this."

"I'm sorry," I rasped, because I was.

Because I'd never wanted anything more than I wanted him to positively unload on me, and I couldn't have it.

"Everything can be fixed," he assured me, letting go of the back of my neck with a shove into the bed. I didn't move because he hadn't told me to. He stood up, one of his knees cracking in my ear. "Go into the living room. Crawl, if it pleases you."

I hesitated, unsure if crawling would please me, but I also didn't want to please myself. I wanted to please *him*. I'd played with dominant partners before who strictly adhered to the whole don't speak unless spoken to mantra, and Dalton didn't seem like one of those, but I wasn't entirely certain. There was still about a hundred miles of gray area between us, but I knew he would stop if I told him to, so I wasn't terribly worried about it. And he was right. I didn't have a lot at home that could cause me too much harm. I normally relied on my partners to provide that kind of thing. I shivered at the thought, wondering what kind of toy bag Dalton kept back home. Then my stomach roiled, wondering if I'd ever get to find out.

For now, not forever.

I gathered the courage to ask, "Would it please you?"

He hummed an appreciative sound, and I didn't know if it was in response to the question or the idea of my crawling through my apartment naked with my wrists bound together.

"I think it's something I'd like to watch," he said.

So I crawled for him.

Dalton followed behind me, close on my heels, and every footfall made me painfully aware of the hardwood against my knees and the cold air of the apartment against my exposed asshole. Between my legs, my cock bumped against my stomach with every shift of my hips, an embarrassing and wet slap of skin.

After what felt like a lifetime, we reached the living room. I slowed to a stop, and Dalton gave my coffee table an unceremonious shove toward the wall. The sound of the legs dragging over the wood after they skittered off the throw rug echoed as loud as a gunshot, and the satisfied hum from Dalton barely registered in my ears.

"I should punish you," he muttered, looking around the room. "For making this so hard."

"I'm sorry," I whispered.

"I know. Now lay down on your back."

I shifted onto my heels and then rolled onto my back, feeling extra exposed considering the giant windows on the far side of the room. Using his feet again, Dalton softly kicked at my legs and my torso until I'd turned forty-five degrees, lying at an angle across the Persian rug in front of my couch.

Dalton made a show of arranging himself on top of me, still dressed as he squatted down over my face and hauled my bound hands above my head. I inhaled deeply, taking in the way his soap and sweat had mingled together with the smell of my laundry soap. With one hand, he lifted the corner of my couch, shoved my hands forward and let it fall. Giving an experimental tug, I realized he'd effectively tied me to the couch, using the short wooden leg as a restraint point. Creative bastard.

He slid down, dropping his full weight on the middle of my chest, making it exceedingly difficult for me to breathe.

"I know you want to fight," he warned. "And I want you to fight me…one day. But if you do it now, you're going to send your couch into the window."

"Understood," I murmured, letting my lashes flutter closed.

He dropped something onto my chest, then started to fidget. Part of me wanted to see what he was doing and the other part wanted to be surprised. I never would have thought to tie me to my own couch, and I was beyond curious what he was going to come up with next.

I shouldn't have looked, though.

Because I opened my eyes in time to watch him attach my favorite nipple clamps to my chest. They were my favorite because they hurt, which was what I wanted, but going in cold, the twin bites of pain were always a shock. I groaned, twisting beneath him. He reached back and slapped the outside of my thigh.

A warning.

Dalton gave the clamps a tug, then let the metal chain connecting the clamps fall against my chest. He ripped the drawstring of his pajama pants out, looped it around the chain, then pulled the chain taut. The drawstring stretched over my head and he tied the end of it to the link on the cuffs. There was no easy position for me to settle into where the nipple clamps wouldn't pull against my skin. They were tight and strong, and my eyes rolled back in my head, the pain almost immediately centering me and drawing out a needy gasp.

"That's a start," he said under his breath, sliding back and standing up.

My eyes were still closed, but I felt it when his pants fell, and I heard it when he moved away from me to take them off. The smell of laundry soap blew through the air above me and then it was just him.

Him and me.

"Spread your legs," he instructed, tone different from before.

Dalton always sounded like he was in charge, but it was different now. There was no argument to be had, every syllable wrapping around my cock like a velvet glove. I shivered, painfully aroused, and my body shifted, tugging the chain on the clamps until I willed myself to settle down.

I spread my legs, and Dalton was between them, fingers curled around my thighs. He shoved my legs up and out, like he was ready to get down low and eat my ass…which I wouldn't have hated. But then his hands were gone, and I pried one eye open to see him reaching behind him for the wooden paddle from my toy bag.

"If you were prepared," he said, testing the paddle against the palm of his left hand. "I would have rigged your legs to the couch too. To make sure you didn't flinch."

"I have neckties," I suggested, dropping my head back against the floor with a thud.

"I'm sure you do," he said. "Maybe next time you'll have rope."

And then he brought the paddle down on the inside of my left thigh.

There was no warm up, no preamble, and the sting of the paddle was so hot and unexpected, I yelped. The nipple clamps twisted, the couch shifted against the floor, and everything hurt. Dalton waited for me to calm down, then right before I took a normal breath, he hit me again.

And then there was no stopping him.

He alternated between my legs, sometimes closer to my knees, sometimes closer to my balls. Every strike made me jump. Every hit *hurt*. Eventually, the pain of wood against flesh did that tricky thing where it turned liquid inside of me, melting into something more like bliss. The edges of my mind went fuzzy, and my whines became moans, my thrashing hips began to undulate, chasing after every ounce of pleasure Dalton had for me.

When he stopped hitting me, the pain sharpened almost immediately to acute swatches across my thighs, and I knew without looking I'd be purple from knee to balls for at least a week. And Dalton hit me again, this time with his hands. His fingernails dug into the soft muscles of my thighs and he spread my legs wider, then did what I'd hoped for all along.

He buried his face between my ass cheeks, tongue licking a hot stripe over my hole before swirling around and plunging in. I could have cried with relief... maybe I was crying. I didn't know. Dalton hummed against me, licking and kissing and fucking me with his mouth, and then two of his fingers were inside of me and I arched so high off the floor, I lifted the couch again.

With his mouth still sealed around my ass, Dalton chuckled and then pulled back. I was cold and empty, so close to the edge of subspace, but not quite close enough to get all the way there. The result was a specific kind of torture that I'd never experienced before, almost like the crest of an orgasm when you know something big is coming, but it's just out of reach. Everything hurt, and everything felt amazing, and I barely even registered the sound of the condom wrapper before Dalton's thick cock breached my already well-prepped hole.

I cried out, and instead of silencing me with a kiss, he slammed his hand over my mouth instead. My eyes fluttered open, rolling back again when I focused on the sight of him above me. He'd gone still. We hadn't even started to fuck, but he was already sweaty, already flushed. And his cock was so fucking hard inside of me.

"If you keep making those noises, Ivey, you're going to make me come, and I'm not done hurting you yet," he warned. "Can you keep it together or do you need help?"

I desperately wanted to know what help from Dalton looked like in that regard, but I also wanted to push myself. I wanted to try.

"I'll be quiet," I whispered, the words muffled against his palm.

"You don't sound sure."

He untied the drawstring that had pulled the nipple clamps tight, then shoved it into my mouth. He'd wound half of it up, so my teeth held the chain tighter than the couch had, and I was again achingly aware of how much my nipples were going to hurt once the clamps came off. Every tug was a reminder of the pressure in my chest, every movement from either of us, a bite of agony.

"I know how much you like your pain," he said, tracing his fingers over my lips. He looked like a man unhinged, a man in his fucking element and damn if I wasn't ready to come on the spot at the sight of him.

Earlier, I'd wanted to see him work with his own toys in his own space, but I found myself faced with the very likely possibility that I hadn't met my match in Dalton—I'd met my victor.

"So you keep that in your mouth until you're coming. You understand?" He flicked mindlessly at the clamps and I bared my teeth at him, drawstring clutched tight. "Hurt yourself for me until you can't fucking stand it anymore."

He leaned down and kissed me, licking and sucking against my lips like we were in the middle of a make-out session that I couldn't take part in. His cock still inside of me, Dalton started to move, moaning against my lips as he fucked in and out of me so slowly I feared I was going to die.

I managed a muffled whimper, and Dalton raised up, shifting back onto his knees. He grabbed my hips, tight enough that I knew he'd leave more bruises. It was impossible to keep my eyes open anymore, so I stopped trying. I focused on the drawstring between my teeth, the clamps on my nipples, and the cock in my ass. Dalton gouged his nails into my hips, and I was aware of him there too. He was everywhere. Not just inside me, but all around me, and then he started to move again.

Slamming into me with snaps of his hips that should have been powerful enough to send me and the couch right through the window. But the hold on my hips was as punishing as the thrust of his cock so I barely moved at all. My spine inched back and forth against the rug, the abrasion from the tight pile turning into a raw and burning ache as he bottomed out inside of me over and over again.

"I love how you look with my marks on you," he whispered, again with the nails. "I'm afraid you bring out the worst parts of me, Ivey."

He sounded almost sad, a contrast to the way he moved inside of me. I shook my head to protest, to tell him that wasn't true, but the cord in my mouth yanked my nipples from one side to the other and I cried out, clenching my jaw down tight. Above me, Dalton shook, upper lip twitching up into a grimace.

"Your ass grabs me so fucking tight. You're such a slut for me, just like you wanted."

I managed a nod, that time enjoying the way the nipple clamps twisted and pulled. Still riding the border between being present and being in subspace, I was happily aware of what was shaping up to be a serious case of rug burn on my back, the dark mottled bruising on my thighs and my hips. I was overjoyed that Dalton was the cause of it all, and my entire body went soft at the knowing of it.

Dalton fucked me until I lost sense of time and thought, until my teeth held the clamps taut because that was their only job, until my balls churned and tightened because that was what Dalton wanted them to do. My cock burned my stomach, leaking and throbbing and so treacherously close to an orgasm that I feared would suck the life out of me.

One of his hands left my waist and curled around my dick, hard and sweaty. He stroked me with long and punishing drags up my length, and I gritted my teeth, fighting the orgasm for as long as I could manage, but he grabbed my balls with his other hand, making a tight fist and it was over for me.

I shouted out, the noise deafening to my own ears as the drawstring fell out of my mouth, soaking wet with spit. Dalton growled and wrapped his fist around the chain, giving one sharp tug that snapped the clamps right off my already tortured nipples. Cum spurted wildly out of my dick, and his hands were back around my waist, hard and demanding as he drilled into me, crying out and going still as his own orgasm peaked.

I tried to watch him, tried to focus on the way his body flowed like a wave above me, back bowing as he emptied into the condom. My own cock had shot off all at once, but my entire body was wracked with aftershocks. Cum dribbled out of my slit, pooling against the puddles already spotted across my stomach.

Above me, Dalton had let go of my hips, his fingers instead dancing across my ribs and my stomach, swirling the cum in meaningless spirals up to my throat. With a wince, he pulled out of me and bent forward, licking the evidence of my release up with long and hot swipes of his tongue. He laved over my tender nipples, laughing against my skin when I whimpered. And then my cock was in his mouth and I fought against him, again dragging the couch across the floor.

Dalton opened his eyes and stared up at me, cheeks hollow as he sucked on my sore and spent cock like it was a pacifier.

"Please," I whispered, shaking my head.

It was too much.

He let my cock slide out of his mouth, pressing a kiss against the tip.

"Are you with me?" he asked, fingers again tracing over me, this time the bruises on my thighs.

I nodded. "Yeah."

Dalton picked up the corner of the couch and dropped it down, pulling my arms slowly toward him. He hoisted me into a sitting position, still situated between my legs, and I dropped my head against his shoulder with a happy moan. His hands moved to my back, making their way up my spine. The pain was searing, and he petted the back of my head with a quiet chuckle.

"Does it hurt?" he asked.

Dalton's arms came around me, and I went lax against his chest before using all my strength to bring my legs around the front of him. I tried my best to curl up in his lap, but I was too tall, too long. He understood what I wanted, though, pressing my legs up and my back closer, doing his best to help tuck me into the cradle of his lap.

"Yes," I whispered, pressing a kiss against the cum-filled reservoir tip of the condom. "Thank you."

I WASN'T A FAN OF WAKING UP IN IVEY'S BED WITHOUT IVEY'S BODY next to mine, but he was an early riser and I…was not. My phone rang before my alarm went off, and I had absolutely no idea who would be calling me before seven in the morning, considering it wasn't even four at home.

I dragged my hand around the nightstand until I found the offending device and answered the call without looking at the screen. "Hello?"

"Are you asleep?"

I scrubbed a hand down my face, flopping onto my back. The shift pulled the charge cord tight, knocking a bottle of lube to the floor. I hoped one of us had the foresight to cap it last night because if we hadn't, it would've made quite a mess all over Ivey's original wood floors. I forced myself to roll to my side long enough to check that the bottle wasn't leaking, then settled onto my back again.

"It's early," I said.

"For me." Barclay sounded smug, and I made a tally of all the times I wanted to hit him in the face once I got back to L.A.

"What do you want?" I asked.

"I wanted to check on my best friend, for one. He kind of

dropped some bombs on us and then took off across the country without another word."

I sighed, the sleepiness taking a fair amount of the fight out of me. Barclay was right. I'd done all those things. And it sounded far more unreasonable when he said it than when I thought about it.

"I'm okay," I told him, before correcting myself to align more with the truth. "I'm actually good."

"In New York."

"With Ivey."

Barclay made an indecipherable noise that was loud enough to vibrate the side of my face through the phone.

"I thought you were doing him a favor."

"I am."

"But?" he prompted for the rest.

"He's attractive and I enjoy being with him."

"You're fucking him," Barclay said, like it was some epiphany.

"I fucked him in Vegas."

"Which time?"

"Both," I snapped.

The call lapsed into silence, and I knew Barclay well enough that I didn't need to see him to know his forehead was wrinkled and creased in thought, deep lines forming an eleven between his brows. His jaw worked back and forth, like he would pop the bottom off if he thought hard enough.

"Stop grinding your teeth," I told him.

"Shut up," he muttered under his breath before letting out a long sigh.

"I'm fine," I promised him. "Everything is under control here."

Everything was so fine, I hadn't even come close to having a panic attack since arriving, which was a miracle in itself. Not that I was always on edge and ready for it, but I was used to them. Being with Ivey seemed to quiet that part of my brain. I wasn't delusional enough to think he cured me of my anxiety, but I knew I felt far less anxious when he was near.

"I hear you," he said, sounding tired. "But I don't know if I believe it."

"If Ivey was some guy in L.A., none of you would be blinking an eye at me shacking up with him and doing whatever he and I are doing. With Rob, Archie, and Flynn's track record, it should be expected at this point."

That earned a soft laugh from my best friend. "Do you think you're the next to get married?"

"I was the first," I reminded him.

Another laugh that sounded a lot more like a concession.

"I promise you that I know what I'm doing." That was half true at least. "Just waiting for a date to meet with the co-op board and then once he gets the sale sorted out, I'll be home."

"And what about the two of you? Whatever is going on in the meantime?" he asked.

"We're worrying about for now," I repeated back the agreement from our conversation the night before. "The rest we'll deal with when it's here."

"Sounds ill-advised," he murmured.

"Not any more ill-advised than you running around pretending you're not head over heels in love with Val," I said.

Barclay's feelings for his longtime friend-with-benefits were the worst kept secret in our friend group. No matter how often or how loud he tried to deny it, the truth was right there for all of us, including Val, to see. I didn't know what went on behind closed doors with them, or rather I did know, but not all the time. What I did know is they had insane chemistry together and not one single shred of commitment to share between the two of them. I was fairly certain they'd never been on a date, but I supposed that wasn't important to them.

Suddenly…

The idea of taking Ivey on a date felt very important to *me*, though.

"We aren't talking about Val," Barclay said. "But if we're talking about people we're fucking, we might as well talk about Drake."

I closed my eyes, groaning. "What about him?"

"He asked about you last night. I thought you were going to talk to him."

"I meant to," I said. "It slipped my mind."

Before Ivey ransacked my life, I'd been sleeping with Flynn's boyfriend's best friend. It wasn't anything serious, but I imagined I owed him a status update.

"I'll call him today," I promised.

"He's an infant. I'm sure you can text."

I wanted to crawl through the phone and throttle Barclay, but he had a point. Drake, and his best friend Rose, were both considerably younger than Flynn and I. There were generational differences to take into account that I didn't ever give much thought to because, at the end of the day, Drake could still take a cock up his ass like a champ and that was the important thing between the two of us.

"Anyway." I kicked Ivey's stupid soft bedding away so I would get cold and have some incentive to get out of bed. "Why are you calling so early?"

"Because I was going to call in a favor for you, but I need the address of the dream house your boyfriend is trying to get into."

"He's not my boyfriend," I protested.

Right?

We'd talked about letting whatever the thing between us was play out, but we hadn't made anything official. There wasn't a name or a title to it, and I barely knew Ivey. There was no good to come from thinking of him as a boyfriend because *boyfriend* felt a lot more like forever than for now.

"That's not the point."

"What's the favor?" I asked.

"Just going to dig up some info on the board before your interview," he said. "So you know what you're walking into."

"That's very obsessive and also thoughtful."

I sat up, swinging my legs over the side of the bed. There was a torn condom wrapper on the floor beneath my toes, shrapnel from the second time I'd taken him after our scene in the living room. I grabbed it and tossed it on the nightstand next to the lube before unplugging my phone and shuffling into the bathroom.

"If it's important to you, it's important to me," Barclay said.

"It's important to him."

"Well…"

He left the quiet part unspoken—that if it was important to Ivey, it was important to me.

"I'll get the address and send it over," I said. "Thank you."

"That's what friends are for." He cleared his throat, the display of camaraderie almost out of character for him but not unwelcome on my end. "Now text Drake and get the hell out of bed. You have a meeting in less than an hour."

"How do you know that?" I put him on speaker and set the phone on the counter so I could splash some water on my face and pray it helped me wake up.

"Because it's with me. Goodbye, Dalton."

The screen flashed white, and the telltale disconnecting call beeps echoed around Ivey's bathroom.

After I was awake enough to think about stumbling into the shower, I fired off a quick text to Ivey asking for the address and one more to Drake, letting him know I was out of town, but I'd started seeing someone seriously. Which felt like an overstatement, but the bubbling in my stomach when I typed it out made me worried that things *were* serious between us.

Drake responded quickly, which was surprising, but not unusual. He answered me with a frown face emoji. Then told me to let him know if things got unserious. I assured him I would, which earned me a smiley face emoji in return, but it was that big water-eyed looking smiley with the flush on its round yellow cheeks, and I just had to assume it was a good response, not a bad one.

"Fucking children," I muttered.

Right before I was ready to step into the shower, Ivey answered me with the address, which I forwarded to Barclay. He sent me a thumbs up. I didn't know a lot, but I knew the thumbs up wasn't ever a good response. But I also knew Barclay was even more behind the times than the rest of us were so I let it slide.

After a long shower and a good wank where I got lost in the way Ivey shuddered but didn't lean away the night before while I inspected all the bruises I'd left for him, I got dressed in real clothes and headed into the kitchen for coffee. Checking my phone, I found two more texts from Ivey, which left me feeling like the coffee I was so eager for would spoil my stomach.

Ivey: Meeting with board tomorrow at three.
Ivey: We need to get our story straight.

He wasn't wrong. But we weren't even supposed to have a story. We were supposed to be a happily married couple with fifteen years of history between us, and while the history was there, it definitely didn't exist in the way the board most likely assumed it did.

But beyond that, there was one glaring oversight about our whole scheme. I stared down at my naked left hand while the coffee burbled a fresh cup's worth of brew for me.

Me: We also need wedding rings.
Ivey: Fucking hell.
Me: We can go out tonight.
Ivey: I'll leave early so we can go to the jewelry district. If I give you instructions, can you meet me? Do you know how to take the subway?

I'd never been on a subway in my life.

Me: I'm a generally capable adult, Ivey. I think I can manage.
Ivey: Then dinner?

That felt a lot like a date.

Me: Then dinner.

He didn't say anything after that, which I read as an agreement.

The coffee pot beeped at me, and I carried the mug around to the counter where I'd set up my laptop to work the day before. Instead of being tucked against the wall where I'd left it, it was centered in front of the stool on the end where I'd sat for dinner. And that was when I realized that not only had we barely eaten dinner the night before, but we'd definitely gone to bed without cleaning up the leftovers.

Which meant Ivey had taken care of it all in the morning before work.

The countertop was sparkling, and the sink showed no evidence of anything being disposed of. He'd left a clean mug next to the coffee pot for me too, and as I opened my laptop, I cursed him under my breath.

While the machine booted up, I thought about how different my life would have been if the first round in Vegas had gone different. If I hadn't walked out on him the way I did. I wondered if he would have stayed in California or if I would have come to New York after him. I couldn't imagine my life without my friends, and I was sure he felt much the same. It almost felt like things had to go the way they had to get us to where we were, but being aware of how many of my boxes he ticked off, it was hard to not look at that fifteen years as wasted time.

By the time I got my email open, I already had at least four contracts that needed red lines, but I also had one from Barclay with nearly a dozen attachments. It was going to be a lot of work to keep the info on the board straight and keep whatever story Ivey and I came up with straight, but I also knew the easiest way to keep a lie straight was to keep it as close to the truth as you could.

So I imagined the life Ivey and I could have had together if things would have been different between us, and then I spent the rest of the day convincing myself it was real.

DALTON SHOWED UP FOR RING SHOPPING LOOKING LIKE HE MEANT business. From the pressed black slacks that hugged his thighs to the white dress shirt that had the top button undone and the sleeves rolled up to his forearms, the man was a sight for tired eyes. When he turned enough to the side to see me coming, a slow, sly smile split his mouth and he stalked toward me like the predator I knew him to be.

"Hey." I tried to greet him, but he cut me off by pressing his lips against mine in a kiss that had no right being as hot as it was. Dalton slid his hand around my waist, fingers splayed across the small of my back, but instead of deepening the kiss, he licked my lips with a moan, then broke away for a breath.

"Hey, yourself," he said, trailing his fingers across my hip before letting them fall away. The gentle touch was a reminder of the bruises he'd left as decorations across my body the night before. From the bruised patches on my thighs to the fingerprints around my waist and the rug burn up my spine, I was basically walking proof of his ownership.

Even with all of that, I hadn't known for sure if we were going to be the kind of couple that greeted each other with kisses, especially in public, but Dalton's broad decision making had made his opinions clear. And that was more than enough for me.

"I wasn't expecting that," I murmured, touching my lower lip with the tips of my fingers.

"I wasn't expecting you," he said, glancing over his shoulder toward the store he'd met me in front of. "Did you want to go in?"

I cleared my throat, tried to clear my head. "Yeah."

"Did you want to hold my hand?" he asked.

What I wanted was to find a good wall to lean against, because everything he had done and said in the last minute was enough to flip my world onto its head. I knew we'd talked about being together *together*, but I hadn't expected any of this from him. Not to say that I didn't like it, because I did, but it had been awhile since I'd had a...

"Are you my boyfriend?" I asked.

Dalton huffed out a quiet laugh. "I'm your husband."

"You know what I mean."

His laugh died off and he licked his lips, giving my face a onceover so strong and serious that it felt like he was tracing my cheeks and my frown lines with his hands, not just his eyes.

"Boyfriend feels...insignificant," he murmured.

"You know what I mean," I repeated.

He wasn't wrong, though. In fact, insignificant couldn't have been closer to the truth.

"Boyfriend works," he said, if not reluctantly.

I swallowed, understanding it was the best we could do considering the circumstances. Suddenly, for now had gone out the window because Dalton didn't strike me as the type to have casual *boyfriends*, and I wondered if I'd gotten us both in even more over our heads than we already were.

"Ready?" he asked, taking my hand in his, like we were boyfriends.

We were boyfriends.

"Ready," I agreed.

I let Dalton open the door for me and I let him lead me around the display cases, and I let him drag me to a stop when he found a tray of rings he liked. I didn't know how, but he already knew what he wanted, for himself and for me.

"Ivey." His voice was a scratchy whisper. "Give me your hand."

I turned so we faced each other, sliding my left hand onto his waiting palm. He had a simple platinum band in his hand, thin with rounded edges. It looked unassuming; it looked traditional. It looked perfect.

His stare flickered up at mine as he slid the ring down the length of my finger. When it caught around my last knuckle, my breath caught in my throat at the same time, but with a little twist it was on and I could breathe again. Dalton didn't look at the ring on my finger. He looked at my face, something indescribable playing across his dark features.

"This one," he said to the clerk, stare still focused on my face. His fingers tightened around mine, and I had to look away from him because I couldn't breathe for how intense his eyes were, for how the way he looked at me made me feel. I twisted the ring around my finger, wondering how something new could feel so familiar at the same time.

How *he* could feel so familiar…

So ingrained in my being, in my life.

"Dalton, I…"

I didn't know what I was about to say, but it felt like there was *something* that needed to be said. And my pants rubbed against the tender muscles of my thighs, reminding me that with or without a ring, whatever this thing between us was, it was real.

"Shit," Dalton cursed under his breath and let go of my hand. He cleared his throat and took a step back. The moment between us was gone, shattered in a syllable, and I kept my hands cradled together, the weight of the ring more noticeable.

He threw a glance down at my hand, then up at the clerk. "We'll take it," he said.

"And for you?" the clerk asked.

"Whatever," Dalton answered at the same time as I said, "I'll choose."

His shoulders tensed, but softened on an exhale. "He'll choose," he confirmed.

The clerk gave me a quick onceover of what rings I could find where, and I left Dalton so I could go peruse the others. Picking a ring shouldn't have been hard because the rings didn't even mean anything. They were just an extravagant prop in our little game of pretend, but that didn't change the fact I had a piece of platinum wrapped around my finger and I definitely wasn't worried about price tags when it came to what I wanted to pick for Dalton.

A yellow gold band in a case near the corner caught my eye, and the clerk made a show of settling it on the velvet display cushion on top of the glass. It was classic and elegant, but it didn't feel entirely right.

"Did you find one?" Dalton murmured, coming up behind me.

"This one is nice," I said, picking the band up and holding it out for him.

"It's nice," he agreed. I slid it on his finger, admiring the way our hands looked with rings, side by side.

"I don't think it's the right one."

He took it off and set it back down on the display pad. "It's not the right one," he repeated.

The clerk put the ring back in the case, then clasped his hands together behind his back waiting for me to make another decision. I couldn't help but think ring shopping would have been better after dinner, when I'd had a chance to learn more about Dalton so I could pick something that suited him. The only things I knew about him were that he liked rough sex, had a private jet on speed dial, and he could make me come harder than anyone I'd ever met in my life.

"Can you give us a moment?" he asked the clerk, who answered with a nod and then left us alone in the corner of the store.

Dalton took my hand in his, sliding his finger back and forth over the ring on my finger. His breath came in heavy exhales and a flush crept up his cheeks.

"I have to admit, Ivey, this is giving me a lot of unexpected feelings," he whispered.

"Like what?"

"I'm feeling very possessive," he said, mouth twitching into a smile. "Also horny."

I huffed a laugh. "I don't know you well, but I think you're always both of those things."

"No." He was quick to cut me off, raising my left hand to his mouth and kissing my palm, right below where the ring sat. "Not like this."

My heart sputtered, banging against my ribs like it was trying to make a break for it. Dalton kissed my hand again, this time right below my knuckle and above the ring.

I knew then that Dalton needed to pick his own ring. Not because I didn't have an opinion on it or because I didn't care, but because that was the nature of our relationship. That was who we were, down to the marrow of our bones.

I made one choice—him.

And he made the rest of them.

"Did you find one you'd like?" I rasped, not sure why I was so overcome. We'd talked about being together, we'd agreed that we were boyfriends, no matter how trivial that sounded at our age, so why did this feel so monumental in comparison to the rest of it?

Dalton nodded.

"Show me."

Why did it sound so breathy and dreamy when I talked? Why were my palms sweating with this stupid ring on my finger?

Even if things between us were real, the marriage was pretend.

Dalton raised his hand and flagged down the clerk, who came over and set a diamond band down in front of us. I picked it up and turned it around, admiring the piece under the light. It was platinum, I assumed, with rows of baguette diamonds aligned vertically around the band with a blue stone inlaid between every few diamonds.

Dalton gave my hand a push toward my eyes, another smile breaking out across his face.

"I knew it," he murmured, sticking his hand out for me, fingers splayed.

I slid the ring onto his finger. "Knew what?"

"The blue topaz matches your eyes."

"It what?"

The ring pushed over his last knuckle with a satisfying stretch, and then it was my turn to hold his hand in mine like he'd just done to me.

Never in a million years would I have picked that ring out of the case for him. Even with as much money as I knew Dalton had, the ring was gaudy and demonstrative, but on his hand…It looked like something that he deserved, something that belonged to him.

Dalton lifted his hand and cradled the side of my face, his dark eyes tracking from my eyes to the ring around his finger. A secret kind of smile ghosted across his lips, and then his hand trailed down, fingertips dancing across my jaw before his palm grazed my throat. He angled his head to the side, expression darkening, and then just like before, the moment passed.

"We'll take them," he told the clerk, not looking away from me.

"How much?" I asked.

"Doesn't matter."

He pulled his wallet out of his pocket and dropped his Amex onto the pad that had previously held both of our rings.

"I don't want you to pay for both of them," I protested.

"It's not up to you."

There was a finality in his voice that sent a shiver up my spine, and I nodded my concession. The clerk took his card and scampered off, undoubtedly pleased with whatever commission he was about to make on the sale.

After Dalton signed the credit card slip and put his card back into his wallet, he turned to me with an expectant look.

"Now that that's finished, we can get dinner."

"Where did you have in mind?" I asked.

"I figured I'd let you choose."

"Now I get a say?"

"You know the area," he answered with a smirk. "But if it's too much for you, I'm happy to take that decision away from you too."

"Can you not?" I grabbed his hand, squeezing his fingers so tight it hurt my own hand to hold him. Dalton laughed, and led me back out to the sidewalk. With it being near six, there were thousands of people navigating their way through the crowds, and I found myself jostled right up against Dalton's chest. He took a step back until his shoulders hit the wall, and he rested his hands against my waist. I could have sworn I felt the weight of his ring there on my right side, but I knew I had to be imagining it. He jerked me closer against him, his cock hot and half-hard against my thigh.

"Can I not what?" he asked.

"I'm…" I trailed off when he shifted to the side, so his erection dragged alongside mine.

"You're what?" He smiled up at me like the arrogant asshole he was.

"I'm so fucking horny right now," I admitted.

Between the ring and the bruises, and the natural way his dominance permeated everything he did, I had no idea how I was going to make it home without coming. There was no way we could go to dinner without getting arrested for public indecency because I didn't foresee a world where my cock was every going to settle down. At least, not as long as Dalton and I were breathing the same air.

My shirt was still buttoned up, and he flicked open the second from the top button with a growl like my shirt offended him, like it blocked him from what he wanted most.

"Do you need to come?" he whispered, pressing a soft kiss at the base of my throat.

"That might be an understatement," I admitted.

His hand trailed down my chest and pressed against my cock. I slammed my body closer to his, hoping that no one around us would see him touching me. Dalton smiled against my throat.

"Where are we going for dinner?" he asked again, using the palm of his hand to shove my whole body away from his. I whimpered, chasing after him, but he sidestepped me, adjusting himself like it was a normal evening and there was definitely nothing out of the ordinary happening.

"I don't know." I couldn't even remember my name, let alone what kind of food I wanted to eat.

"Well, figure it out, Ivey," he said, again brooking no argument. "Then call a car to get us there and make sure it has a privacy screen in the back or you're going to have a really fucking uncomfortable night."

CHAPTER 23
DALTON

Tucked into as much of a ball at Ivey's feet as I could manage, I had his wrists pinned together against his chest and his cock halfway down my throat. He made the most delicious noises as I sucked and bobbed up his measurable length. I stretched a finger out from the hold I had around his wrists, searching out the smooth platinum band around his finger. It was as much a mark as any of the bruises I'd left on him and feeling it wrapped around his finger had an urgent sense of ownership swelling inside my chest.

I sucked him harder, letting my teeth graze his shaft as I made long and wet pulls up his shaft. He knew he had to hurry. He knew that even with traffic, the restaurant wasn't far and it wouldn't be long until our cordial and grandfatherly driver pulled up alongside the curb and came around to open the door. If Ivey didn't come soon, Cliff was about to get more of a tip than he'd bargained for and I, for one, wasn't into public displays of sex without willing and vocal consent.

"You better get on with it," I warned, coming up for air and sliding my tongue through the leaking slit of his cock.

"I'm trying," he moaned, bright eyes dark and hooded, even as the lights of the city flashed by through the tinted glass.

"Try harder."

It was the last thing I said before I swallowed him back into my throat. I tightened my hold around his wrists, giving them a shove against his chest. It took another minute before his breathing turned frenzied, hips bucking off the seat. I sealed my mouth tighter around him and swirled my tongue... and that was it. Ivey's shoes scrabbled against the carpeted floor of the car, kicking at my legs as he bit back a cry and came in my mouth.

He tasted like everything I'd ever wanted.

I sucked down every drop, swallowing with his dick still lodged in the back of my throat. I milked the rest of the cum out of him, going on a little longer than necessary because it made me hard when he squirmed, then I collapsed onto my ass and let go of his arms.

He looked as debauched as I'd ever seen him, still dressed for work but with his spit-soaked cock out, still twitching against his leg. There was going to be a cum smear against his dark slacks, but I didn't think either of us cared too much about it in that moment.

The car rolled to a stop and his eyes went wide. I chuckled, crawling back up onto the seat and praying that my throbbing erection wasn't as noticeable as it felt. Ivey made quick work of tucking himself back into his pants and smoothing his hair, then he turned to me and did something unexpected.

He kissed me.

The crash of his lips against mine caught me off-guard, but the insistent intrusion of his tongue past my teeth flicked my attention on. I pressed into him, taking his head into my hands and taking control of the kiss. I wanted to fuck him right there in the back of the car, bystanders be damned. I'd never wanted a man as much as I wanted him, and I didn't understand why the ring on his finger had dialed that want up to eleven.

I'd never wanted to get married. Though I wouldn't have hated the tax break, I found the whole idea of marriage to be archaic. It wasn't like I was a religious man, so there were no eyes of God to worry about, but still...Ivey was my husband on a technicality, and that was causing some new and complicated kind of feelings in my chest that I couldn't make sense of.

The door to his left pulled open, and I kissed him harder before giving him a push away. Cliff, for his part, paid us no mind.

"Gentlemen," he said.

Ivey climbed out of the car first and I followed after, taking time to make sure my cock wasn't getting ready to pitch a tent in the middle of a Manhattan sidewalk. After ensuring both of us were presentable enough for public, we went into the restaurant he'd chosen for us. It was a cute little Italian place with fake vines decorating the ceilings and red and white checkered cloths on the tables.

"This is quaint," I remarked, taking the menus from the hostess after she walked us to a table near a window in the far corner of the restaurant.

"They have delicious Chianti," he said.

I passed him a menu, but before he took it out of my hand, he frowned. The expression felt so out of place on his face I stopped and leaned back.

"What's that for?" I asked. "You have a wedding ring on your hand, you just had an orgasm in the back seat of a town car, and I'm about to ply you with food and wine. What on earth could be wrong with any of that?"

Ivey inhaled sharply, shoulders raising like a shrug. "Nothing," he lied.

"Try again," I warned.

"It's embarrassing."

I leaned toward him, setting the menus down and crooking my finger to draw him closer so I could whisper. He leaned in, face still flushed, but his stare evasive.

"Tell me."

Ivey worked his jaw and looked down at the table. "I just…you can order."

I huffed out a laugh, in love with Ivey in a way I'd never be able to put words to.

Shit.

Shit.

Fuck me.

"You want me to order for you?" I asked, angling away from him because I worried I was about to admit my deepest and darkest truth to him right there in the middle of whatever cute and kitschy nightmare of a restaurant he'd picked for dinner.

"Yes," he whispered.

"That's not embarrassing," I told him, gesturing for him to lean back and get comfortable. "That might be one of the sexiest things you've ever done."

The flush from his orgasm turned a darker and violent shade of red on his cheeks. He almost matched the tablecloth, and I was certain my dick was just as colorful.

After my comment, everything about his demeanor changed. His shoulders went down and the lines around his mouth went soft like I'd taken a burden off of him that I wasn't even aware he'd been carrying. I'd suspected it about him from my first night in New York with how willing and eager he'd been to take care of me, but every day I found myself surprised at just how deep his submission went.

"Alright," he said, clearing his throat. "But I do want some Chianti."

I laughed, shaking my head at him and turning my attention toward the menu so I could decide what we were going to eat.

"Of course you do," I said.

The service was the kind I loved the most, a quiet waitress who didn't try to make conversation beyond what her job required. She got us wine and bruschetta and salad. I ordered us pasta and chicken, and she was gone unless our wine needed to be topped off.

"So," I decided to broach the important conversation after our appetizer had arrived and my erection had started to wane. "Tomorrow."

"Tomorrow," he murmured.

"I want to make sure that you and I have our story straight so if they ask us any questions about our relationship, we'll have the same answer."

"Agreed." Ivey took a small sip of his wine.

"What have you told them about me so far? About us?"

He scoffed, taking a larger sip. "I've told them nothing because I didn't know you existed until last week."

"Am I so forgettable?"

"You know what I meant."

I pushed the plate of bruschetta toward him, and he slid one of the slices of toasted bread onto the small white plate in front of him. It hadn't gone unnoticed that he hadn't eaten, hadn't even taken food, until I indicated he should. Ivey's submission was far beyond anything I'd ever encountered before, but it came so naturally to him I couldn't imagine it being any other way.

Grayson, Rob's boyfriend, would've had a fit over the whole thing.

"I told them about going to school in California and coming back home to take the bar. About working and just everything I've been doing here," he said.

"What *have* you been doing here?" I asked.

"I did a fair bit of moping after the bar. I would have preferred to do it before, but my father was insistent that I start working as soon as possible, and he didn't know about you or Genevieve." He shoved a huge bite of bruschetta into his mouth, eyes downcast while he chewed. "So I got all of that in order and then kind of spiraled a bit, behind closed doors of course."

"Spiraled how?"

"Nothing I'm proud of. I'd gone out looking for…looking to get hurt. You know?" His eyes flickered up to meet mine before returning to the half-eaten piece of bread in his hand. "That was when I met Ford and Perry, and then the rest of them."

"The rest of who?"

"My friends." Ivey shrugged and finished off the bruschetta.

"Kale moved back with me after graduation, but he wasn't...he didn't used to care about some of the things I like sexually."

"But now?"

A flare of jealousy surged up the base of my spine at the implication that anyone besides me cared about the ways Ivey wanted to get off. Even though I knew it was absurd, because it wasn't like I'd been celibate since college, but still...

"It's not like that." A smirk played across his mouth. "Are you jealous?"

"I want to know who left rope marks around your wrist before you came to L.A.," I admitted.

"No one you need to care about."

"That wasn't what I said." My back molars actively tried to grind their way out of my jaw, and judging by the somber mask that washed over Ivey's face, he could see how serious I was about the question.

"I think name is Alex."

"You think?"

"I did more than one scene that night. I didn't know one of the men, the other I do know. So let's just call it the latter and say it was him," he said.

"Do you play with this Alex often?" I asked.

"Yes."

"Do you play with strangers often?"

"Sometimes," he whispered.

I swallowed, dropping my hands onto my lap so Ivey didn't see how white my knuckles were. I'd never fancied myself to be an overly controlling kind of man, at least not outside the realms of what my role in relationships called for, but something about Ivey brought it out in me. And, again, the fucking rings didn't help. The diamonds around my finger caught the light, and I brought my hand up onto the table, a clear display of propriety that didn't go unnoticed.

"Not anymore," I said.

He nodded.

"Not as long as you and I are…" I wanted to say married, but that was wrong in a thousand different ways.

"As long as we're together," he said softly. "I'm yours."

I was going to have to run into the bathroom and jerk off into the sink or something because there was no way in hell I was going to make it out of the restaurant without coming in my pants.

"I know," I said, even though hearing it had done more for my jealousy than I'd ever admit. I cleared my throat. "Is there any way your little co-op board knows about how you like to fuck?"

"I don't think the background check was that thorough," he murmured.

Our wine glasses were empty and the waitress was there to refill us. She cleared away the empty plates and was gone again.

"How are we going to explain your missing husband? Fifteen years is a long time."

"I figure that maybe we've done things long distance. You got a great job offer out of college, so you wanted to stay," he suggested.

"I did get a great job offer out of college," I reminded him. "Thanks to dear old Dad."

Ivey made an unhappy sound. "Yeah. Where would we be without our good old parents?"

It was rhetorical, but the answer was a fantasy. We'd be anywhere besides where we were, I knew that much.

"And is our plan that I'm moving to the city now? Working remote?" I asked.

"Maybe for a few months. We can play it by ear and see how they respond."

"Alright." I committed the first half of the plan to memory. "Are they going to ask me your favorite color? Your favorite movie?"

"It's green, if they do," he said, rolling his eyes. "And it's *Vertigo*."

"Of course it is."

"What about you?"

"Blue," I answered, daring a glance at the topaz stones in my ring. That particular shade had been a favorite of mine for years, but I'd never put any thought as to why. "And it's *Euro Trip*."

Ivey clutched his chest and let out the loudest laugh I'd ever heard. People turned and looked. Our waitress scowled.

"That's positively shocking," he said.

I shrugged dismissively.

"Tell me about our wedding," he said, a quick change of subject. "What was it like?"

Briefly, I allowed myself to indulge in the dreams that I'd ignored when we were in the ring store.

"If we waited until we were older, I would have wanted to give you a big wedding," I said, still staring down at my ring. "I always want to give you everything that you want."

That part, at least, wasn't a lie. Whether it was allowing him onto his knees so he could take off my shoes for me at the end of the day or making him come in the back of a rented town car, I had yet to run across a single thing I wouldn't want him to have if it pleased him.

"I love that about you," he murmured.

"But you wouldn't want it." I looked up and found his stare locked on mine, heavy and wanting. I pulled my lips between my teeth, rubbing them together while trying to maintain myself.

"I wouldn't," he said, like it was a confirmation that I knew him so well, so soon.

"You know, when we got married, we were so young." I knew we had to stay as close to the truth as possible, but it was fun to weave some of my dreams into the story. The way I would have done things, if I could. "Still in college. We hadn't even talked about getting married, but the stress of exams and the threat of bar prep had gotten to us."

"We went to Vegas," he chimed in, knowing where I was going. "To blow off some steam."

"To blow off something," I countered.

Ivey laughed, quieter this time, like it was just for us.

"We had too much to drink, ended up at a drive-through chapel, and we got married in the back of a white '57 Chevy."

He arched a brow. "Did we?"

Then it was my turn to laugh. I shrugged. "I have no idea."

"It's a good story."

"We got married and then just…went back to life. We did what we had to do."

"Didn't we, though," he agreed under his breath. "What did our parents think?"

"We never told them." Not a lie. "Because it was for us, not for them."

Ivey slid his hand toward mine, and I threaded our fingers together, turning our joined hands so I could admire the pale spread of his skin against mine. I swallowed, giving his fingers a squeeze.

"For us."

CHAPTER 24
IVEY

I had a problem.

I was in love with my husband.

In less than two hours he'd created a reality so tangible I could almost taste it. If I closed my eyes, the life he'd talked us around to flashed on the backs of my eyelids like I was really living it. And maybe it was because I had lived parts of it that it felt so real to me. Dalton was my husband, was my boyfriend. He was also my Dom, and the way he leaned into that with such an easy comfort had me ready to worship him for the rest of my life.

I know I'd been the one who told him for now, not forever, but forever didn't feel as impossible as it used to.

"I think we'll be fine," I rasped, unsure if I meant for the interview or for the duration.

"I won't let you down," he murmured, letting go of my hand and leaning back. I frowned at first, unsure of why a promise like that would come with *less* contact, but the waitress appeared beside me with two steaming plates of food. She set them down with a practiced efficiency, offered us grated cheese, and then was gone. My wine was half full and that would be more than enough because Dalton already made my head float enough without the liquid help.

"Royce."

Hearing my name was the last thing I expected. Seeing Alex and Kale at the side of the table was the second to last thing.

"Alex," I sputtered, cheeks burning.

Dalton's stare burned two holes in the side of my face, but he otherwise remained silent.

I turned my attention to my other friend. "Kale."

"Beamer," he greeted, mouth pulled into the smuggest and barely-contained smile that I'd ever seen.

"Beamer?" Dalton asked, brow arched.

I knew Kale and Alex would look at him and find it amusing that the stupid nickname was what he fixated on. Kale telling people the story of why he called me "Beamer" was something that brought him immeasurable amounts of pleasure, but one look at Dalton confirmed the nickname was the least of his concerns.

He eyed the two of them carefully, chin tipped up and chest swelled out. He would have pissed on me to mark his territory if it was even remotely socially acceptable for him to get up and do it, but the restraint he demonstrated was impeccable.

I cleared my throat. "Dalton, these are my friends, Kale and Alex. This is Dalton."

"The infamous Dalton," Kale said with a smirk.

Dalton's eyes narrowed. "The infamous Alex."

"Kale." All three of them looked at me. "Do you remember Dalton from school?"

"The name not the face," Kale said, staring Dalton right in the eye.

Dalton lifted his left hand from beneath the table, scratching under his eye and making what I assumed to be a deliberate show of his wedding ring while he had Kale and Alex's attention.

"I don't remember you either," he said.

"Can we not do this, please?" I whispered, stretching my leg out and kicking Dalton's shoe. The warning look he shot me was deadly enough to let me know that I'd pay for the overstep later, but the tension between my husband and my two best friends was more than I wanted to handle anywhere, let alone in public.

Wait.

My husband…

"Where'd you go?" Dalton murmured, clearly focused on me finally and not the two of them.

"Nowhere." I shook my head. "I'm here with you."

His proud chin dipped toward his chest and the hint of a smile flickered across his face before his entire expression settled into something far calmer than before.

"That's a nice ring," Kale said, tone laced with antagonism.

"He asked you nicely," Dalton warned.

Kale shifted his weight, letting out a low laugh.

"I just want to see if my feelings should be hurt, Beamer. You've had a house guest for days and you haven't invited him out."

"He's kept me entertained plenty at home," Dalton answered that, and the flush on my throat and cheeks burned hotter.

"He's good at that." Kale grinned, and I knew what he was going to say next before the words left his mouth. "Isn't he, Alex?"

Dalton was up faster than I could blink and he had Kale's shirt in his fist before I could even ask either of them to stop. For his part, Kale laughed, stumbling backward until Dalton put both of them back on balance.

"He's feisty," Alex said, and I rolled my eyes, far more focused on Dalton.

He had his back to me, and I slid my hand around his waist, bringing my chin to his shoulder and our faces almost side by side.

"Dalton," I whispered his name, lips pressed at the soft spot on his neck just below his ear. "Stop."

He sucked in a breath that dripped with unspoken protest, then he shoved Kale off, taking us both back a step toward the table.

"Down boy," Kale teased.

"Fuck you," I snapped, leveling a shaking finger in my best friend's direction. "You know who he is to me and you know why he's here. You're trying to make it a pissing contest, and I won't have it."

Kale raised his hands in surrender, at least having the decency to look somewhat chastised. I turned to Dalton, who hadn't looked away from Kale.

"He's just trying to get a rise out of you," I said.

"Mission accomplished," he muttered.

"It's like passing a test." Kale smoothed out the crumpled material around the center of his chest where Dalton had grabbed him. "If you hadn't reacted at all, then it would have been safe to assume you didn't care about him at all."

"I care about him plenty."

"So much so you forgot you were married to him?"

Dalton opened his mouth like he was about to offer up another scathing reply, but he snapped his lips back together and scrubbed a hand down his face. He took a slow breath, then sat back down at the table and settled his napkin back across his lap.

"Sit down, Ivey," he said, not looking up. "Eat your dinner."

"Ivey?" Alex asked.

"He said not here." Dalton kept his sight trained at the wine glass in front of him, tension rolling off his shoulders in waves.

I sat back down at the table, spreading my napkin out over my lap and reaching for my fork and knife.

"Well, well, well," Kale said like a taunt.

I glanced up and he traced his tongue back and forth across his lower lip, and I shot him a pleading look.

"Come on." Alex grabbed Kale's arm and gave him a tug toward the door. "We just wanted to say hi."

"You didn't," Dalton said. He wasn't wrong, and I couldn't stop myself from laughing at the simplicity of his observation. "But you're more than welcome to try and say goodbye now."

"You're more than welcome to stop ordering me around like a little bitch," Kale snapped.

Dalton sucked in a sharp breath, the tightness in his jaw making it clear—to me, at least—that he caught the barb.

"Has anyone ever told you that you make a killer first impression?" he asked.

"More than once."

I huffed, rolling my eyes.

"Alex, please help," I wasn't above begging the one neutral party to help me out a little, since Kale and Dalton seemed content to verbally spar with each other for the rest of the night. Dalton, at least, had tried to get himself under control. He'd gotten us both back down at the table and tried to get Kale and Alex to leave.

I didn't know what had come over Kale.

"Eat your dinner," Dalton warned again.

Kale knew who I was. Alex did, too. So when I tucked into my pasta without another word to either of them, I didn't expect them to be surprised. We were friends. Hell, Alex and I were lovers even, but Dalton was...Dalton was Dalton. And even if he was only my husband on paper, his ring was on my finger and...

Fucking hell, this was a dangerous gray area.

"I'll call you later," Kale said, and I didn't look up.

Beyond putting Dalton's commands ahead of my friendship, I was mad at Kale. More than *mad*, I was furious. He was the one who'd been the first to know about things with Dalton and me. He understood how important the penthouse was to me. He knew the fucking game. I didn't know if he was trying to posture or pretend he was superior in some way, but the way he'd treated Dalton just now was absolutely deplorable.

"Sorry about him," Alex muttered, giving Kale a shove toward the front of the restaurant. Dalton didn't look up, but he also didn't move. It wasn't until the two of them were gone that he let out a breath, jaw tight and eyes dark.

"I'm sorry," I said, setting down the fork. "I don't know what his problem was."

"I said eat your dinner."

"Are you upset with me?" I asked.

Dalton leaned back in his seat, taking a decent drink of wine before chasing it down with another. After the longest minute, he shook his head.

"Are you sure?"

He shook his head again, closing his eyes and quickly changing the motion into a nod.

"I'm not upset with you at all," he said, stare flickering across my face. "Though I do question your choice in friends."

"He's not normally like that."

"I'm sure he's always like that," Dalton corrected. "Just not with you."

I didn't know what to say to that, but I knew I didn't have an excuse for Kale or for the way he'd treated Dalton.

"I'm sorry I got physical with him." Dalton finished off his wine and set down the glass. "That was out of character for me."

"You can apologize to him for it after he apologies to you for that."

"He doesn't strike me as the type."

"He's not, but he'll find it," I said. "I'm sorry he ruined our night."

At that, Dalton scoffed. "He hasn't ruined our night. He gave us a questionable five minutes."

"Your words are contrary to your reaction," I hedged.

"I am allowed to be upset when someone insinuates that I don't care about you or that you're lesser than because you get on your knees for me," he said, sounding tired.

"Is it bad if I admit that I kind of like it?"

Dalton looked at me then, dark eyes sparkling under the ambient candlelight of the restaurant. The waitress came to refill the wine and he had her pack up both of our entrees, correctly sensing that our appetites had seen better days. I was full enough from the bruschetta, and the adrenaline that spiked through me had my hands feeling shaky and my throat dry.

"What about it did you like?" he asked softly.

It was a complicated answer because I'd never been a fan of dramatic and traditionally masculine shit like that. Dalton and Kale were both trying to stake their claim on me, and that should have made me feel very small and insignificant, but it actually had me feeling quite the opposite. It was almost like pride had surged through my chest when Dalton came to my defense, and then when he'd ordered me back to the table, something else had surged somewhere more between my legs.

There was such a nuance to the kind of relationship I wanted to have. It was one thing to get on my knees and strip a man naked and suck him off, to make him dinner and clean up after him. Those were all important parts of the things I enjoyed about submission, but so often my dominant partners—Alex included—didn't understand the silent expectations that sat on their shoulders. Being a Dom didn't only mean that they were in charge, there was also a level of care and protection that came with that, and without even a second thought, Dalton was on the attack.

Defending my honor.

"How it made me feel," I answered, because it wasn't a lie, but it wasn't all the details either.

But Dalton was relentless.

"How did it make you feel?"

I raised my left hand, palm toward my face. "Like this was real."

Dalton's mouth parted just enough for me to watch him trace the bottom of his teeth with the tip of his tongue. He stretched his left hand out and I slid my palm against his. He turned them both, admiring the differences in the rings we'd chosen, understanding that even though they looked different, they meant the same thing.

Dalton was my husband, and I wasn't sure if it was still just for show.

CHAPTER 25
DALTON

It took every ounce of sanity in my body to not put Ivey's friend through a wall, but all of that energy quickly shifted after his departure. The way Ivey looked at me, the way he looked at our rings, to say it affected me would have been an understatement.

Things had moved fast between us.

From enemies in college, to husbands, to strangers, to something that almost felt like friendship, to…whatever we had turned into.

I paid our bill, got Ivey back to his apartment, and then as soon as the front door closed behind us, I was on him. Even though his apartment was large for the city, the entryway was small, and I slammed him against the wall and crashed our mouths together before he could catch his breath.

He slid his hands around my waist like he'd done earlier at the restaurant, like he did often when he wanted my attention, and I bucked against him. Using my hips to square him up against the wall, I kissed the corner of his mouth, his cheek, his eyelids, his jaw, his chin.

"I need you right now," I murmured against his neck.

"Please," he whimpered.

I tore away from him enough to get my belt off, to get his belt off, to start on the buttons of his shirt. But the way he looked at me with a narrow and needy intensity almost made me shoot off right there in my pants. I growled, shaking my head, nowhere near ready to be done with him.

"Get into the bedroom," I demanded, giving his shoulder a spin.

He was off like a rocket then.

"Get naked," I called after him.

Ivey was out of his shirt before he reached the bedroom, jumping on one leg to get his pants off. But I intercepted him and shoved him backward onto the bed. He groaned, shifting his weight and yanking out the coil of rope I'd left under the pillows earlier in the day.

I'd almost forgotten.

"Plans?" he asked, lids hooded.

"It's going to have to wait," I said, climbing on top of him. I'd gotten my pants off and my shirt unbuttoned, but I needed to touch him again.

"I thought you worked during the day," he trailed off when I sank my teeth into his clavicle. Beneath me, he kicked out of his pants and we shimmied him out of his underwear. With our mouths pressed together, tongues tangling, he shoved my shirt off my shoulders and I wiggled out of it.

"I did work," I told him. "Worked on finding a store that sold some fucking rope so I could pin you down like a butterfly and take you apart."

"I'm not sure that's how it works," he whispered, eyes closing.

"No?" I grabbed one of his arms and stretched it toward the far corner of the bed, and then the other. "Isn't it? One wing at a time? Piece by piece until you look just how I want?"

"Fuck."

"That's why it has to wait," I said, reaching between our bodies to push my underwear down enough to expose my throbbing erection.

There wasn't much in life that I wanted more than to get Ivey naked and splayed out, with rope of my choosing and toys that I knew he would love, but the need to claim him rang louder than everything else in my life. The fun would have to wait. I needed to stake my claim.

Even though that felt petty and juvenile, even though it was more for me than him, I needed to remind myself that no matter what his smartass friends said or implied, no matter how handsome that fucking play partner of his looked, Ivey was mine. He was mine and it wasn't temporary, it wasn't pretend.

Grabbing the lube off the nightstand, I was near frantic while I slicked up my fingers and reached between his legs. His hole was hot and tight, but it made room for me, just like he had. I fucked him with my fingers, slow and easy, until he was as desperate and needy as I was.

"Kiss me," he pleaded.

Fuck, I loved when he asked for what he wanted.

I slanted our mouths together, wide and messy. Swirling our tongues, I tried to coat my cock with as much lube as I could get off of my hands and from the well-prepped crack of his ass. I teased his hole with my tip and he whined into my mouth, fingers digging into my waist and pulling our bodies closer together.

"I'm not wearing a condom," I warned.

The insistent hold he had on me didn't let up.

"I want you bare. I want to feel you come inside of me."

I huffed, pressing our foreheads together and trying to catch my breath. Everything about Ivey was like a drug, overwhelming and consuming. It was so easy to lose myself entirely around him, and I wanted more of it. I wanted it all.

"Don't you feel it normally?" I asked.

He made a sound in the back of his throat.

"You know what I mean." He spread his legs wider. "I'll beg, Sir."

My muscles locked and it took every bit of control I possessed to not bury myself to the hilt inside of him at his use of the honorific. "Ivey."

"What?"

"That word does things to me," I cautioned.

"It does things to *me*." He gave a little thrash beneath me and I yanked his hands off my waist, pinning them above his head. We were sideways on the bed and our wrists hung over the edge. His feet were barely planted on the closer side, making room for me between his legs. I was half on the floor, levering myself over top of him, the last semblance of control and propriety ready to snap at any second.

His cock burned like a poker against my stomach, and I didn't want to wait any longer. I aligned myself as best I could and then pushed into him.

Ivey wasn't the first man I'd fucked without a condom, but I sure hoped he would be the last. Because it didn't even take all eight inches for me to realize that no one would ever feel as good as he did. No one would feel as right.

I forced my entire length into him and then pressed up onto the bed so I could get a better angle. With a rough snap of my hips, I fucked him toward the other edge, wrists still held tight between my fingers.

"You're mine," I whispered, eyes scanning his face for even the slightest sign of protest or unease.

I found none.

His features were slack and happy, his jaw loose and his eyes half-open. When I fucked into him, his teeth clattered together, wringing a smile out of his mouth with every withdrawal. He huffed and he panted, body going pliant. At least, as pliant as a man of his size and musculature could ever manage. Ivey was a brick wall of a man, and he was defenseless around me.

I couldn't think of a single thing that had ever made me feel more powerful than that.

"You're mine," I said again.

He tipped his head back and moaned.

I licked along the underside of his jaw, stretching my fingers out to get a better hold on his wrists while I fucked him. My fingertip dragged across the cool shape of the wedding band around his finger and heat exploded in my spine, radiating out through every limb, every nerve.

"You're my husband." I nipped his jaw, his ear. "You're my fucking husband."

"Yes, Sir," he rasped in return. "I'm your husband."

I wanted more from him. I wanted everything.

"I'm your husband," he said again, repeating it over and over until the syllables turned into nothing more than ragged and panting breaths.

Sweat dripped off my forehead, spattering onto his face, his chest, the bed beneath him. I kept hold of his wrists and shifted back, hauling Ivey onto my lap. He was so fucking big in this position, practically towering over me.

"Ride your husband's cock," I demanded. "Ride your Sir's dick."

I let go of his wrists, only to regather them at the small of his back. His head tipped toward the ceiling and he started to ride me. His cock bounced between his, slapping against his stomach with every thrust. I had no idea how I hadn't come yet because every pump of my hips made my balls ache, like the precipice of this orgasm was going to shatter my bones into pieces once it came.

With my other hand, I reached between our stomachs and made a loose fist around his cock. Every slide of his hips fucked his dick through my fingers, and it didn't take long for him to lose the pace and falter.

"Just like that," I coaxed, sealing my mouth around the exposed base of his throat. "Come for me, Ivey."

His mouth opened in a silent shout, and then hot spurts of his cum coated my fingers. His release splattered across my stomach and the top of my hand, and I wanted to watch him come, but I couldn't get my face out of his neck. He was warm and he smelled like home, and then I was over the edge after him.

I let go of his wrists, and Ivey tumbled onto his back. I managed a half-dozen rough thrusts before my cock swelled and spilled inside of him. With my forehead pressed into the sheets next to his ear, I rutted through the aftershocks of my orgasm until my muscles gave out and I collapsed on top of him.

After a few minutes, I managed to roll off of him, barely aware of the rope beneath my spine or the wet spots our sweat had made all over the bedding. A few minutes after that, it was still hard to breathe, and I sought out his hand, threading our fingers together with a quiet sigh. More time passed, but I still didn't feel like I'd quite returned to my body, even with Ivey's heat and presence beside me.

"I think we need to talk about some of the things we just said," I finally choked out. The words were quiet and cracked, my throat aching from how loud I must have shouted when I came.

I angled my head to the side, studying Ivey's god-like profile.

"What about them?" he asked.

"Well…"

Being a Dom meant a lot of things, one of those things being that you were sometimes the person responsible for initiating awkward or hard conversations. And it wasn't that Ivey was being evasive, but he and I had spent enough time *not* talking that I wasn't interested in carrying on the trend. I, for one, had meant everything I'd said to him since we got home.

I meant everything I'd said to him, ever.

Apparently I owed his asshole friend Kale an apology and a thank you, because it was his snarky little attitude at dinner that had drawn everything into sharp focus for me. I wasn't interested in playing a game with Ivey and then going back to a normal life in L.A.

"Do you want to start with the husband or the Sir?" I asked.

"You're both of those things," he said softly, matching the angle of my face so we could see each other almost head on.

"I know we'd talked about pretending I was your husband, or pretending the marriage was real." I scrubbed a hand down my face. "And that we were boyfriends and that was fine."

"I don't want to divorce you," he said.

"For now or forever?"

"I want to be your husband." His cheeks were already flushed from the sex, but they darkened, the color rising up to the very tops of his cheeks and even his forehead. "For as long as you want me to be your husband."

"Then you'll be my husband."

I didn't foresee a day when I wouldn't ever want this man to be mine, whether it was legal in the eyes of the law or not. I raised our joined hands to my mouth and kissed his wedding ring. He reached across my chest and grabbed my left hand, repeating the gesture with his kiss-swollen lips against the stones in my ring that matched his eyes.

"And I'll be your Sir," I said.

Ivey's lashes fluttered and he nodded, lips still pressed against my wedding band.

Another title, another promise.

=I woke up the next morning with Dalton's mouth against the back of my neck and his lubed up cock poking my ass.

"I want you," he murmured against my skin.

The room smelled like sex and sweat, and I flung one of my legs back over the top of his to give him room.

"I'm yours."

He eased into me, slower than he had the night before, like he wasn't scared anymore of losing the right to be inside me. When he seated himself fully, he brought his arms around my chest, fingers splayed as he levered himself in and out of me. The burn was a slow and delightful stretch that made my already hard cock tingle. Dalton took my hand and slid it down, curling both of our fingers around my dick in a loose fist. Every pump of his hips fucked my cock against my palm and I dropped my head back against his shoulder with a sleepy—and satisfied—groan.

My thighs and balls were sticky with lube and cum from the night before, and it wasn't more than five minutes before Dalton added some more to the mix. He bit down hard on back of my neck as he came, the shock of pain being more than enough to empty my own balls onto our joined fingers.

His cock had barely stopped pumping into me before he pulled out and shifted me onto my back. He slanted his mouth over mine and kissed me until the sour taste of sleep was gone and the only thing left was him.

"Is it too much if I told you now that I'm falling in love with you?" he whispered against my mouth.

I shook my head, breath leaving my lungs in a rush.

"I love you," he said, whispering the words as he dropped kisses across the lower half of my face. "I love you. I love you. I'm in love with you."

I hooked my legs around his waist and tilted my head so he could continue his professions up my jaw.

"I love you," I said back to him.

It was as much the truth as anything about us ever had been.

"Can you call out sick today?" He licked the shell of my ear and I shivered. "I want to fuck you again."

"We have the interview at three," I rasped.

"That wasn't what I asked."

I hummed, closing my eyes and trying to call up a mental image of my calendar. I had already cleared the afternoon to make room for our interview with the co-op board, but I knew there was at least one call on my calendar for the morning that I couldn't get out of.

"I don't think so," I said regretfully. "But I can be a little bit late."

Dalton smiled against my neck. "Good. Go make me some coffee."

I shivered, eyes rolling back as he moved off of me.

"I love when you talk dirty to me."

"Go." He smacked me with the pillow, and I laughed before climbing out of bed.

My entire body was sore in the best ways, but it didn't stop me from shuffling awkwardly out of the bedroom and into the kitchen. My thighs shook from the stress of holding my body weight and my hole throbbed like Dalton was still inside of me. He just had been, and he'd spent plenty of time there the night before.

Which I was only reminded of when a bubble of cum leaked down the back of my thigh.

I was halfway back to the bedroom with a cup of coffee for him when he called out, "Make one for yourself too, Ivey."

I stopped in my tracks. I hadn't even realized I *hadn't* made one for myself. Did listening to Dalton really come so naturally to me that I didn't do something I did *every* morning? My routine didn't really vary. Even the past days with him at my apartment, I'd get up first thing and make coffee, so why hadn't I now?

Swallowing back the question that felt a lot heavier than it should, I finished the journey back to the bedroom and handed him the coffee I'd brewed at his request.

"Did you hear me?" he asked, taking the mug and sitting up with his back against the headboard.

"I'll go back and do it now," I said.

His mouth twitched as he took a drink, then I went back into the kitchen to make one for myself, trying to ignore the implications of the fact I hadn't done it the first time. It wasn't a surprise or a shock to me that I had submissive tendencies—more than most—but what did surprise me was how naturally I slipped into the role. It hadn't ever been like this with Alex or any boyfriends before, so what about Dalton called it out in me? I got lost in the thought, lost in the reflection of the wedding band around my finger, when the coffee pot sputtered out the last of the liquid and beeped angrily at me to announce it had finished its job.

I carried the coffee to my bedroom and climbed back in beside Dalton, who had his coffee in one hand and his phone in the other.

"Your phone has been buzzing like mad," he said, not looking up from his screen.

"Who is it?" I asked.

That earned me a look from him, one brow raised right up into his hairline. "I didn't check. I can if you'd rather."

I shook my head, biting my lower lip between my teeth.

"I don't have anything to hide," I told him, grabbing my phone off the charger and finding messages from Kale interspersed between work emails.

"I trust you, Ivey," he said, turning his attention back to his phone. "Or I wouldn't be here."

"It's work," I told him anyway. "And Kale."

"He has about as much emotional intelligence as a head of lettuce," Dalton murmured, taking a drink of his coffee. "Why does he call you Beamer?"

I'd been waiting for the ask since Kale had done it the first time. Thankfully, it wasn't some dramatic or shameful story.

"Because I used to drive one," I said with a shrug. "He found it hilarious that my last name was Royce, but I drove a BMW instead of a Rolls."

Dalton scoffed, rolling his eyes. "That's as good a nickname as any, I suppose."

"I know why you call me Ivey," I said to that, "but I don't know *why* you call me Ivey."

"Do you mean why I call you Ivey instead of Royce like everyone else?"

I nodded.

"I used to call you Royce. Ivey was…I don't know. It was intimate. It was mine." Dalton's lip twitched like it couldn't decide if it wanted to smile or frown.

"I am."

That tugged his mouth up into a smile, and he set his phone and coffee back down on the nightstand. The air was somehow sucked out of the room, and I struggled to breathe, putting my phone and coffee down as well.

"Rightly so." Dalton swung his legs over the side of the bed and picked up a coil of rope from the floor. "Let's get you cleaned up."

I followed him into the bathroom, ready for whatever he had in mind, but unsure of what he was going to do. Dalton detoured into the closet, unzipping my toy bag and pulling out a sizeable butt plug that he tucked under his arm. In the bathroom, he kept his back to me while he turned on the water and unwound the rope. I leaned against the wall, catching my breath as the sound of the rope sliding through his fingers echoed off the walls.

"Are we good with sensory games, Ivey?" he asked.

"Yes, Sir."

He rolled his head around, cracking his neck. The hand holding the rope fell down to his side, and I worried I'd said the wrong thing. But then he turned around and faced me with a leaking, hard cock and I knew my words had the exact opposite effect.

"More pain?"

"Please."

He rubbed away something from the corners of his mouth, stare dragging over me like his eyes were hot coals and every inch of my body burned from the perusal.

"Piss?" he asked.

I breathed out a laugh, not sure whether to be relieved or turned on. I knew he'd wanted to mark his territory the night before, and if he wanted more than the bruises and the teeth marks and the ring on my finger, I didn't see the harm. He already—somehow—owned me completely.

"If you like," I whispered.

"Do you like?"

"I've never tried it."

"Okay." He nodded, crooking a finger and beckoning me closer.

He pushed the butt plug into my mouth, then grasped my wrists and did some knotwork that had me bound together faster than he'd managed with the cuffs before. His talent was impressive, the speed even more so. He used the end of the rope as a leash, pulling me into the shower, then he looped the ends around the shower head and tied me to the wall.

My cheek pressed against the cool tile, my arms raising above my head as he pulled on the rope. I was a tall man and I'd had the shower custom designed, but my arms were still higher than the shower head, and Dalton let out a low curse, dropping my arms back down. He added some more knots, looping his way down my forearms until he reached my elbows.

"Is that too tight?" he asked.

I shook my head, telling him no around the intrusion he'd put into my mouth.

He hooked one of his fingers between the knot and my forearm to check, then hoisted my hands back toward the ceiling. He secured me around the head, somewhere near my elbows, content at the stretch.

"Don't break your shower head off," he warned.

I rolled my forehead against the tile, but I was already so hard and hot, there would be no cooling me down until the water heater ran cold. Dalton reached out and poked at the control knobs, turning on some of the side sprays. The water sluiced over me, warm and welcome, melting my already liquid muscles and bones. I leaned into the wall with a happy groan, and then Dalton touched me.

Barely.

His fingertips traced over my ribs, down over my waist and around to the bruises that still darkened the fronts of my thighs.

"Who do you belong to?" he asked, digging his fingertips into the marks.

I did my best to enunciate around the plug. "You."

There wasn't a lot of space between my body and the wall, but Dalton still managed to find a way to slap my thighs and make it hurt. The bruises throbbed and my knees trembled. I tried to press against the wall to stop from sliding down, but he hauled me back by my waist and slapped my bruises again.

"Damn right," he muttered, moving behind me and pushing his still hard cock into my very tender and used hole.

He slapped one hand against the tile in front of my face, growling into my ear as he tunneled in and out of me, over and over. The pace was far from punishing, but it was hard and it was steady, and it didn't take long until I was shaking beneath him uncontrollably.

His cock swelled and he pulled out, spreading my ass cheeks apart with one of his hands. I cried out at the loss of his cock, whimpering as hot jets of his cum landed against my hole without going in. I tried to buck back against him, and he settled me with a sharp slap against my hip. My own cock pulsed in time with my heartbeat, skipping time completely when Dalton pushed his softening cock back inside of me.

"Was last night and this morning not enough for you?" he whispered, pulling out and using his fingers to scoop some cum into my hole. "Are you my dirty little cum slut, Ivey?"

He reached around and yanked the plug out of my mouth. Spit trailed from my lips to the toy and he pushed it inside of me with a surprising amount of ease. The stretch of the plug was wider than his cock and consistent, pushing at my muscles…and my prostate.

"I am," I answered, hips jerking and chasing after friction I didn't think he was going to give me.

"You're a mess back here." Dalton made a tutting sound with his tongue against the roof of his mouth, the pad of his finger tracing around my swollen rim. "All puffy and used, covered in cum."

I whimpered.

A steady stream of heavy and liquid water landed against my rim, sliding down the flared base of the plug and my balls. He didn't say anything, but I knew he was pissing on me. Claiming me, once again, as his. I didn't hate it, but I was already so gone for him he could have looked at me the right way and I would have given him anything he wanted, even if it was something I hated.

It was a new thing, to trust that even if it wasn't for me, Dalton would make it that way. I wondered if he understood how much power and control he truly had over me. It went far beyond the rings and the honorifics and the endearments. Dalton Fox owned me, body and soul.

"You're so fucking perfect," he murmured, after the stream had died off. "I love hurting you, Ivey. Is there something wrong with me, do you think?"

Dalton twisted the knobs on the shower controls and stepped away from me. The water ran ice cold and I shouted, my immediate reflex to try and get away. But the rope tugged at the shower head, the plug pressed against my prostate, and I forced myself to go still.

"Nothing wrong," I whispered, even as my teeth began to chatter from the icy water that ran over my naked body.

I repeated it, half to him and half to myself, as my muscles started to tremble of their own accord. I flexed my toes against the floor, my dick still painfully hard while the rest of my body screamed for a reprieve. Over and over, until the cold wasn't so cold anymore. My body still twitched and twisted, but the water didn't hurt. I didn't feel much of anything, save for the soft ghost of Dalton's burning hot skin against the backs of my legs.

Between the heat of his body and the frigid spray of water, my brain was going sideways. I didn't know which way was up and I started to ramble, mumbling things that didn't make any sense to my own ears, beyond I love you, I love you, I love you. Over and over and over. And then Dalton slid one hand around my front to brace himself, the other sliding to that very sensitive strip of skin between my ass and my thigh.

"I love you," I said again, and he spanked me so hard I saw stars.

I didn't think he'd really hit me so hard, but I was freezing cold and my muscles ached like they never had before, and his hand just *hurt*. He spanked me again and again and again. He spanked me until I stopped trying to talk, until I stopped trying to fight. Dalton rained his hand down against the back of my thighs until the sensations became too much and I came.

My cum was so hot, it burned as it shot out of my dick, painting the wall in front of me and I cried out in relief and agony all at the same time. I didn't know how much more I could take, and I didn't have to find out.

"Perfect," Dalton whispered in my ear, turning the water from cold to tepid, then lukewarm, and finally warm again. He kept his body pressed against mine as sensation returned to my limbs. I shivered violently against him, and when he unwound my arms from the shower head, my knees immediately gave out.

Like he'd expected it, Dalton was there. He caught me in his arms, gingerly lowering us both to the floor of the shower. He tucked me against his chest, half my body in his lap, my legs sprawled in front of us. I didn't have any control over my muscles at that point and as much as I hated to admit it, neither did he.

He brushed my soaking wet hair out of my face and pressed a tender, worshipful kiss against my forehead, and he held me in his arms until the water turned cold again on its own.

CHAPTER 27
DALTON

After I got Ivey out of the shower and dried off, I had no interest in keeping my hands off of him. It had taken me well over an hour to get him dressed because I had to stop to suck his cock on the floor of his closet before I bothered to put him into underwear. Then I was kind enough to let him return the favor when it came my turn. I wasn't sure how I had any cum left inside of me, but in that way he had, Ivey always managed to find a little more. We stumbled through lunch, a prolonged make-out session against the front door of his current apartment, and finally we made our way to the Upper East Side to meet the board for his penthouse interview.

I'd kept the plug in him because we both liked it there.

Standing on the sidewalk, I tipped my head back to look up at the building. "This is a lot."

Ivey squeezed my hand. "It's honestly perfect."

I rubbed the shell of my ear with the side of my finger, wanting to argue the point, but knowing the time wasn't right. It might have been perfect before, but was it perfect now? Did he still feel the same way, considering we were both all in with each other? Considering we wanted to stay married and be together, and knowing that I had a life of my own on the other side of the country. There were lots of logistics that didn't involve our cocks that needed to be considered.

Eventually.

Maybe after dinner.

"If you say so."

"You should see the view." Ivey angled his head toward the doorman, who'd been eyeing us patiently while we talked on the curb. "You'll love it."

"I'll take your word for it," I murmured, letting him lead me toward the front doors.

"Good to see you again, Mr. Royce." The doorman tipped his hat and made room for us to step into the lobby.

I had to bite the inside of my cheek to stop from rolling my eyes. The whole thing was ludicrous. I didn't understand how New York could be a real city. Sure, I had more money than I would ever know what to do with. Some of it was mine and some of it was thanks to my family name, but the appeal of New York living had always evaded me.

"And this is…" The doorman turned his attention to me, trailing off.

"My husband," Ivey said, his tone sure and brooking no argument. "Dalton Fox."

"Mr. Fox."

"A pleasure," I said.

"We're here for another interview," Ivey explained.

The doorman gave him a knowing smile. "They'll be waiting for you on the twenty-first floor."

He called the elevator for us and then leaned in behind us, pressing the button that read twenty-one in some slim modern font. The doors slid closed, leaving us together in the small and surprisingly delightful-smelling space.

"Is that a perk of the building?" I asked. "Someone to push the buttons for you."

"It's a perk of having a doorman."

The elevator was fast enough to tumble my stomach, and the doors slid open before I had enough time to settle myself. We stepped out into a well-appointed lobby with white walls, thick carpets, and white furniture, and I sucked in a steadying breath. I knew I'd gone fifteen years without even speaking Ivey's name in any of its forms, but now that I had, none of this seemed like him.

I also knew it didn't matter what I thought about it, though. It was what he wanted, what he'd wanted before me and what clearly still mattered to him. Even though there were conversations we needed to have. Because while we'd spun a tale about living separate lives because of work, that wasn't the reality I wanted for us.

Not now.

"Mr. Royce." A frail-looking blonde woman met us in the lobby, her arm outstretched. He gave her a gentle shake, then pressed his hand softly against the small of my back.

"Ms. Vanderlin, this is my husband, Dalton Fox."

"Mr. Fox," she greeted me, and I gave her a similar handshake to what Ivey had offered.

"We've been expecting you. Please, right this way."

Ivey shot me a reassuring look that fell flat, but I pasted on the smile that I used for work and dialed up all the feigned interest I could manage. My heart hammered against my sternum, but Ivey's hand in mine kept my breathing steady.

I don't know what I was expecting with a co-op interview for a penthouse apartment in the middle of a city that I hated, but it played out pretty much the way I imagined it would. They asked me about my family history, my education, my philanthropic interests. Ms. Vanderlin seemed to be the most concerned with our love story and she kept most of her questions focused around that.

How did you meet? College.

How long have you been married? Fifteen years.

When is your anniversary? Thankfully, Ivey had given me the date and I recited May 12th back to her like it was an anniversary I'd known my whole life.

Is it hard being apart from each other for so long? Extremely, but now that we're getting older, maybe our schedules can align better.

You know this is unconventional, right? It was more than that, but I gave her an answer that she'd want to hear. Ivey was the love of my life and I'd known it all along. Even though our lives had taken us on different paths, I wanted to walk with him.

At that answer, he reached over and patted my thigh. I took his hand in mine and raised them to my mouth again, dusting a kiss over his wedding band. Ms. Vanderlin paid very close attention to that, her collagen-stuffed lips stretching thin at the display of affection. I wanted to make it worse, but I knew this penthouse mattered to Ivey, so I let go of his hand and folded mine neatly in my lap.

We answered another laundry list of questions and then we were done. Escorted back to the elevator lobby as fast as we'd been collected, but this time there was no one around to push the button for us. Ivey did it, because of course he did. Back in the ground floor lobby, we said a pleasurable goodbye to the doorman, and then we were back on the street.

I leaned against the wall of the building and unbuttoned my coat then worked loose my tie. Ivey crowded against me and popped open the top button of my shirt, smiling softly at the exposed V of skin that he revealed.

"Did I do okay?" I murmured, feeling suddenly tired.

I wondered if it was the interview that had drained me or all the orgasms.

Probably both.

Maybe it was the subconscious work I'd done holding off the frayed edges of a panic attack on top of it.

"You were perfect," he said, coming in closer. "So perfect I could kiss you."

I smiled, eyes closing. "You should."

Ivey softly pressed our lips together, offering me one of the most tentative kisses we'd ever shared. The sound of taxis and car horns racing through the street kept me grounded in the present, and I tangled my fingers into his hair and deepened the kiss. I wanted to drown out everything that wasn't him, but an incessant buzzing started to overtake the traffic chatter and I broke off the kiss with a groan.

"Someone needs to talk to you," I whispered against the corner of his mouth.

"It's probably Kale," he said, fishing his phone out of his pocket, but his expression quickly fell when he saw the screen.

"Is it Kale?"

He shook his head. "It's my father."

The ringing ended, and then promptly started up again.

"You should get that," I suggested.

"I know." He sighed and turned, leaning against the wall beside me, so close our shoulders touched. I waggled my fingers against his and he waggled them back, answering the call, "Hello."

I could hear the deep timbre of a voice on the other end of the line, but not loud enough to make out the words.

"Not yet," Ivey said. "Just met with the board again…No, everything is fine. They just had some more questions is all….I'm sure it is very unusual…Oh."

The *oh* sounded like someone had taken a baseball bat to his chest, and I shifted, pressing my shoulder against the wall so I could look at him. Ivey's brows knit together as his father rattled off on the other end of the call. I wasn't an expert at reading people, but I was better than most, and the tone didn't sound happy.

"Fox," Ivey said, clearing his throat. "Yes, that Fox…I didn't tell you be—"

Ivey closed his eyes, scrubbing his free hand over his mouth and his chin.

"Yes, sir," he muttered, and I frowned at that. I was as familiar as he was with the term of respect expected during a dressing-down by a parent, but in light of what had transpired between us recently, I hated to hear it said with such disdain.

"Yes, sir," he said again. "Yes. I understand."

He ended the call and fisted his phone without another word. I tried to wait him out, but the silence stretched on for miles, and I could see the distress darken around his eyes with every second that passed.

"Are you all right?" I asked.

He nodded, keeping his eyes closed.

"Do you want to tell me what happened?"

He let out a tired breath and opened his eyes. Staring out at the traffic, I watched his eyes track back and forth following cars and people as they passed by.

"Ms. Vanderlin and my father are apparently friends," he said. "They sit on another board together. She called to ask why he'd never mentioned my husband to her before."

"Do your parents know you're…"

"Bisexual? Yes."

"Well." I huffed a laugh. "At least there's that."

"He asked who you were. Who your family was." Ivey frowned. "He has already committed your net worth to memory."

"And they said the devil works fast."

"But Carter Royce III works faster."

Ivey's phone buzzed again, a text message not a call. He dared a look down at the screen, then rolled his eyes and cursed Kale's name under his breath. He fired off a quick text message and then shoved his phone into his pocket.

"My father says if we're legally married, that there needs to be…" he trailed off again, gesturing vaguely.

"A postnup.."

Ivey nodded.

Things between Ivey and me were getting very real very fast. We'd gone from a game of pretend to a serious commitment to a conversation that necessitated the merging and separation of our finances and our families' finances. This trailed right behind the fact we needed to talk about living situations, but that felt such a small concern now…considering.

"Do your parents know you're attracted to men?" he asked me.

"They suspect it."

My brother had been so dutiful about getting married and producing little Fox heirs, they had to be aware of my resistance to the whole idea. I'd never brought anyone home for the holidays and I hadn't mentioned anyone serious to them since I'd made the mistake of telling my mom about Genevieve when I was in college.

"Do they know you're married?"

"We don't talk that often," I said.

"My father is already having our attorney call, so...I don't know if you need to let anyone know." He chewed his bottom lip between his teeth, stare flickering toward me while not quite being able to hold my eyes. "I'm sorry."

"For what?" I shifted again, boxing him against the wall like he'd had me earlier.

There was no doubt that the past week, the past half an hour, had been a lot more than either of us had bargained for, but I'd meant it earlier when I told him that I loved him, and my love didn't come with stipulations and it sure as fuck didn't get scared about an overzealous attorney on someone else's payroll.

"You didn't ask for this," he said.

I grabbed Ivey's face in my hands and held him steady until he looked at me. The rich blue of his eyes shone with unshed tears and he worked his jaw back and forth, fighting against my palms.

"I asked for you," I told him. "I wasn't lying when I told you that I was in love with you, and there isn't anything your father or his attorney can say or do that will scare me off."

"He'll ask for millions." Ivey let out a mocking laugh. "As if we don't have enough of our own."

"As if *I* don't have enough on my own. Your father can ask for whatever he wants to protect his assets. I don't care. But he's not the only one with an attorney and he can bulldog all he wants, but at the end of the day, this is you and me."

"You know it's not that simple," he whimpered. "There's more on the line than just us being together."

He wasn't wrong, and it was one of the main reasons I'd avoided getting *really* serious with anyone in the past. Getting married when you had the kind of money our families did was more like a business deal than a proclamation of love, and it took a special kind of person to see that, understand it, and take it in stride.

I'd never met anyone I felt could bear the brunt of that without falling out of love with me, so I'd never worried about it.

But then... Ivey.

"I'm not scared of your father or his attorney," I promised, swiping my thumb beneath his right eye. Tears had escaped, but I didn't want to call attention to them. I just wanted to wipe them away.

Carefully, I leaned in and pressed a kiss against his mouth. I wasn't looking for anything, but I wanted him to taste the truth of the things I'd told him. We could deal with the postnup and the parents, and then we could deal with where we were going to live.

"I love you," he whispered, barely louder than a breath.

"I know. And I love you back." I kissed him again. "What did Kale want?"

Ivey scoffed, sniffling and rolling his eyes simultaneously. I dropped my hands away from his face and he replaced them with his, giving a quick wipe across his face. If it wasn't for the red splotches on his cheeks, he would have looked good as new.

"He wanted to go to the gym."

It was almost laughable, but at the same time, it sounded like it might be exactly what Ivey needed. I wasn't going anywhere and there would be plenty of time for me to deal with Ivey's best friend and his smart fucking mouth.

"You should," I said, taking his hand and flagging a cab. "It'll get your mind off things for a bit, and then we can talk about it all with more of a level head over dinner."

"The three of us?" he asked.

"That's up to you."

"You know I hate making decisions."

A cab stopped alongside us on the curb and I pulled open the door, stepping out of the way so Ivey could get in first.

"I know," I said, climbing in after. "But you can manage it this once, I think."

It was too late.

The adrenaline rush from the meeting with the board and the call from my father had worn off by the time I reached the gym, only to spike a third time when I opened my locker. I didn't need to take my slacks off to know my legs were covered in bruises, I'd seen it when I stopped in the bathroom to take the plug out. And thanks to an ill-timed laundry run, I only had black nylon basketball shorts in my locker.

"What are you waiting for?" Kale asked with a rich laugh. He came around the corner and sat down on the bench beside me. He'd already changed and was eyeing me expectantly. I didn't even hear him in the other row, and I'd hoped to have more time to get myself ready and situated before facing him. "Did you want an invitation?"

"No." I closed my locker and sat down next to him, shoulders sagging.

What I wanted was my best friend to be my best friend, someone who understood what my life was like and wasn't going to give me shit for my family or my choices. But after how he'd acted toward Dalton at the restaurant, I wasn't sure I would get that from him.

My face must have made my worry clear because he bumped

his shoulder into mine softly. There was no humor in his tone when he cursed under his breath. "Was the interview bad? Do you need to talk instead? We don't have to work out today."

"The interview was fine. My father knows about Dalton now, which is less fine, but…" I trailed off.

Dalton had taken the news about our marriage being outed to my father in stride, and the calm, collected way he had talked to me about it should have been reassuring, but instead it left me unsettled. Was he *so* sure about us that he wasn't intimidated by my father's threats? He'd never met the man, and that had to be the only explanation because if he had, he wouldn't have been so dismissive. He would be more worried. I wouldn't be alone in my concerns.

At the end of the day, this is you and me.

"What does he know exactly?" Kale asked.

"He knows we're married."

"Well…" Kale dragged his tongue across the front of his teeth, leaning back against the bench and kicking the toes of his sneakers against the lockers. "That doesn't matter because it's just pretend, right?"

He was calling my bluff, and we both knew it. He saw the way Dalton had acted at dinner, the rings on our fingers that had price tags far beyond a game of pretend.

"I'm in love with him," I admitted.

I'd barely confessed the truth to Dalton and it felt beyond weird to share it with Kale. The relationship with Dalton and the feelings were so new, it didn't feel reasonable to be as invested as I was. The emotional involvement was mutual, though. Dalton reminded me of that every time he looked at me, every time he touched me. I stared down at the platinum band on my finger, and Kale held his hand out for me, clapping his fingers together.

With a huff, I dropped my hand onto his waiting palm. He raised my hand to the light, twisting it this way and that, making a show of examining the ring.

"Is this Cartier?" he asked, returning my hand to my lap.

"I honestly have no idea."

"His looks like it cost more money than yours," he said, confirming my suspicions that he had been sizing up more than just Dalton when he and Alex had run into us.

I snorted and rolled my eyes, not even surprised. "Dalton and I have different tastes. His suits him. It wouldn't have been right for me to have one like that."

"I'm glad he let you pick something less showy," Kale said.

"He didn't *let* me pick anything."

The accusation was so thick in Kale's comment that the adrenaline rush from earlier headed right toward another crest. I was so fucking tired, and it would be a wonder if I made it through the rest of the evening without collapsing on the spot.

"Did you buy your own rings, then?"

"He bought them both." I spun the band around my finger. "He picked this one for me."

Kale let out a noise that might have been a combination of shock and confirmation. He wanted so badly to dislike Dalton, and it was going to be a problem for me if he didn't get over whatever his issue was. Exhausted of worrying about other people, I decided to rip the band aid off and get it over with.

I stood up and undid my belt and fly, then let my slacks fall to my ankles. The bruises on the front of my thighs were still dark and mottled, but patchier than they had been at first. The handprints on the back of my thighs were dark pink with a few stripes of yellow mixed in, and Kale was going to have to get used to seeing them if he wanted to continue being my friend.

It wasn't news to him—or any of our friends—that I was a submissive, that I enjoyed pain. They'd watched me on more than one occasion and this would be far from the first time they'd seen bruises on me.

"What the fuck?" Kale growled, grabbing my leg just above my knee and yanking my body so I faced him.

I smacked his hand away and hung my slacks up in my locker before pulling out my basketball shorts and stepping into them.

The thin nylon covered almost all of the marks, but when I sat back down, they rode up, exposing more.

"Don't act so surprised," I muttered.

He tried to grab my leg again and I smacked his hand again. At my rebuff, he narrowed his eyes, using the tip of his finger to slide the hem of the shorts up so he could study the marks on my thighs. I sighed and closed my eyes, giving him the chance to get the eyeful he was so clearly after.

"Who did this to you?" he asked, voice low.

"Who do you think?"

"I knew I didn't like him."

"What's not to like?" I snapped, throwing my hands up in frustration.

My entire life had been fighting for the things I wanted and walking away from them when it was too much work. But I wouldn't walk away from Dalton. I wouldn't walk away from this.

"He put his hands on you."

I barked out a sharp laugh. "That's generally how it goes, or did you forget what it's like to be a Dom?"

"But you're not!"

"No shit, Kale." I gestured broadly to my thighs, yanking the hems up higher so he could get a look at the extent of the marking. "That's the point."

"But—"

I cut off his protest before he could even find the words for it. "No buts."

He huffed out a breath that sounded like a growl, and he folded his hands together in his lap, which I knew was a defensive move so he didn't touch me again without my consent.

"Dalton and I are making a go of this," I said, voice low. I let go of my shorts, but didn't pull them back into place. "I love him. He loves me. And we're staying married."

"Beamer!" Kale practically shouted at me. "You can't be serious."

"I'm allowed to fall in love, you asshole." I shoved his shoulder and stood up, walking away so I could put space between us. The air around Kale was stifling, and it was already hard enough to breathe when I thought about a future with Dalton.

"I never said you weren't," he called after me.

"Would you rather I got involved with someone who wasn't a Dom? A man who couldn't give me the things I need. You know what it's like to need this, so I don't understand why you're so put off that I've found it."

"Beamer, come on."

"You don't care when it's Alex giving me marks, but you're all up in arms when it's Dalton? When it's my husband?"

"He's your husband on accident," Kale reminded me, but there wasn't any malice in the accusation.

"Not anymore."

Kale let out a breath, steepling his hands together in front of his nose before scrubbing them down his face. He muttered something under his breath and shook his head, then dropped his hands in his lap.

"Alright," he conceded, holding his hand out for me again. "Let me see your ring."

I wasn't sure that I was ready to be close to him again, but I shuffled across the locker room anyway. At the end of the day, Kale was one of my longest running and best friends. Even if he had a possessive and controlling way of showing it, I knew he only wanted the best for me. The bossiness came with the territory when my four closest friends were all dominant men, but it was the first time I'd had their judgement aimed at me in a way that mattered.

It was important to me that they accept Dalton because, for better or worse, I was in it for the long haul with him. There were a lot of things Dalton and I needed to sort out, namely the postnup my father had undoubtedly already drafted, but the living situation was a very close second. If our marriage had us split between the coasts, that was another fight for Kale and me.

I tried very hard to not be upset with him. He wanted the best for me. All of my friends did, and my preferences in the bedroom made it so they were all inherently protective of me in a way they weren't with each other. It was like having four more older brothers, which…

Pass.

I slid my hand into his and Kale again lifted it to the light, examining the slender platinum band.

"That's a nice ring," he said, barely louder than a mumble.

"Thank you."

Half-dressed for a workout, I stripped out of my button-up and hung it up in the locker. I knew Kale caught sight of the hickeys that decorated my neck and my shoulder, but he smartly bit his tongue and didn't make a comment about them. I shrugged into an old college t-shirt that had seen better days, then slammed the locker closed with a little more force than necessary.

"The bruises are nice too," he grumbled. "If you're into that kind of thing."

I loved Kale, and it was nearly impossible to stay mad at him. I hoped that he'd be able to get his shit together before dinner, because I didn't have it in me for him and Dalton to piss all over each other again. Last time it had happened, Dalton had pissed *on me*, and while I wasn't against a repeat of that sometime in the future, the circumstances had left something to be desired.

"I am," I reminded him.

"Paddle?" he asked.

"Some of them."

He sucked his teeth again and then shoved off the bench to stand. He was shorter than me, closer to Dalton's height, and he looked up at me, eyes scanning my face for any hint of discomfort and fakery. I exhaled loudly, letting him know just how ridiculous I thought the whole thing was, but I let him finish his appraisal, and when he was satisfied with what he saw, I was happy to collapse into the hug he offered me.

"I'm sorry," he mumbled into my neck.

"I know," I told him, slapping him against the back. "All is forgiven on my end. Dalton is going to be some work, though."

"Can't you soften him up for me?"

"Not after the stunt you pulled at the restaurant," I said.

Kale unwound his arms from around my neck. "That's fair."

"You have until seven to figure out how to make it right with him," I said, checking my locker to make sure the lock had engaged.

"Seven? Why?"

I jerked my head toward the doors and Kale headed out behind me. "Because we're getting dinner after we're done here."

"With Dalton?"

"Obviously, Kale." I threw a look over my shoulder at him, ready to test him. "He's my husband. You need to get used to him."

He worked his jaw back and forth before squaring his shoulders and clearing his throat. I saw it, the moment the argument and the fight went out of him, and I let out a breath I didn't realize I'd been holding. It was so important to me that Dalton and my friends get along, and Kale's quiet acquiescence was the first step in making sure I had that.

"I'll be on my best behavior," he promised me, drawing an X across the center of his chest. "I hope when the time comes, his friends give you the same courtesy."

I swallowed, adding another thing to the list of potential problems Dalton and I had to work though.

"Yeah," I agreed. "Me too."

I'D BARELY MADE IT BACK INTO IVEY'S APARTMENT BEFORE MY PHONE started ringing. I knew who it was without looking at the screen.

"Hi, Dad." I kicked the front door closed behind me and then toed off my shoes. Using my feet to arrange them side by side, I put my phone on speaker and cradled it in the palm of my hand.

I'd never planned on coming out to my parents. Not because I was afraid of their reactions. My older brother had done his job. He'd married well and his wife had produced a son and all was well for the legacy of the Fox name. I was a spare and any children I had would trail even further behind. I hadn't intended to come out because I'd never planned on getting serious enough with anyone to warrant it.

"Dalton." He sounded as buttoned up and smug as he ever did. "How's New York?"

I climbed onto a barstool at the counter and dropped my phone onto the marble with a tight sigh. "Busier than I prefer," I said.

"When do you imagine you'll be back in L.A.?"

Okay, so that was how the conversation was going to play out. He was going to play dumb about the whole thing until I confessed it on my own. Well, joke was on him. I enjoyed dragging things out, well past the point of pleasure and enjoyment. "Couldn't say."

"I can pick a date for you," he offered.

"I'm closer to forty than eighteen," I reminded him.

"Are you done being cute?"

"I think it comes quite naturally."

"You can be home in four days and you can bring Carter Emerson Royce IV with you, or you can watch how your bank account changes when you don't fall in line," he snapped.

"This doesn't have anything to do with Iv—" I cut myself off, stopping before I used the endearment that I never wanted to hear in my father's voice. "This doesn't have anything to do with Royce."

"His attorney says differently."

"His father's attorney says differently," I corrected.

"Then the two of you have at least one thing in common, which is a relief to me considering today is the first I've heard about this…this *man*…that you're married to."

I sighed again, drawing a figure eight on the counter with the tip of my finger. "I don't want to do this with you."

"I don't blame you."

I had half a mind to ask him how much of my trust fund he would call back if I didn't give him his way. The curse of being born with a name like Fox or Royce meant that you didn't get to turn eighteen and set out on your own. Things were bought for you, paid for, and then leveraged over you for the rest of your life. You were raised up accustomed to a certain kind of life and so the threat of loss always hovered around the periphery.

I think it was more a problem for Ivey than for me because the way his face had blanched when his father called him was enough to have my heart skipping beats itself. I wasn't scared of my father, though. I'd done enough for myself that I would be far from poor, even if he took back all of his financial support. But that wouldn't change the fact I'd built what I had on his name—my name—and his money.

"Marie, calm down," my father said, and I knew he was talking to my mother. I closed my eyes, folding my arms and dropping my forehead on the cushion they made. It had been so long since I'd seen either of them. On purpose, because my father was exhausting and my mother was a worrier, and it was a lot.

They were a lot.

My life…was a lot.

But as much as I hated New York, being with Ivey made it much more tolerable.

"Everything all right over there?" I asked, even though I hardly cared.

"Your mother is just…hold on."

The line went deathly silent, and I knew I'd been put on hold.

I didn't think that was a normal life experience for most people either. Being put on hold by your own father? I couldn't help but laugh at the absurdity of the whole thing. Rolling my head back and forth across my forearm, I waited for him to come back on the line, but when the call resumed, it was my mother's voice on the other end of the call.

"Dalton?" she asked.

"I'm here, Mama."

"Ignore your father," she said. "Stay in New York as long as you want."

I chuckled. "I was going to."

"He's just being dramatic."

"I know," I said.

"It was a little unfair of you, though," she went on, voice soft as a hug. "He was caught off-guard earlier."

"So were we," I told her. "I didn't think that it would escalate that way."

She made a thoughtful noise. "There is paperwork."

"I know," I said again.

"But it will keep."

"Thank you, Mama," I whispered.

"Don't make him wait too long," she warned. "And bring the boy home with you when you come."

"He's not a boy."

"Even better." I could hear the smile in her voice. "I love you."

"I love you."

"We'll be seeing you, Dalton."

She disconnected the call before I could say goodbye, which was her way. My mom was far softer and kinder than my father ever had been. She tempered him in most ways, but at the end of the day, she stayed in line and she kept us there too. She was the living embodiment of the old saying "you catch more flies with honey than vinegar," but even after almost fifty years together, my father hadn't learned the lesson from her.

Either way, I got the impression she had talked some kind of sense into him, and that was enough. I had more important things to worry about anyway, namely getting my shit together and meeting Ivey and Kale for dinner after their little jaunt at the gym.

I'd hated to send him away after the interview and the disastrous phone call with his father, but when shit went wrong for me, I wanted the support of my friends above almost all else. I loved being with Ivey, and I enjoyed sharing with him, but there would always be things better suited for Barclay or Flynn. And that was no shortcoming on his part. It was only the nature and the beauty of friendship.

With that in mind, I called Barclay who answered on the third ring.

"Is the prodigal son ready to return?" he asked as a greeting.

"Not quite yet, but soon." I groaned, forcing myself up off the counter. The screen on my phone was still bright from the call connecting, and I was relieved to see I had plenty of time to get ready for dinner.

"How did it go today?"

"The interview went fine, I think, but the board incidentally outed both of us."

"That feels illegal," he murmured.

"You're not wrong, but you know how money talks."

The only point in pursuing legal action against Ms. Vanderlin and her mouth would be if I could afford better lawyers than she could.

And I couldn't.

My father, maybe. Ivey's father, definitely. But I didn't think either of them would feel inclined to help us in that regard.

"Anyway. It happened, and now we're waiting for the board to make their decision on whether he gets the penthouse," I said.

"Do you know how long?"

"No, but…it doesn't really matter."

"Why not?" Barclay balked. "You said you were staying in New York until he was sorted and then you'd be home."

"Things…have changed."

"You stupid son of a bitch," he cursed, laughing at me at the same time. "You fell in love with your husband."

"Shut up."

"Oh, that's rich." He laughed again, louder. "I can't wait for the guys to hear about this."

"Archie is the gossip, not you," I reminded him.

"Archie is right here," Archie said, his voice tinny.

"Am I on speakerphone?"

"Obviously," Flynn chimed in, and I wished Ivey's windows opened so I could throw myself out of one.

"When are you coming home?" Archie asked.

"I said I don't know."

"If you don't come home soon, we'll have to come out there," he threatened.

"You best not."

I had enough to deal with, between Alex and Kale and whatever other friends Ivey had ready to come out of the woodwork. The last thing I wanted to do was throw him under the scrutiny of *my* friends.

Not until things were more settled, at least.

"Are you scared we won't like him?" Flynn asked.

"You'll love him." I'd never been as sure of anything as I was of that.

"Have you met his friends?" Barclay asked. "You have to be doing more out there than just fucking."

I snorted a laugh, shaking my head. "I've met two of them."

"And?"

"And it's complicated," I said. "I'm having dinner with one of them later tonight."

"Complicated how?"

"Complicated in that he makes Grayson look like he has self-esteem issues," I said. "He's a lot."

"Sounds like a handful," Grayson said.

"Oh, my God. You're there too?"

"The gang's all here, bestie," Flynn teased.

I rubbed at the bridge of my nose, grabbing my phone off the counter and standing up. My hip cracked, and I staggered into the bedroom, feeling surprisingly aimless.

"I miss you assholes," I muttered, plugging my phone into the charger and flopping down on the bed.

My foot dragged across a coil of rope that I'd half shoved under to get it out of the way the night before. I flicked it up onto the bed beside me and started making loose knots at the ends and picking them apart to repeat the process over again.

"Very sentimental," Barclay teased.

"I didn't call for this abuse."

"Why did you call?" he asked.

"I don't know. I'd just talked to my parents, and Ivey is out with Kale, and—"

"I'm sorry, what did you just say?" Grayson interrupted.

I knew it would be him. I knew I liked him the most, even though he was the newest.

"Ivey's best friend is named Kale," I said.

"Like the lettuce no one likes to eat?"

"Correct."

"That's unfortunate."

"He is," I agreed.

"Well..." The sound of the call changed, and I would guess

Barclay had taken me off speaker. I heard the rest of them complaining in the background and then a door closed and it went silent. "Sorry about that. They saw your name on the screen. It was unavoidable."

"It's fine."

"Is everything okay?" he asked.

"Yeah, honestly. Everything is better than okay. It's just… complicated now."

"You'll manage it," he said, which was apparently exactly what I needed to hear. I dropped the rope on top of my legs. "Are you sure?"

"Very." He laughed. "At least, as long as you don't murder his friend tonight."

"I don't think I can promise that. He's just such a prick. The way he acts like he owns Ivey—"

"I'm going to stop you there," Barclay interrupted me, and I groaned. "Putting aside the fact you've been married to him for most of your adult life, when was his last serious relationship?"

"A while back."

"And how long as he known this friend of his?"

I knew where Barclay was taking the conversation, whether I liked it or not.

"Since college," I mumbled. "Don't say it."

"I won't, but you know it."

"He can be protective of Ivey without being such a prick about it."

"As if we've treated Grayson, Owen, or Rose any different," he said.

It felt like an overstatement to me. I didn't think we'd given any of the new boyfriends as shit of a time as Kale had given me, but I wasn't going to argue the point.

"You should be happy about it," he said quietly.

"Why?"

"Because it means that he had people watching out for him before you came around."

I exhaled loudly, hating how right he was.

"But you're there now," Barclay went on, so arrogant I could hear the smirk in his voice. "So get your head out of your ass and go prove to them that it's safe for them to step aside. He's your husband, Fox. Make sure they know what that means to you."

CHAPTER 30
IVEY

A game of handball had settled Kale's attitude and by the time we pulled up to the restaurant, he was acting much more like himself and far less like an arrogant piece of shit. The only give-away that he still had it in him was a questionable noise in the back of his throat when Dalton climbed out of a cab half a block down from us. I barely registered the sound because Dalton looked better than he ever had.

The time alone at the apartment had done him good, and my breath skittered when he stood to his full height. He hadn't seen me yet, but I watched him as he smoothed a hand down the front of his shirt, looking around to take the city in. Dalton wore a pair of shiny black dress shoes, his usual, with a pair of slacks that looked more tailored than normal. Instead of pairing them with a white button-up, he had on a black one, top button undone and the sleeves rolled up toward his elbows. It looked gorgeous against his tanned skin and dark hair, and the way the diamonds in his ring glittered when he finally saw me almost matched the shine in his eyes.

A slow smile crept across his mouth like he knew a secret that existed only for the two of us. He headed for us, hand outstretched and I slid my palm against his, letting him pull me into an embrace that should have been too decadent for public. Instead of kissing me, he buried his face in the crook of my neck, sucking in a deep breath.

"You smell different," he murmured.

"Gym toiletries."

He hummed and kissed the underside of my jaw, stepping back without letting go of my hand.

"Kale," he said, polite as I'd expect him to be when meeting a client or a judge for the first time. "Good to see you again."

Dalton switched our hands and stuck his right hand out for a shake, which was ridiculously overdone, but he was *trying* and I had to appreciate that. I gave him a squeeze as Kale returned the gesture with minimal reluctance.

"Good to see you again," Kale repeated.

A knot of tension that had taken up residence in my chest slowly started to unwind, loosening even further when Kale and Dalton both tried to be the first one inside the restaurant. Dalton conceded, letting Kale take the lead, shooting me a fond smile that I returned by pressing our arms together so we could fit through the door side by side.

The host led us to a booth, and Dalton slid in next to me with Kale on the other side. Together, we formed the most imbalanced triangle, but I knew it would take time for the weight and the responsibility to shift around.

"So, Kale." Dalton cleared his throat, fingers still wrapped around mine beneath the table. "Ivey says you went to college with us?"

It was almost a dig, but defendable. I chuckled.

"I did."

"And you moved back here after graduation?"

"I prefer the city," Kale said. "Easier to cater to varied tastes out here."

Kale shot me a knowing look that had heat flaming up my throat. At the same time, a waiter appeared with three paper menus, and Dalton intercepted the one meant for me. It was a fluid move, and both sheets of cardstock were in his hand and my hands were in my lap.

"I'll have a gin and tonic," he said to the waiter, angling his head toward me. "And he'll have a whiskey and water."

Kale's nostrils flared, but he ordered himself a whiskey with no spoken protest. He did raise an eyebrow at me while Dalton perused the menu, and I shrugged at him. We'd talked about this at the gym, about the way I was, the things I wanted. They'd never been a secret to him, so the performative outrage wasn't necessary. Dalton didn't give me anything I hadn't vocally and excitedly asked for.

A small silence fell over the table, and Kale pursed his lips before asking, "How do you find Los Angeles?"

Dalton finished his scan of the menu, setting them down on the table.

"I can't imagine living anywhere else," he said.

As the words left his mouth, Dalton patted my thigh reassuringly, but the unspoken problem hung over our heads like a storm cloud. I looked up, the pressure of it so heavy, I would have sworn it was a real and tangible thing threatening to open up and pour all over us.

"That's...interesting," Kale murmured.

"Nothing you need to concern yourself with," Dalton said, giving him a sharp look. "Wherever Ivey and I end up will be a place we both want to be."

"But you don't want to be here," Kale said.

"I want to be with him."

I swallowed, the answer so honest and simple that some of the storm clouds felt like they dissipated. The way Dalton and I wanted each other hadn't faded after fifteen years, and both of us had tried to walk away from that Vegas trip and failed. Even with a country separating us, I was confident we would figure out something that worked.

"Alright then," Kale conceded, tossing his menu down on the table.

The waiter returned with our drinks and we ordered our dinner. Dalton, of course, ordered for me, which drew another pinched expression from Kale, but he was trying. I saw it, and I hoped Dalton saw it too. Dalton was still posturing in front of Kale, but it wasn't in a demonstrative, pissing match kind of way like before. Dalton was acting the same way he'd act if it were just the two of us. He wasn't trying to hide the dynamic between us. If anything, he tried to emphasize it.

He ordered for me, which he knew I liked. He kept his hands on me, a possessive touch that burned beneath the table like fire. When he turned to look at me, his stare was strong enough to strip me bare, even though I was fully dressed. It unmanned me in a different kind of way and, admittedly, it made me horny as all fuck. I didn't know how I was going to make it through dinner because every time Dalton spoke, he oozed confidence and propriety, and my body ached to show him just how right he was about all of it.

How right he'd been about us.

The conversation after that came easy enough, talking about generally mundane topics like law and the weather. The three of us managed to avoid anything that could spark a debate or an argument, which to me felt like a step in the right direction. By the time we finished our entrees, Dalton and Kale were even laughing at each other's jokes.

It was a win.

It was a relief.

We were waiting for the check, our last round of drinks half empty in front of us, when Dalton cleared his throat and spoke up, "So, how many more like you are there that I need to prove my worth to?"

"You don't need to prove yourself to anyone," I said.

"Four," Kale answered.

Dalton swirled the melting ice around his drink, mouth pursed into a thoughtful frown. "Four including Alex or four plus him?"

"Including."

"Who are the other two?" he asked.

"Ford and Brooks," Kale said.

Dalton nodded, tongue darting out back and forth across his lower lip.

"What about on your side?" Kale asked.

"It really feels like the two of you are discussing my dowry and I'm not sure I like it," I murmured.

Dalton chuckled, grazing a kiss across my temple. The soft wetness of his mouth was enough to silence any other protestations that had started to form on my tongue.

"It's important that I meet your friends." Dalton dropped another kiss against the shell of my ear. In my pants, my cock jerked violently. The whole meal had felt like foreplay, every touch, every secret decision he made on my behalf enough to kick start my arousal to out-of-this-world levels.

"And that they like you," Kale added.

"Is it?" Dalton left another kiss on my ear, then glanced at Kale. "I don't really care if my friends like Ivey or not. I mean, it would be nice, but it's not a deciding factor for me."

The overwrought tension started to creep back in, and I swallowed, grabbing Dalton's thigh to steady myself. The emotions were too much, half nerves, half arousal. I didn't know how I was going to make it through the rest of dinner without screaming, either in pleasure or frustration.

"What's not to like?" Kale pressed.

"Not a single thing," he said. "I'm only saying it doesn't matter."

"Don't you value their opinion?"

"They don't make my decisions for me." Dalton leaned across the table, and instinctively Kale did the same. "And even if I was a submissive, they wouldn't make the decisions for me then either."

Kale's gaze darted up, and Dalton held his stare, jaw tense.

It was a kind of assertion of ownership and dominance I could be okay with because it wasn't overdone. It was fair. It was Dalton reminding my very jealous but well-meaning best friend that I was my own man and capable of making my own choices. And it just so happened that I'd chosen Dalton.

For better or worse.

Kale cleared his throat and leaned back, breaking away from Dalton's stare to finish off the rest of his drink. Kale looked at me, and I smiled at him…imploringly. It was important to me that my friends liked Dalton because I didn't want to have to choose. I wanted them to see all the things I saw, and understand all the good he brought to my life.

"I'll make sure they understand," Kale said, setting his drink down on the table. He fished his credit card out of his wallet and held it out, just as the waiter came back with the check. "Dinner's on me."

"That's not necessary," Dalton protested.

"I know." It was Kale asserting himself, and I couldn't fault him for that. "I'll be right back. Men's room."

After I'd lost sight of Kale's back in the restaurant, I turned to say something to Dalton, but whatever the thought had been vanished as soon as he grabbed my face with both hands and crashed our mouths together. For as much force as he put behind the kiss, it was relatively chaste. His lips were barely parted, tongue dragging across my lower lip like he was trying to wet it instead of getting inside. Helpless, I grabbed his arms and whimpered into his mouth.

"I love you," he whispered, and I took the opportunity to try and get my tongue deeper into his mouth. In response, he bit my lip and my entire body trembled.

"I'm so close to coming," I whined softly.

Dalton worried his tongue over the place he'd bit me, not bothering to pull away when Kale returned to the table. I was too far gone to care, body slack in Dalton's hold as he continued his slow and torturous assault on my mouth.

"Better not," he warned, finally breaking away.

I covered my cheeks with my hands and groaned, looking at the wall instead of him or my best friend. It wasn't the first time

I'd shown my tendencies in front of Kale and I somehow knew it wouldn't be the last. It wasn't the display that embarrassed me, it was the desperate and unflinching way that Dalton was able to command me. With a look, with a kiss, with a touch, I was his in every sense of the word. The waiter came back with Kale's card and he signed the receipt, shooting a look across the table at me that felt like a pre-emptive apology.

"What?" I asked, a sense of dread curdling in the pit of my stomach. I thought things had gone so well. I thought we'd made progress.

"I had a message from Ford when I went to piss." Kale scratched the side of his neck, and I shook my head, telling him no. "He's at The Black Door with Brooks and Alex if the two of you were up for a nightcap."

"The Black Door?" Dalton glanced at me, question on his face.

"Sex club," Kale answered helpfully, a recognizable and playful grin dancing across his face.

It was a relief to see my best friend back in his usual, smug form, but a trip with Dalton to the club was not how I envisioned my night ending.

"Are you up for that?" Dalton asked me.

"Up to you." I gave him a half-shrug.

Across the table, Kale angled his head to the side, clearly watching the whole exchange for weak points that he could use against Dalton later. That was also very much like his normal self. It wasn't a competition anymore; that was just how Kale was with everyone in his life.

He always needed the upper hand, and with Dalton…he didn't have it.

"It is up to me," he agreed. "But I don't want to go if you're not comfortable with it."

"It's fine with me."

Dalton studied my face for any sign of a lie, then lifted my left hand to his mouth and again kissed my ring. It was something he did often, and it felt as much a proclamation of love and dominance as his words did. The unbearable pressure between my legs built toward a breaking point, and I grimaced, shifting my hips to ease the ache.

"Sounds perfect." Dalton slid out of the booth, pulling me with him, my glaring erection be damned. I pressed against the back of his thigh, trying to hide my arousal from everyone else trying to enjoy their dinner. "Are you ready?"

I pressed a kiss against his shoulder. I was ready as I'd ever be.

CHAPTER 31
DALTON

New York wasn't anything like Los Angeles, and The Black Door wasn't anything like Rapture. Tucked inside a surprisingly nondescript building surrounded by far more popular and bustling clubs, The Black Door was the definition of discreet. Inside was much the same, if not more open. Lots of exposed brick and frosted glass giving the illusion of privacy when there wasn't much to be had.

The clientele looked to be an even split of genders, with most people milling around and drinking. Where Rapture had a bustling dance floor, The Black Room had a well-appointed lounge with small tables and overstuffed couches and chairs designed for conversation. There was music and there were people dancing, but it looked to me like the kind of dancing that led to sex.

The point of a sex club, I imagined.

"Do you want a drink?" Kale asked after we'd made it past security.

"I'm good," I told him. He looked at Ivey, and I answered before he could ask. "Water for him."

Kale worked his jaw back and forth, but went to the bar without a word of protest. I took his absence as an opportunity, pulling Ivey's chest against mine and sliding my arms around his waist.

"We need to talk," I said.

"He's trying."

"Not about Kale." I huffed a laugh. "But you're right."

His shoulders sagged with relief, and I leaned closer to kiss his chin.

"I wanted to talk about tonight. What you're comfortable with," I said.

"I trust you," he answered.

"I know. And I love you for that. But we've never really talked about limits. It's always kind of been stop if you need to stop, and that's been careless and irresponsible of me to not press it before."

I'd known the whole time that it was bad form to not have a more serious conversation with him before things developed between us, but I honestly trusted Ivey enough to tell me to stop if I went too far. He liked to serve and he liked to be hurt, and I liked giving him both of those things. The night I'd taken him in the shower, I'd brought him as close to the edge as I'd ever taken anyone, and I had no plans to ever go further than that.

But still…

"You've always asked before you've done new things," he reminded me. "Like with the pissing."

Maybe I was imagining things, but I would have sworn his body heat spiked at least ten degrees at the comment.

"You did like that, didn't you?"

"More than I would have expected. So that's why I don't want to give you limits. I trust you to not do things that won't bring me pleasure in the long run."

It was a heavy burden he was trying to put on my shoulders, but the responsibility was something I'd asked for. Something I'd demanded.

Tracing my fingers across his cheek, I shivered when he melted into my touch. The trust he had in me, after everything we'd been through, was overwhelming sometimes. I didn't want to lead him astray or treat him wrong. Ever. That was why the criticism and judgement from Kale had been as hard for me to deal with as it was. Because the thought, the insinuation, that I would ever hurt Ivey was so far out of the realm of possibility for me. It was only a shortcoming on me as a partner and as a Dom if that wasn't immediately clear to everyone else.

"What if I make you cry?"

Ivey hummed and leaned against my palm. "As long as you make me come."

I slid my hand around the side of his head and hauled his mouth against mine, kissing him much more intent than I had at the restaurant. Ivey had been hard since dinner, and his erection pushed insistently at my hip as I deepened the kiss, digging my fingers into the back of his head until he grunted into my mouth.

"Am I correct in assuming all of your friends have seen your cock?"

He nodded.

"How many of them have you fucked?" I asked.

Our mouths were still aligned, lips dragging and wet with saliva as we whispered to each other.

"Just Alex," he said.

I didn't know if it was better or worse that he'd only slept with one of his friends. Did that mean Alex was special? Shoving the unnecessary jealousy to the back of my mind, I kissed the corner of Ivey's mouth.

"Thank you for being honest."

"Always."

I wanted to go home.

Back to L.A.

And I wanted to take Ivey with me, his stupid penthouse and friends be damned. I wanted him to meet my friends, and I wanted to take him to my club. I wanted to fuck him in the darkest hallways of Rapture, and then I wanted to tie him up to the rigging in *my* house. The way I wanted—no, needed—him to leak into all of the corners and crevices of my life so thoroughly that I'd never be able to get him out was very nearly a tangible thing for me.

I tightened my hold on his head and grabbed his waist with the other, bracketing his body against mine so we were touching in all the places that our clothes would allow.

"Would you be upset if we didn't play here?" I nipped my teeth against his chin hard enough to make him wince.

"No," he answered quickly. "But why not? Is something wrong?"

"Nothing's wrong," I promised. "I just...I'm having a lot of feelings about you and about my life, and I don't want to play unless I can get them all back under control."

Ivey leaned back and peered down at me, brows knit together in the most adorable look of concern I'd ever seen.

"Are you okay? We can go..."

"I'm fine." I tightened my hold on him until the tension between his eyebrows softened. "I promise."

"Okay."

He didn't look like he believed me. I caught movement over his shoulder and found Kale leaning against the bar, his stare trained on the back of Ivey's head. He had two other men with him. Alex was nowhere to be seen, but I recognized the other two from the pictures Ivey had out at his house.

"Would you get on your knees for me?" I whispered.

"Always."

"Right here?"

It was partially hypothetical, but Ivey took it to heart and sank down to the ground without being asked. He was a big man, tall and broad enough for anyone to take note of in a crowded room. And when he slid down to the floor, Kale and the other two, Brooks and Ford, all three of them watched with rapt attention, unsure of whether to look at Ivey or me.

I didn't watch them any longer than I had to, instead looking down at the top of Ivey's golden hair and threading my fingers through it so I could tip his head back. He gazed up at me, nothing but love and want in his eyes. His pupils were already broad, dark pools, and I tapped his cock with the tip of my shoe. He was harder than before, even though I didn't know how that was possible, and his entire body trembled from the pressure.

"If I haven't told you lately, you're perfect."

"Thank you, Sir."

I hummed, stroking my fingers down the side of his face.

"If you keep that up, you're going to make me come," I warned.

An easy smile settled on Ivey's face and his lashes fluttered. He sank lower onto his knees, ass resting on his heels and his hands drifted upturned toward his thighs. Even in the middle of a busy and crowded club with his asshole Dom friends looking on, Ivey was the perfect picture of submission.

And he was mine.

Kale, of course, picked the opportunity to show up, passing me the water I'd asked him to get Ivey. He had their other two friends flanked on either side of him, and the way they both sized me up was commendable, but lacking. There wasn't anything they could do or say that would take away the power that surged through every cell in my body when Ivey was on his knees for me.

"Thank you," I told him, twisting open the cap and holding it down low for Ivey to take a drink from.

He did.

Without using his hands.

When he finished, I twisted the cap back on and tucked the bottle under my arm, repeating the same formalities from dinner with Ford and Brooks.

"I'm Dalton Fox," I said, holding out my hand for two sets of handshakes.

"Ford Carlisle," the dark-haired one said.

"Astor Brooks," the other said. "You can call me Brooks."

I chuckled, unable to ignore the similarities.

"You go by your last name?" I asked.

"Not a fan of the family name," he answered.

"I have one of those back home too," I said, thinking of Barclay. "My best friend, Perceval."

"Don't blame him for that one," Kale said.

"That's rich coming from someone named after lettuce," Brooks teased, and I looked down at the top of Ivey's head to hide my smile.

He hadn't moved since I'd offered him the water. The tops of his hands still rested against his thighs and his eyes were so focused on my cock it was as close to a hands-free blow job as I'd ever had. Was an eye job a thing? Because the heat rolled off of Ivey in waves, sloshing me closer and closer to the very dangerous edge of a cliff.

"Ivey." I scratched the top of his head and he blinked up at me. I wondered if he was even aware of his friends joining us because when Ivey went into subspace, he went hard.

I'd played with people before who only got off on pain, but I'd never met someone like Ivey, who *truly* got off on the service side of submission. Like, I could wake up on Saturday morning and tell him to make me breakfast, demand that he bathe me, make him ride my cock until I came, then fuck off and make me lunch, and he would do it all gladly with his very own erection.

He made a soft humming noise, blinking slowly. I waited until I was sure he saw *me*.

"Your friends are here," I said. "Did you want to stand up and say hello?"

Ford's mouth twitched into a smirk and Kale groaned, shifting his weight from side to side. Brooks watched the two of them before looking directly at me. I didn't bother making eye contact with him because my focus was solely on Ivey, who had managed a weak nod of agreement.

Shifting the water bottle out from beneath my arm, I helped him to his feet. With his back to his friends, I passed him the water bottle, then busied myself with his belt. I pulled the leather strip out of the loops, then popped the fly and shoved my hand into his pants. He sucked in a tortured breath when I curled my hand around his cock, the desperate noise turning into a whimper when I tucked the head of his cock up behind the elastic waistband of his underwear. I buttoned him back up and redid his belt, using the next available hole so I didn't strangle his cockhead, though the longer I thought about the idea, the more appealing it sounded.

"Are you good?" I asked him, deciding to go ahead and tighten the belt after all.

Ivey's back bowed and he fell forward, dropping his head against my shoulder. I laughed softly in his ear, rubbing my hand up and down the length of his shaft through his slacks.

"I'm so close," he whispered.

"Did you want me to make you come before you said hello?"

The tip of his cock poked out from his waistband, and I dragged my fingertip back and forth across it. He shivered and groaned, and there was no longer doubt in *any* of our minds about who I was to Ivey and who he was to me.

"I want to wait," he said.

"That's good." Another press of my thumb against his leaking slit. "I want you to wait too. Now say hello to your friends, Ivey. They're waiting."

I could feel the arrogance dripping out of their pores, but after Dalton helped me back to my feet, I greeted Brooks, Ford, and Kale as I normally would have. With Dalton's hand burning hot against the small of my back, I felt more at ease in my natural state than I had in longer than I could remember.

Having a herd of dominant men as best friends was great… until it wasn't. Even after Alex and I had started to play together, I'd never truly felt comfortable showing that side of myself around them. They all knew I was submissive, but it was one thing to know it and another to see it.

With Dalton, they were seeing it for the first time.

"It's just me," I told the three of them, hoping it would alleviate some of the wariness in their faces. "You're not unfamiliar with how this works, so stop looking at me like anything that just happened is so far out of the norm."

"It is for you," Brooks said.

"But it's not." I lifted my hand and rubbed his shoulder reassuringly. "I promise you, it's not."

"Did you want to show me around?" Dalton asked in my ear.

"That would probably be a good start," Ford said. "Alex is around here somewhere, so we'll go find him and you two can get more comfortable."

Dalton tipped his chin and the three of them headed off in search of trouble. Dalton's hand was still against the small of my back and I swiveled toward him, nose dusting across his forehead.

"Are you good?" I asked.

"Never been better." He sounded like he meant it. "Your friends don't scare me. Neither does your submission."

A strangled laugh fell out of my mouth. "Well, I'm glad you feel okay about it."

"Do you not?"

"It's not that. It's just…it comes so easily with you."

Dalton's mouth quirked into an almost embarrassed smile, and I would have sworn his cheeks darkened in the dim light of the club.

"I don't think that's a bad thing," he said.

"Neither do I. Can I show you around?"

"I'd like that." He kept his hand against the small of my back, but instead of steering me, he followed close enough behind to never break contact.

"This is obviously the main lounge area," I said, gesturing around us at the familiar brick and glass space. "There's some rooms down a hallway in the back for other interests."

"What interests?" he asked.

"More public demonstrations." I cleared my throat. "Free use. That kind of thing."

He hummed, fingers pressed possessively against my spine.

"You can use them privately, but they're generally more free-for-all situations than you get out here. Not that you need the rooms. Pretty much anything goes as long as both parties are consenting," I explained.

"As it should be."

"There's another floor." I took a small step, waiting for him to follow, then I led us toward the hidden elevators. They were on a weight sensor, and there were no buttons to press. After a matter of seconds, the stainless steel doors slid open, revealing an otherwise glass box that was completely exposed to the club space on three sides.

We stepped into the car and the doors whooshed closed behind us. The elevator rose, sliding into a concrete encasement so the occupants would be hidden as they passed through the floors that weren't owned by the club. When the elevator reached the top floor, the concrete disappeared and the lights of the city sparkled off the glass as the doors slid open.

"Jesus," Dalton muttered under his breath, following me out. "And I thought Rapture was nice."

"Rapture?"

"It's the club we go to at home," he explained.

"Interesting name."

"It's in an old church. Private rooms in the organ loft, original stained glass." Dalton chuckled. "Very blasphemous."

"It sounds like a good time," I said.

He pulled me closer, kissing my shoulder. "I can't wait to take you there."

And again the unspoken problem between us surfaced, but the sharp sound of a whip cracking through the air washed it away. At least for the time being.

The top level of The Black Door had always been my favorite. With the giant panes of plate glass instead of concrete, patrons on the top floor had an unhindered view of the city. There was a patio off the back that was lovely when the weather was nice and sometimes even when it wasn't.

The mood on the top floor was generally a lot more hedonistic than the main floor, and as soon as we stepped into the space, the air changed. I'd already been painfully aroused through dinner. The kneeling downstairs hadn't helped matters at all, and if I closed my eyes and listened to the sounds of sex echoing around me, I was practically ready to explode.

"You're tense," Dalton whispered with a sadistic little laugh in my ear.

"Yes, Sir," I agreed.

Dalton gave me a push into the crowd. I was clearly done leading him around, and the two of us moved around together with him taking the lead. I'd been coming to The Black Door for so long I didn't really remember what my impression of the place had been the first time I visited, but I was jealous of Dalton for getting to experience it for the first time. He didn't seem overwhelmed or out of place, which only spoke to his comfortability with his role in our relationship.

Through and through, Dalton was a dominant man.

"Excuse me." We'd come up to a cluster of couches around a low wooden table, two couples spread out over the seating. Dalton leaned down closer to them so he didn't have to yell. "I hate to intrude, but do any of you have a paddle or a tawse I could borrow?"

One of the women grimaced, and her partner let out a low and dangerous laugh.

"Unfortunately, no," the man said, patting his partner's leg softly. "I'm woefully unprepared, but he has some canes in his bag."

Dalton grinned, turning his attention to the other couple on the couch, two men.

"This is terribly bad form," Dalton went on. "But I'm from out of town and I wasn't planning on coming out tonight."

"Say less." The smaller of the men held a long and thin leather case out to Dalton. "You're welcome to anything in here as long as you don't take it out of my sight."

He gave me a slow onceover, and Dalton paused.

"What do you think, Ivey?" he asked me, unzipping the case.

"I think that's very kind of them, Sir."

"I agree."

After some rearranging, there was room for us on the couch and Dalton sat down, holding up a finger indicating for me to wait.

It was like a switch with me, the way I could go from equal partner to submissive around him. A single word, the flick of his finger, and it was as if my synapses misfired before clicking back into place and working the right way. The way Dalton wanted them to work.

"Unzip your pants," he said softly, selecting a bamboo cane from the case and testing the flexibility against his palm.

My fingers fumbled the zipper, but I managed to do as I was told.

My cock was still pressed up into my waistband, the belt applying enough pressure that I genuinely worried after he moved it I would come on the spot. Which was, of course, what he wanted. Dalton gave me a small nod, and I wrestled my cock out through the hole made by my undone zipper. The cool air sent a shiver up my spine and I fisted my hands at my sides, trying with all my might to not pop off without being touched.

"Do you want to come?" he asked.

"Yes, Sir."

"I bet." He reached out and pinched the tip of my dick so hard I saw stars. "It looks painful."

When Dalton let go, my legs gave out and I went right to my knees, which seemed to please him. He petted a hand down the side of my face and smiled down at me.

"Good boy," he whispered. "My very best pain slut."

He set the cane across his knees and loosened his own belt and zipper, pulling his cock out and making a tight fist around the base. Even in the low light, I could make out the glistening precum around the head of his dick and without knowing, my body lolled forward, wanting to taste him. Again the right move, because Dalton cradled the side of my head in his hand and guided me down until my lips sealed around his dick.

Beneath me, his thighs tensed, and he pulled the cane out, giving me more room to settle in between his legs and suckle. I teased his hot length with my mouth and my tongue, taking him halfway down before working the muscles of my throat around him. Dalton grunted, fisting my hair and yanking my head back. Trails of spit connected my lips to his shaft and he slapped me across the face so hard my teeth chattered together. His fingers were tight in my hair and there was nowhere for me to go as he slapped his palm across my cheek a second time.

"My cock isn't a security blanket," he warned. "Do better."

He wasn't messing around and I returned my attention to his cock with a more intense focus than before. He made a pleased noise and I slid more of him into my mouth, grunting happily when he grabbed my wrists together in the middle of my back like a harness and used the leverage to guide me up and down his length as he pleased.

That would have been enough for me, at his feet on my knees with a mouthful of cock and a stinging memory of his touch against my cheek, but then the sharp bite of the cane landed against my still bruised ass. It wasn't a direct strike lengthwise, but as Dalton swung the cane through the air vertically, the end landed against my skin over and over, delivering pinpoint precise marks with every swing.

As far as the pain he'd given me in the past, it wasn't much, but paired with the eyes I knew were on me and the cock that stretched my jaw to the point of discomfort, I was painfully close to coming. Precum leaked against my tongue, and Dalton whispered some praise that didn't quite register, and then he shifted. Folding himself over me, his cock pushed into the very back of my throat, nose buried against the trim hair around his base.

I choked and sputtered, and he smacked his hand against my freshly bruised ass, dragging lower to the backs of my thighs. One, two, three, four… I lost count and I lost air, and Dalton's hips lifted off the couch when he came. My vision blurred around the edges, the city lights twinkling in my periphery like far away fireworks. He fucked his cock as deep as it would reach in my mouth and gooseflesh raced up my arms and down my sides.

He untangled himself from me, leaning back with a content grunt as his cock slipped out of my mouth. My eyes were screwed shut and my breath came in hard, rough pants. Even though he'd let go of my wrists, I kept my own arms pinned behind my back, and when he pressed the toe of his shoe against my chest, I rocked back and rested on my heels.

"Very nice," he murmured.

I wavered, falling forward and dropping my forehead against his knee. Dalton smoothed his hand over the back of my head, fingers working through my hair until I was able to focus.

It was the sounds that came back first, the low thump of the bass drums that reverberated through the floor, the conversation and the moans around us. Then Dalton's voice next, a rumble in my chest as he talked to the other couples around us. The smooth slide of his slacks against my skin, the cold air against my sticky and soft cock. Because I'd clearly finished off at some point, which should have been embarrassing, but my sense of self-preservation had yet to return so I wasn't there yet.

Taking a deep breath, I lifted my head and immediately Dalton's proud and smiling face filled my line of sight. He petted my cheek, tracing his thumb over my lower lip. He'd put his cock back into his pants, the only proof that he'd gotten off himself was a small smudge of cum next to his zipper. He followed my line of sight to the stain and chuckled, picking at it with the edge of his fingernail.

"You did make a bit of a mess of me," he said.

"I'll take them to be dry cleaned, Sir," I murmured.

Dalton nodded, another slow smile settling on his face. "I know you will, Ivey. I know you will."

"I'm sorry I came," I whispered, turning my eyes back toward my own soiled cock.

The woman closest to us made a sweet sound like I had just performed a trick, and I felt my cheeks flood with heat and shame at her observation. Dalton and I hadn't talked about whether I was allowed to come during our scenes or not, but when I was so deep in my head, it felt wrong to have done it without his approval or permission.

"Never apologize for that." He curled his fingers around the outside of my arm and pulled me up, then he bent over and busied himself putting my still sensitive and leaking cock back into my pants.

"I didn't have permission, Sir," I whispered.

"I always want you to come," he said against my ear, patting my cock after zipping me up. "If I'm not done with your dick when you come, then you'll just have to come again."

I swallowed, the taste of him still rich and salty against my tongue.

"I want to take you home and really hurt you." He pushed up from the couch and lifted me to my feet. My legs were shaky, and I leaned against him, his arms coming around my waist to support me. "But your friends are across the room and I think they want to talk."

The last thing I wanted to do after that scene was see my friends. The second to last thing I wanted to do was see them in the headspace I was in after that scene. Even though I'd played with Alex in the past, he'd never gotten me even close to the places Dalton sent me, and there was something extremely vulnerable about being revealed that way, especially to people who *thought* they knew me better than most. And to be fair, they did, just not in the ways Dalton knew me.

"We got you a drink," Alex said, elbowing Kale in his ribs.

"Whiskey," Kale said, eyes narrowed, but more wary than judgmental.

With one arm still curled protectively around my waist, Dalton reached for the drink and took a sip before tipping his chin and raising it up.

"Thank you," he said.

Dalton set the drink on the table and helped me back down into a seat. I was sore and shaky, but being off my feet felt better than standing ever would.

"Did you want to join us awhile?" Dalton asked, sitting beside me.

"Yeah." Ford was the first to sit, Kale, Brooks, and Alex following soon after. There wasn't a lot of space at the table and we were smashed in pretty close. Before Dalton, that wouldn't have been an issue, but I found myself achingly aware of how on top of each other we all were, the way their different colognes mixed together in the air even as the only thing I truly wanted to smell was Dalton's sweat and skin.

"So." Brooks cleared his throat and stretched his arms along the back of the couch. "Dalton, why don't you tell us about yourself, and while you're at it, tell us your intentions with our friend."

"My intention is to love him," Dalton answered quickly, head cocked to the side in challenge. "In whatever way he needs."

I swallowed and set my hand on his knee. He threaded our fingers together and raised our hands to his mouth, kissing my wedding band before returning my hand to his thigh with a soft pat.

"Is that going to be a problem?" he asked.

All I'd ever wanted was a man like Dalton, and my friends knew that. They watched as I'd tried and failed to find a man who could treat me the way I wanted all while loving me in the ways I deserved. I had that now, and I wasn't going to lose him, least of all over their childish posturing about who owned me.

Kale cleared his throat, shoulders sagging as he exhaled.

"No," he said, having the courtesy to look almost ashamed of himself. "It's not a problem at all, Beamer."

"Good," Dalton murmured, situating himself beside me like he planned to stay awhile. "So, what about me did you want to know?"

After our night out at The Black Door, things moved fast.

We hadn't heard back from the co-op board, but work—and my father—called me back to California. My mom had tried to hold him off as long as possible, but every day Ivey's finances sat on his desk with the unsigned postnup, the testier he got. Before I went home, Ivey and I had come to an agreement that we weren't going to let our fathers bully us around when it came to the terms, but that was also easier said than done. Our lives were, and had always been, more complicated than most.

Being back in my house—alone—didn't help make things easier either. I missed Ivey and all the subtle ways our lives had already begun to blend together, and across the country, he was positively aimless. Even Kale couldn't keep him entertained for more than an hour or two.

My friends hadn't fared much better.

"Why don't you just fly him out here?" Barclay asked me after I'd been home and apparently unbearable for four days straight.

"I plan to." Gratefully, I accepted a glass of gin from our usual waiter at Cunningham's.

It was a Thursday, and we were early.

Barclay raised a brow, and I sighed.

"I plan to," I said again, with what I hoped was seventy-two percent less vitriol than before. "But it's the one thing we never talked about."

"You're joking."

I sipped at my drink, avoiding my best friend's very judgmental stare.

"You two decided to give your fake marriage a real try, Dom/sub roles and all, but you never talked about where you were going to live?" The admonishment in Barclay's tone rang loud and clear.

"That sounds stupid," Flynn said from behind us. He walked around and slid sideways into one of the chairs that circled the low cocktail table in front of us.

"That's what I'm saying," Barclay said.

"Not as stupid as fucking the same man casually for years on end and expecting it to last forever," Archie chimed in, taking a seat beside Flynn.

"While that was a low blow, I appreciate the support." I raised my glass to him in a toast.

"Don't bring Val into this."

"He's not going to wait for you forever," Flynn said.

"Who?" Rob was the last to arrive, taking the chair closest to me.

"Val," I said.

He scoffed, rolling his eyes and flagging down our waiter for a full round.

"I'm not saying you have to put a ring on it." Archie laughed, a patronizing smirk on his face. "But—"

"Val understands what this is," Barclay snapped, holding up a hand to silence them.

I studied his profile, making note of the way the muscle at the corner of his eye twitched and how his jaw tensed while he ground his molars together. It wasn't a nervous habit, but it was a frustrated and angry one.

"Enough about Val." I waved my hand in the air, drawing everyone's attention back to me because, for some reason, Barclay looked woefully unequipped at handling it. "We were talking about me and my bad decision making."

"Ah, yes." Rob folded his right leg over his left and leaned back in his seat. "Your pretend marriage."

"It wasn't pretend. Just forgotten."

"Clearly an important differentiation," Flynn murmured.

I flipped him the bird, and the waiter came back around with drinks for the three of them. Barclay and I were still holding steady with our first ones and passed on a fresh refill.

"You've been terribly cagey since you got back from New York," Rob said. "I wager Grayson's feelings are a little hurt over it."

"Your high-maintenance boyfriend will have to survive it."

"He's fond of you."

"I like him too," I agreed. "But I've had other things on my mind."

"Like how you and your husband never talked about what coast you were going to call home," Barclay said.

I shot him a glare, wishing that I hadn't bothered deflecting the attention from whatever the hell it was he had going on with Val.

"You hate New York," Archie said.

"I do, but he's there."

"And you'd go?" he asked. "For a man?"

"He's not just a *man*." I spun my wedding ring around my finger, fighting back a very unnecessary wave of anger that had come over me at his statement. Archie gave me the same patient look Barclay had offered me earlier and I groaned, throwing my head back and scrubbing a hand down my face. "I'm sorry."

"You're forgiven." Archie chuckled. "But, respectfully, you know you can still jerk off, right? Because you sound as high-strung as Owen gets when I don't let him come for days."

"I know I can still jerk off," I grumbled.

I just…hadn't.

Well, I'd jacked off once, and the orgasm had been so unsatisfying and hollow, I hadn't bothered since. When I'd told Ivey about it on the phone, he gave me a tired and sad look that made it clear to me he was in the same boat.

"He's waiting to hear about the penthouse he wanted," I explained. "They're on a tight schedule, so if he gets it, he won't have time to fly home because of the time difference and the travel time."

"So he's going to sign the deal on a multi-million dollar home in New York while you're here?" Flynn asked.

"In your own multi-million dollar home," Archie said.

"We'll figure something out." I polished off the rest of my gin right at the same time my phone buzzed against my thigh. I fished the device out, expecting it to be Ivey, but instead finding my father's name on the screen. "Shit."

"What's wrong?" Barclay leaned over and frowned down at my phone.

"I'll be right back."

I made it to the curb just before the call went to voicemail.

Unfortunately.

"Hello?"

"Dalton."

"Father." I leaned against the wall and stared up at the streetlights.

"I know you're as eager as I am to put this marriage mess behind us—"

"I'm not putting my marriage behind me," I interrupted. "Ivey and I are staying together."

"All the more reason for you to act like the man I raised you to be and come home and deal with the legalities of your choice."

"I don't need to see whatever his father's attorney or ours have drafted up to tell you that I'm not going to sign it," I said.

"That's absurd."

"He's not entitled to anything and neither am I," I repeated to my father what Ivey and I had agreed on before my departure. "Unless the paperwork reflects what's mine is mine and what's his is his, neither of us is signing."

"I hoped you wouldn't be so stubborn."

"And I hoped you would see reason," I said back. "What better outcome could there be than he doesn't get anything of mine if this goes wrong?"

"When," he corrected.

"If."

I held my left hand out, studying the baguette diamonds and blue topaz nestled into the heavy band around my finger. The ring was as solid as Ivey was, of that I was certain.

"I'm confident he's told his father the same thing, so you two can either redraft the paperwork or it's sitting unsigned," I told him.

"His father indicated as much, but I think he has a little more bargaining leverage than I do." My father let out a low and cruel-sounding laugh.

"What does that mean?"

"I'm sure you'll find out soon, and then you can let me know how insistent you are about not going after him for anything."

Sometimes, talking to my father was like talking to a brick wall. Like he didn't even hear the words I was saying, which was a feat because I'd gone to school specifically to learn how to persuade people to see things the way I wanted them to. I was a lawyer, a damn good one, and my father was out of his mind if he thought he had any control over making me sign an overdone postnup.

When we first found out about the whole idea, I told Ivey I'd sign anything, that it didn't matter to me what his parents felt he deserved if things didn't last between us. But as our connection deepened, we both saw the folly in that approach. Signing the post-nups as they'd been presented felt like letting our fathers win, and we both agreed they'd already gotten more than enough from us.

"Is there anything else?" I asked.

"I expect to see you before the end of the weekend, Dalton."

"I'm sure you will."

I hung up on him and rolled my eyes, groaning at the absurdity of his control over my life. It had been years since he'd flexed himself in a power play like this and I was not impressed or amused.

I called Ivey and he answered on the first ring.

"It's late," I said when the call connected.

"I can't sleep," he muttered. "I miss you."

"I miss you," I said. "I just got off the phone with my father."

Ivey laughed. "I'm sorry."

"He seems to think that you're going to cave and sign the postnup."

"I don't know what on earth would give him that idea. He doesn't even know me."

I pushed off the wall and headed toward the corner. Maybe a brisk walk around the block would do me good. Clear my head a little bit before going back inside to face my friends. I hoped they'd been kind to Barclay in my absence, but there was never any telling with them.

"I believe he's talked with your father," I said.

Ivey cursed under his breath.

"Have you not heard anything about it?" I asked.

"Not yet, but I can imagine the chain of events."

"Bad?"

"He'll threaten my job," Ivey said. "Probably yank some money from my account. Who knows with him."

I scratched the side of my nose. "Are you sure this is all worth it?"

"More than."

"Well..." Relief washed over me at how easy he was taking the whole thing. "Like I said, it's late. Maybe tomorrow will bring you news from the king."

He groaned, and I knew if we were together, if we'd been in bed together talking, he would have tried to smack me with the pillow. I would have stopped him, rolled him onto his back, and then kissed him until he remembered who was in charge.

"Have you heard back from the board yet?" I asked, rounding the corner onto a quieter side street. "I want you here."

"Not yet," he said. "Hopefully before Friday."

"If not, come out for the weekend."

"Are you asking?" I could hear the smile in his voice.

"I'm telling."

He moaned into my ear so loud and guttural that I slipped into an alley to fist my aching cock through the soft wool of my slacks.

"God," I rasped, pressing my forehead against the concrete wall. "I miss you so much."

"I'm desperate without you here," he whispered.

"You're home?" I asked.

"Of course."

"In bed?"

"Yes," he murmured.

"Touch yourself," I told him. "Let me hear how it feels."

Ivey whimpered. "Not as good as you."

"Of course not."

"Are you touching yourself too?" he asked.

I fought open my belt and fly, then shoved my hand into my underwear.

"I'm in an alley outside of a bar," I said, breath catching in my throat. "My friends are inside and my father has just threatened us both and you're making those sounds in my ear. Of course, I'm touching myself."

"I miss the way you hurt me."

My eyes rolled back in my head and I groaned, giving a tight and long tug down the length of my erection.

"I miss hurting you," I assured with a grunt. "Once you're here, I'm going to tie you up and spread you out, penetrate you with everything except my cock."

Ivey sighed happily on the other end of the call.

"I'm going to spank that perfect dick of yours with my belt while I'm inside of you. Spank your legs, flip you over, and beat your ass while I fuck it…" I sucked in a breath, orgasm already there and ready to go.

It turned out that I enjoyed hurting Ivey just as much as he liked to be hurt.

"What else?" He exhaled a trembling noise into my ear.

"Greedy little cum slut."

"Yours, Sir."

Cum shot out of my dick, splattering against the wall and the tight grip of my knuckles. I grunted and groaned into the phone, the aftershocks of my orgasm threatening the strength of my legs with every wave that rolled through me.

"You're damn right you're mine," I told him, voice hoarse. "My husband, my submissive, my fucking man."

On the other end of the call, Ivey forced out a strangled cry that sounded like a melody to my ears. I knew he was coming, and I closed my eyes to picture him in bed, cock in hand and phone against his ear, back arched as cum sprayed across his belly.

"You're mine, Ivey. And nothing is ever going to change that."

"I know," he whispered, words shaking. "I know."

CHAPTER 34
IVEY

MS. VANDERLIN CALLED ME THE FOLLOWING DAY. I HADN'T LET MY phone out of my sight since Dalton had left to go home, so I was able to answer her call on the first ring.

"Hello?"

"Mr. Royce."

She wasn't asking. She knew who she'd called.

"Ms. Vanderlin," I greeted.

"The board has approved your tenancy."

A month ago, the news would have been the best part of my day. I'd spent so long working toward my dreams and that penthouse was one of them. But now there was Dalton, and all of it seemed hollow without him. I hadn't been attached at the hip to my phone because I'd been waiting to hear about the application. I'd been attached to it because I didn't want to miss Dalton's calls and texts. Since he'd gone back to California, the silly little mobile devices had become our lifeline. From sunrise to well past sunset every day apart, we'd been connected with more than our wedding rings.

"Mr. Royce." She cleared her throat, tone dripping with disdain. "Don't you have anything to say to that?"

"Right. Uhm…thank you."

She scoffed, but carried on. "Considering you're married, we would normally need you and Mr. Fox on the application, but your family attorney has provided the board with a copy of your nuptial agreement, so that's not necessary…"

Ms. Vanderlin droned on, but I'd already completely zoned out.

What did she mean she had a copy of my nuptial agreement? Dalton and I hadn't signed anything, and even if we had ever agreed to, it most assuredly wouldn't be whatever draft my father's attorney had on hand.

I interrupted her, "Can you repeat that, please?"

"Which part, Mr. Royce?"

"The whole of it."

"We've reviewed the nuptial agreement so we'll only need your signature on the paperwork for the residence," she said, which was more of a summary than the first time, but I wasn't trying to pick it apart.

Admittedly, Dalton and I hadn't even thought about the necessity of him being present to deal with the paperwork. Even after I'd started the process in the first place and even after they'd interviewed him, there hadn't been any talk about including him on the agreements. I hadn't thought…but he *should* be on them. He was my husband and what's mine was meant to be his, so what angle was my father playing if he was soliciting paperwork that indicated otherwise?

"Why not?" I managed to ask.

"Because he won't be living there, of course."

She said it so matter of fact. The sky is blue, grass is green, you don't have a future with your husband.

"Perhaps not full time," I countered.

Her reply was sharp and biting, "Not at all. Not at all, according to the paperwork."

"I have to admit, Ms. Vanderlin, I'm not sure what paperwork you're talking about. My husband and I don't have a signed nuptial agreement, so I don't know what my father has provided you…or why, for that matter."

"Your father and I are old family friends," she said.

"So I've been told."

"You see, we were going to reject your application, Mr. Royce, but after your father assured us that your husband was not truly in the picture, we felt better about it."

My breath hitched in my throat, and I sat down on the edge of my couch so I didn't fall over. New York was a liberal city, and Los Angeles was too, but that didn't mean I hadn't experienced my fair share of homophobia once people realized I was bisexual. But there was no way she was implying what I assumed her to be implying.

"That's odd," I said slowly. "Because just a couple of weeks ago, you wanted to make sure he *was* around."

"Yes, well…that was before we were aware of your…unconventional living arrangement."

I closed my eyes and sank into the couch with a groan. "You're giving me whiplash, Ms. Vanderlin."

"I'll be plain."

"Please."

"We don't make a habit of allowing non-traditional couples in the building."

That was the other shoe, and it had just dropped.

Slowly, the pieces fell into place.

"But you'll make an exception for me," I said.

"The Royce family…"

I didn't need to hear the rest of whatever she was about to say. I'd heard enough and I didn't want any more of it.

"Ms. Vanderlin," I cut her off and she made a disgruntled sound very unbecoming of her stature. "Thank you, but I'll pass."

"You'll what?"

I would have put money down that I was the first person to ever turn down a spot in that building and, admittedly, I would probably be the last.

"I'll pass," I told her again. "But feel free to tell my father thank you for his efforts."

I disconnected the call and rang Dalton. I didn't know how I managed to dial him, because I was half-numb and trembling until I heard his voice.

"Ivey."

His voice was low and smooth, calm.

His voice was everything to me.

"I heard back from the board," I blurted.

"Congratulations."

He didn't sound excited. He sounded like we were on the verge of divorce.

"I told her no," I said.

"Why?"

"A lot of reasons, I think. One of which being she's a homophobic piece of shit who is in too deep with my father to make me comfortable."

Dalton chuckled. "Two?"

"Two…it's here."

"And?"

"And you're not." I put my phone on speaker and dropped it onto the coffee table, then I leaned forward with my elbows on my knees. With my head hanging low, the blood rushed quick and everything immediately became clear.

"You're not," I said again. "And I don't want to be anywhere without you."

"I've been meaning to have this conversation with you," he said quietly. "We've been fools for avoiding it."

"No. It's okay to enjoy being in love for a little before you have to start worrying about real life."

"Loving you is my life," he said. "There's no separation of that from anything else."

I pressed my fingertips against my eyelids, unsure if I was about to cry or laugh at the circus that my life had become.

"This is a conversation best had in person, Ivey. Will you come to L.A. a while and stay with me?"

I didn't even have to think about the answer because, for Dalton, it was always a yes.

"Of course," I whispered.

"I'll book you a trip," he said, voice going tinny as he put me on speakerphone. "Can you leave tonight?"

I smiled, tears leaking out of the corners of my eyes at the easy and meaningful ways he loved me. Suddenly, for the first time since our very first kiss so long ago, the idea of being away from him pained me beyond reason. When Dalton had left me the first time, there was no place I wanted to be besides as far away from him as possible. There had been too much between us for me to see a way forward back then. Still reeling from Genevieve, on top of whatever feelings hooking up with him had trudged up, I had been too far under my father's thumb to see the sense of it.

"I can leave right now," I told him.

"You have two hours." He was off speakerphone and my phone vibrated against the table. "I sent you the info. You don't even need to pack a bag. Just...be here."

"Before you know it," I whispered. "I love you."

"I love you too." He let out a soft laugh. "Now get off the phone and get downstairs. Your car is coming in ten."

I swallowed, spit lodged in the back of my throat like a softball. "What do you mean?"

"I booked your flight," he said. "I booked your car."

"Why did you book me a car?" I choked out, the tears falling freely now and I was thankful he couldn't see me.

"To get you to the airport," he explained it like it made perfect sense. And maybe it did, to him. "There was only so much I could do when I was in New York, Ivey. I wasn't in my element out there. I could learn it for you if I had to, but here in L.A...I'm going to take care of you the way you deserve."

"But...I'm the one who—"

"It's a two-way street and you know it," he said, cutting me off and saving me from my pathetic stammering. "You serve me so I can take care of you. That's the way of it, Ivey."

"I love you," I whispered, because I didn't know what else to say to him besides that. I hoped it was enough for him to understand the depths of the feelings that had developed for him in our very short time together.

"I love you." I could hear the smile in his voice. "Now get here, Ivey. Don't keep me waiting."

———

The car ride took forever and the flight took even longer. I hadn't bothered to pack a bag, so when the plane landed on the tarmac in L.A., all I had were the clothes on my back and the cell phone in my pocket. Dalton was at the bottom of the stairs and before both feet hit the asphalt, I was in his arms.

"I missed you." He breathed into my neck, arms tightening around me like a vise.

I stumbled off the last step taking us both backward, but he caught my weight and steadied us both on our feet.

"I missed you," he said again, like he didn't believe how much. "I missed you."

"I'm here," I said, tears falling again.

I sniffled and Dalton pulled away, snatching my face into his hands and furiously swiping the wetness off my cheeks. He angled my head this way and that, studying me. But for what, I wasn't sure. I looked him over in return, noticing the way his facial hair was more unkempt than I'd ever seen it, a little long around his cheeks. There were bags under his eyes that made his complexion appear darker, his eyes more tired.

The stones in his ring scraped against my cheek and I sighed happily at the bite of pain.

"I'm here," I repeated, like *I'm here* and *I missed you* were the only things we were capable of saying.

Dalton scanned my face once more, then took my hand and pulled me toward a waiting car. My body clock was a mess, convinced it was well past midnight when it was barely just. He ushered me into the back seat and the leather was cold, even through the material of my clothes. Dalton slid in after me, pulling the door closed and then tucking me against his side.

It was something he did often, and I wasn't sure if he realized it. But on more than one occasion, he'd tried to fold me up and pull me onto his lap. Most of the times it happened after we'd done a scene together, so I knew it was only *half* him. I was so tall, but I liked feeling small and protected with him wrapped around me, and so I didn't fight it. I pulled my legs up, pressing my entire body against his side. His arms went around me and as the car pulled out toward the road, Dalton pressed a kiss against the top of my head.

In our days apart, I'd been aware of the fact that I missed him. Though, I hadn't realized how vital and tangible the feeling was until I was back beside him. Like as soon as we were again breathing the same air, all of the gaps and holes in my chest filled back up and I could breathe again. I could think again.

No wonder the other times he'd left me had sent me on such terrifying spirals. In college, I hadn't realized the cause, though. We'd both been so young and stupid, so overwhelmed with embarrassment and arousal that there were a thousand different feelings between us that we couldn't make proper sense of. I'd been angry at his absence, but thankful for it, even if blissfully unaware of the ache that it caused. And that pain had bloomed in my chest for years and years, and then Dalton was back and he watered it and nurtured it...

I felt whole for the first time in my life.

"You can rest, Ivey." He held me tight, so tight that it was easy and hard to breathe at the same time. "We're together, and you're safe here."

It was the truth.

In fact, nothing had ever been truer in my whole life, so I closed my eyes, breathed in the scent of him, and slept.

Ivey was a beast of a man and hustling him through my house and into bed while he was boneless with exhaustion was no easy feat. He collapsed onto my sheets with a tired grumble, and I set to work stripping him out of his clothes.

The man really had dropped everything and gotten on a plane for me, I thought as I carefully untied his shoes and set them on the floor. His socks were next, then his belt, his slacks, and his shirt. I kept him in his underwear because it felt reasonable. There was no way in hell I was going to get him under the blankets, so I covered him with a throw from the couch and then slipped quietly into the bathroom.

It was beyond late, and I needed to sleep, but after brushing my teeth and rinsing my face, I was too wired to keep my eyes closed for long. Ivey was here. Not just in L.A., but in my house and in my bed. He was too big to ever be in my clothes, but tomorrow I would buy him his own and that would be good enough.

At some point around three, sleep finally took me, and the last thing I remembered before losing consciousness was wrapping my arms around Ivey. Holding him close. When I woke the next morning, I wasn't convinced I hadn't slept for a week, and with Ivey missing from my bed, I was worried I'd dreamed the whole thing.

I rolled onto my back with a groan, kicking the blankets off and flinging my legs out of bed. My feet landed on Ivey's shoes, right where I'd left them, and I breathed a sigh of relief. He was in my house *somewhere*.

After a stop in the bathroom, I stumbled into the living room, where I found Ivey on the couch in his underwear, mug of coffee resting near him and his phone in hand.

"Good morning." I came around the couch and sat next to him, and he startled, jumping up so fast I worried he was going to fall over the table. "Settle down now. It's just me."

"You scared me."

"Never meant to."

Ivey rubbed his ear nervously, and then it was like a switch flipped. He sidestepped away from me toward the kitchen, muttering under his breath about coffee. I chuckled, waiting for him to return, which he did promptly with a fresh mug of coffee for me. I thanked him and waited for him to settle back down on the couch to my right.

"Thank you," I said, taking a slow sip. It was fresh, piping hot, which I hoped meant he had gotten some sleep and hadn't been up too terribly long.

"You know, it's hard to get a feel for you in this place," he finally said, squinting at me. "At least I have some pictures out."

"I have pictures on my phone," I said. "And the frame thingy in my office. They cycle through when it's on."

"It's not on," he said.

"Are you spying?" I arched a brow.

"If you want to call it that, sure." He shrugged and raised his coffee to his mouth, taking a small drink. "I call it getting to know my husband."

"I'll answer any question you have," I told him.

At that, Ivey let out a sarcastic-sounding chortle.

"Alright," he said, mouth twisting into an arrogant smirk that was more befitting me than him. "What next?"

I barked out a laugh, leaning against the back of the couch and wrapping one of my arms around him. Ivey scooted closer and leaned against me, resting his head on my shoulder. We both stretched our legs out and propped them on the coffee table, each crossed at the ankles. His legs were longer than mine, his feet bigger, and his toes more slender. I caught myself admiring the shape of his body as he wiggled his way into the crook of my arm, and I kissed the top of his head.

"Any question but that," I murmured into his hair. "I haven't thought that far ahead. I just knew that I needed you here."

"Selfish," he teased.

"In love," I corrected.

"Same thing maybe."

"Oh?" I pinched the outside of his ribs and he elbowed me in mine. "Do I not take care of you? Make sure you have everything you need? Everything you *want*?"

Ivey angled himself around and dropped a kiss against my chest. "I suppose when you put it like that, you did get me a penthouse."

"Too bad you changed your mind and didn't want it."

Ivey grunted and threw one of his legs over my lap, dropping his considerable weight onto me in a straddle. He flattened his hands against my chest and frowned. "Too bad?" he asked.

And just like that, we were back to the what next question. I shook my head, resting my hands on his narrow hips and tracing swirls over the bone and muscle with my thumbs.

"It's the second best thing that's ever happened to me," I corrected.

"What's the first?"

"You."

He tipped his chin toward his chest, giving me what on any other face would have been a coy smile. But Ivey was so broad, so chiseled, it almost looked out of place on him. I jerked him closer, aligning the hottest parts of our bodies because it was what we both needed. Not just the emotional connection, but also the physical.

"Do you want to stay in New York?" I asked.

He scoffed. "It would be a lot easier if you made the decisions on this one."

"I can't."

As much as I *wanted* to, there had to be limits in the power exchange between us and there were just some things I didn't feel right deciding without his informed and willing consent.

"Will you at least tell me what you *want?*" he asked.

I breathed in deeply, well aware of the way he was trying to coax the right answer out of me, if not in as many words as all that.

"Don't be sneaky," I warned.

"I'm not. What you want matters too."

"Your happiness is what matters to me," I said.

"What would make me happy is you answering the question." Ivey raised a blond brow toward his hairline, and I smacked his ass. Or as much of it as I could reach at the angle.

He didn't ask me for much. Beyond asking me to pretend to be his husband, he hadn't asked me for anything.

"Of course I want you here," I said quietly, smoothing my hands up and down the lower half of his back. "I want your clothes in my closet and your scent on my sheets. I want my cum in your ass."

He hummed, wiggling in my lap.

"And I do love you, but I am a selfish man. I want all of that *here*. I want my friends to become your friends. I want you here," I whispered the sentiment again, swallowing down the selfishness that tasted like acid in my throat. "But I want you happy and your life is in New York. Your friends. Your job. Your apartment."

"Before I found out we were married, I couldn't imagine a life anywhere else." Ivey drew feather-light designs across my chest, making me shiver and hold him even tighter in my lap. "My friends, the penthouse. It was everything for me."

Ivey leaned in and brushed his lips against mine. The barest tease of a kiss that had my hands moving up his back, fingers splayed out to keep him still, to keep our mouths pressed together so I could deepen the kiss and lick the real truth right out of him.

His cock spasmed against my belly and he groaned, going soft in my arms and letting me take control of the kiss, which I slowly and reluctantly brought to a close so we could both catch our breath.

Lips still touching, Ivey smiled.

"But now you're everything," he said. "And if you're here, that's where I want to be."

Fighting back a primal urge to whoop and celebrate at the concession, I searched out the right thing to ask.

"Are you sure?"

It wasn't eloquent and it wasn't demanding, but…

"Getting out of New York will be good for me," he said, pressing his lips against the corner of my mouth. "My father has his hands in too many things. I don't think he can reach here as easily."

My father was a nightmare on his best day, but he was nothing compared to Carter Royce III. I sympathized with Ivey and his need to get away from that kind of control, but the conversation reminded me that we still had the pending postnup to contend with, in one way or another.

"If you say the word, I'll have your things crated up and on a truck before the end of the day," I told him. "If here is where you want to be, then here is where I'll have you."

"I don't want strangers packing up my butt plugs, Dalton."

"Oh." I laughed, feeling light and free at his decision. "Now it's Dalton? What happened to Sir?"

I lifted my hips off the couch and slanted our mouths back together, kissing the answer right out of him. We kissed until Ivey's back was on the couch, one leg bent on the floor and my body nestled between his spread legs. I braced myself against the back of the couch, as if there was ever a threat of me smashing him under my weight. I rutted against him, driving his other knee back toward his ear and grinding my cock into the crease of his ass.

Precum leaked out the head of my dick and I shifted back so I could tug my underwear down below my balls. I did the same to

Ivey, then gathered his wrists in my head and pinned them above his head against the arm of the couch. It was one of my favorite ways to hold him. Moving onto my knees, I took both of our dicks into my other hand, tightening my grip around our shafts and giving a slow tug from root to tip.

"Oh fuck, Sir," he whimpered.

Pride exploded in the center of my chest at his easy use of the honorific. I'd only been teasing him with the earlier chide, but this was what I'd asked for. It was what *I* wanted.

"That's better," I mused, tightening my fist around the heads of our cocks. Our precum mixed together, smearing against my fingers and my palm. "But are you sure this is what you want? To pack up and move across the country tomorrow? To just…be here with me?"

"Very."

"What will you do for work?" I asked.

I didn't know why it mattered, but Ivey's job had been such a big part of his life for so long and I was already asking so much of him. He didn't need to work if he didn't want to. His position at his firm was already on the line with the stance we'd taken on the postnup, and I worried losing it *and* moving would be too much too fast.

"I'll take care of you," he whispered, lashes fluttering and cheeks turning pink. "I'll serve you. I'll be yours."

Ivey blinked up at me with clear eyes, vibrant as the topaz in my wedding band. I couldn't believe my luck. Couldn't believe how one bad relationship, one mistake, had turned into the greatest love of my life. That I'd stumbled onto this man who would give up anything to give me everything. I needed him to know the feeling was mutual. That if the conversation had gone another way, I would have had us on a plane back to New York before he had a chance to get clothes on.

"Do you mean it?" I asked, kissing his forehead, his cheekbones, his nose, his jaw.

"As much as I've ever meant anything."

My friends were never going to let me live it down once they knew the story between us. And I found myself beyond ready to tell them about the recent turn of events in my life. But more than that, I wanted them to meet him. Wanted them to come over and see how perfectly Ivey fit into my home and into my life. I wanted them to love him as much as I did because it was the least he deserved.

I loosened my grip on our shafts and Ivey shuddered, hips chasing after me as I let both of out dicks slip out of my hand. I had to grind my jaw together to stop a violent tremor from tearing through my body at the loss of touch, but I wasn't ready to come and I sure as shit wasn't ready for Ivey to come.

"Sir," he whined, trying to slide his cock against my shaft.

I answered that with a sharp slap across his cheek, which in hindsight was probably not the most suitable way to punish a masochistic submissive who was already right on the edge of orgasm.

Just as I opened my mouth, ready to warn him not to come yet, he did.

A hot burst of cum splattered across our stomachs, and Ivey yelped in agony thrashing beneath me. The orgasm had been ruined by the loss of contact…and the lack of permission. I shoved his wrists harder against the arm of the couch and laughed, using my other hand to scoop from the dismal puddles that had formed in the grooves of his belly. Letting go of his wrists, I traced his cum across his still shaking lips and then I kissed him until the only taste left in my mouth, in my mind…was him.

AFTER AN ORGASM ON THE COUCH, WE FINISHED OUR COFFEE, cleared our calendars, and went back to bed. Dalton fucked me long and slow until our bodies were slick with sweat and when he spilled inside of me, I thought for sure I was dreaming. Everything about being in L.A. with Dalton was surreal. Less than twelve hours earlier, I'd stepped onto a plane and walked away from all of the things I thought meant the most, right into the arms of the man who truly did. I fell asleep with my head pillowed on his chest, and when I came around later, the bedroom was far too bright for it to still be on the morning side of noon.

And much to my dismay, Dalton once again gave me a choice.

"Meet my friends or deal with the postnup and my father?" he asked.

"Can't we just stay here?"

"Not forever, unfortunately." He kissed the top of my head, hand stroking up and down the length of my spine.

I propped my chin on his chest so I could see his face. "Can I get you cleaned up first?"

"You don't have to do that."

"I know. But I like to. You know that." I licked my lips and turned my stare downcast. "I like to serve you. It...it makes me hard. It makes me feel good. And you said that was what you wanted."

I flattened my palm on the bed beside his ribs and pushed up, ready to shuffle off into the bathroom without him. Maybe the things he'd said the night before were just talk in the heat of the moment, trying to convince me that it wasn't an impulsive decision to put everything in New York on hold to come be with him.

He grabbed my wrist, but I was already up, feet on the floor and back to him. He angled my arm back, pulling it straight so I couldn't move away without hurting myself.

"Ivey, stop."

I stopped, shifting my shoulder to alleviate some of the strain.

"That is what I want," he said. "I want that so very much, but I've never had someone willing to give as much as you are. I need to get used to it."

His answer made a lot more sense than the first place my mind had gone on its own.

"And it's my responsibility to take care of you too," he went on, stroking his thumb over my wrist bone until I lifted one leg onto the bed and turned toward him. "So we have to share that sometimes. But as your husband, as your Dom…I'll make sure you have everything you need."

"I know."

Dalton pulled me back on top of him and kissed me slow and sensually, like maybe he'd changed his mind and we didn't have to go deal with his friends or his father. But when I tried to chase after some friction for my now always-hard cock, he shoved us both up into a sitting position and swung his legs off the bed.

"Don't drop me," I murmured into his mouth, not willing to end the kiss.

"I'd never."

With a groan that sounded like there was at least a five percent chance he might not be able to keep the promise, Dalton stood. I wrapped my legs around his waist and continued to kiss him as he carried me into the bathroom. With my back against the tile wall of his shower, I kissed him more, only breaking away when he tapped my legs and turned on the water.

"You're up," he said with a smirk.

It was always like that with him. So easy to be any part of myself at any given time, and the flow between the pieces was steady as my next breath. There was never pressure or expectation. Well, there was expectation, but that was part of the whole thing. That was what I loved the most about it, sometimes.

I'd never been in his shower, but it was muscle memory to find the soap and his washcloth, and then to map the planes of his body with my hands. I forced myself to not linger on his cock or his balls, even as they burned and pulsed beneath my soapy fingers. Dalton groaned and sighed as I cleaned around the broad muscles of his thighs and down to his feet. In his shower, on my knees, with water raining down onto the top of my head, I kissed his feet.

One.

Two.

Back at my full height, Dalton slid his hands around my waist and dragged his soapy torso against mine. I laughed, and he swiped soap off my collarbone to nibble and suck at the thin skin there. It was one of his favorite places on me, and I loved the attention he paid it.

I loved *him*.

He took the soap and washed me, then he let me rinse us both. He turned off the water and I wrapped a towel around his shoulders, drying off as much of him as I could before tending to myself. Through every step, Dalton eyed me silently, fingers dancing in the air like he was itching to touch me.

"Are you okay?" I finally asked, knotting the towel around my waist and following him out to the bedroom.

"I just keep waiting to wake up," he admitted. "I can't believe you're here, that you're staying...that you're my husband. I can't believe I wasted fifteen years without you."

"Hardly a waste." I unwound the towel from around my hips. "You used the time to learn how to tie all those fancy knots."

"I knew how to tie the knots in college." He stripped off his own towel and handed it to me.

"Then it was a waste, indeed."

He laughed, and I threw the towels in his hamper.

All the things he'd said were feelings I shared, the slight tingle of disbelief that vibrated through my arms with every move I made didn't show any indication of going away.

"Can I dress you?" I asked, watching him finger through the collared shirts on matching hangers.

He answered with a thoughtful hum.

I picked out a short-sleeved, plaid button-up that stretched across his chest like it was a size too small for him and a pair of khaki-colored chinos that fell just above his ankle. With a pair of clean white sneakers, Dalton looked almost as good as he did in a suit.

"Thank you," he whispered, pressing a kiss below my ear after I'd tied the last bow on his shoes.

"You're welcome, Sir."

"I hate to ask you to wear the same clothes from yesterday, but we can make our first stop at the store and I can get you a few outfits to hold you over," he offered.

"Thank you, Sir."

"Jesus." He palmed his cock, following me back out to the bedroom where my clothes had been left the night before. "You make me so hard with that."

"With being myself?"

He sucked in a breath and nodded.

I dressed myself and let him fuss over me, catching his left hand between my fingers and kissing his ring.

"We have to go," he said, tangling our fingers together before I could drop his hand. "If we don't leave, we never will."

"I don't hate that." I laughed.

"Trust me, if we don't go to them, they'll come to us," he said.

"Don't let them in?" I suggested.

"They have keys." Dalton snatched his keys, wallet, and phone off the small table by the front door. "We're overwhelmingly connected. It's not healthy."

"You care about each other," I countered. "My friends are the same way."

"Speaking of your friends…"

I followed Dalton onto the porch, stepping out of the way so he could lock the door. "Have they said anything about me?"

"Ford said it takes a hell of a man to bring me to my knees. And that's as much of a compliment as you'll get out of any of them."

He opened the passenger door of his car, and I sank down into the seat. Before buckling up, I reached over and popped his door for him. He grabbed it and pulled it the rest of the way, smiling at me as he settled behind the wheel.

"Alex brought you to your knees," he said under his breath, pushing the ignition on.

I thumped my head against the leather headrest and dropped my left hand on top of his thigh. The sun shone through the windshield, making my ring almost blinding in the reflection.

"I said he and I used to play together," I corrected. "I never said I kneeled for him."

Dalton looked like he had something to say, but whatever it was, he swallowed it back.

"Are you all right?" I asked.

He cleared his throat. "I'm good. Let's get you some clothes."

I admittedly took as long as I could at the mall because I wasn't looking forward to facing his father. Even though Dalton and I were clear on what we would and would not sign, men like our fathers were always formidable. So, with enough clothes to last me a week, we headed to Dalton's parents' house.

The house turned out to be a mansion, which didn't surprise me in the least. Tucked into the hills outside of the city, it was designed to mimic a sprawling French estate, with a Mercedes G-wagon and a Rolls-Royce Spectre parked in the driveway.

"You've got to be joking," I muttered, thinking about Kale and his atrocious nickname for me.

Dalton chuckled and flicked the hood ornament on his way past. "It's my mom's. I bet she would let you drive it."

"I bet she wouldn't."

He scrunched up his nose, brows pinched. "Why wouldn't she?"

"It's a four hundred thousand dollar car." I gave him a pointed look in return before adding, "Sir."

"And you're my husband," he said, taking my hand.

Like it was simple.

He dragged me to the front door, not bothering to knock. It was unlocked, because of course it was, and a woman half his height with all his brooding facial features was headed right for us.

"I saw you coming down the drive," she said, wrapping her arms around him. He tightened down his hold on my fingers and I stumbled forward, halfway into their hug. "Is this him? Is this your husband?"

"This is him." Dalton's voice was muffled in her hair. "Mama, this is…Carter Royce."

"Carter." She said my name with a smile, shoving Dalton out of the way to give me a hug that felt as thorough as his had looked. "It's so lovely to meet you. I'm Miranda Fox."

"It's nice to meet you, ma'am."

"None of that." She huffed. "You can call me Mama like Dalton does or Miranda."

"Miranda," I said.

The soft kindness of Dalton's mother was so far removed from my own upbringing, I had to fight back an unexpected surge of jealousy. I knew no one was as horrible as my father, but Dalton's was close, and how had someone as gentle and loving as his mom survived for as long as she had without losing that kindness?

"Dalton." A sharp voice rang out from down the hall, and

Dalton's shoulders went tense. His mom scoffed, waving off the man I assumed to be her husband.

"Father," he said.

He still hadn't let go of my hand, and his father's stern brown eyes flickered to me and down to the place our fingers were joined.

"My office," his father said, turning on his heel and stalking down a hallway.

"Don't let him scare you," Miranda whispered. "He's soft on the inside."

"He's not," Dalton corrected. "But we'll be fine, Mama."

Fine was debatable, but with Dalton by my side, I was pretty sure I could do anything.

CHAPTER 37
DALTON

The only thing that made my father's office bearable was the reassuring presence of Ivey on my right. Even if I wasn't looking at him, I could see his imposing form in my peripheral. I could smell him, taste him…

But I couldn't allow any of that to distract me from the task at hand.

My father had one palm atop a manila envelope that looked very much like the one I'd recently been served. Except mine, of course, had been stuffed with divorce papers.

"Father, I don't believe you've met my husband," I said, "Carter Royce IV."

The societal imprint of Ivey's upbringing was unavoidable, and Ivey held his hand out for a shake.

"Mr. Fox," he said.

My father shook Ivey's hand and didn't offer him a name or a more casual manner of engagement.

Ivey settled into the seat next to me, and I reached for his left hand, finding it dry and steady against my clammy, nervous one. There was so much on the line for us. Not that I had any doubt about whether Ivey and I would come out of it together or not; I knew we would. But money and family and standing, career prospects…there were so many things that could go wrong.

My father sat back down in his giant leather desk chair and tapped his fingers against the manila envelope on his black leather desk pad.

"Your mother has indicated you're not going to sign this," he said.

I hadn't told her that, but I liked that she knew. It gave me some hope that Ivey and I would make it out of this whole meeting unscathed.

"We aren't," I confirmed.

"But we are amenable to signing something much simpler," Ivey said.

My father scoffed. "Amenable."

"Let me be clear, Mr. Fox, that we use the term amenable in the most direct interpretation of the definition. We are willing, but that doesn't mean anything about our agreement is final."

"Spoken like a better lawyer than my son," my father said, eyes narrowed. "Or I imagine this would have been done fifteen years ago."

"Unlikely," I muttered under my breath. I was still in shock an officiant in Las Vegas married us considering how blackout drunk the two of us were, though we must have presented sober enough to pass muster.

"Your son graduated magna cum laude, if I remember correctly," Ivey said, giving my hand a squeeze. "I was only cum laude."

I snorted at him. "Only."

"None of that is the point." My father pulled the surprisingly thick stack of papers out of the envelope and I inhaled a sharp breath as he tried to pass it to me across the broad expanse of his desk. When I was a toddler, I'd played on this desk, on and around it. At his feet, and he'd laughed when I tied his shoes into knots during meetings. It was impossible for me to reconcile the version of my father that I remembered from my earliest years with the man that I remembered from my pre-teen years. Even harder, the man I knew once I'd become an adult. Sometimes, I caught glimpses of him through my mother's eyes, but they were fleeting.

"We're willing to sign an agreement that in the event one or both of us decide to dissolve the union, anything earned or owned before the first of the coming month remains separate."

"And after the first?"

"Half," I said.

He opened his mouth to protest, but I gave the postnup a shove across the desk and it slid into his lap, papers fanning out as it fell over the edge.

"Half is out of the question," he said.

"Half or nothing," I countered.

Ivey and I had agreed that the entire concept of splitting anything would have been tiresome and unnecessary. We both had enough on our own, at least financially, but we'd thought the concession would soften the blow of rejection when it came down to the expectations of our families.

"What does your father's attorney think of this?" he asked Ivey.

"Frankly, it doesn't matter," Ivey said. "This is what Dalton and I will sign, so it's this or nothing."

"Do you think that a man who sends over a stack of legalities and loopholes this thick..." He shook the stack of papers at us before dropping it onto his desk. "Is going to accept half of the future and nothing from the past?"

"He can take it or he can spend his own money trying to fight me for something more." Ivey gave my father an uninterested shrug that might have been one of the sexiest things I'd ever seen him do. "If he wants to try and strip my trust or my properties as punishment for my rebellion, I'd like to see him try. The attorney in question is the one who drafted all of those up. I'm as protected from him as he wants me to be from your son. The only difference is your son wouldn't ever try to take what's mine from me."

"And you from him?"

Ivey didn't look away from my father's intense stare when he answered, "The only thing I want is him."

My father cleared his throat and looked down at the postnup

on his desk, scanning through the pages with a tired look on his face. I could see the weight of his years in the deep grooves around the corners of his eyes and the hollows of his cheeks. He'd worked very hard for his whole life, half driven to provide for my mama, half because that's what his father had expected of him, and his father before, and on and on ad nauseam.

Ivey and I hadn't ever talked about having kids, but watching my father weigh the options in front of him, I knew that if we did, I wanted it to be different. My father hadn't been a bad parent, not by any means. A strict one, sure. An expectant one, absolutely. And I knew he loved me, in the ways he could, which were far more material and financial than the ways Ivey and I loved each other.

"Fifty-fifty after the first." He glanced at his watch and sighed. Resigned.

"Yes," I confirmed.

"I'll have it drawn up." My father leaned back in his seat and dumped the postnup into the wire trash can beneath his desk, then gave Ivey a pitying look. "But I'm not going to deal with your father's bulldog of an attorney about it. I'm too old."

"We'll take care of it," Ivey agreed.

It was a win.

And there hadn't even been a real battle, no bloodshed. At least not from my side. It was still to be determined how things would go for Ivey, but if I knew anything, it was that he wasn't going to face it alone.

What our parents seemed to forget was we were both accomplished attorneys in our own right. I knew my father wouldn't come back to me with a document that went against what we'd asked for, and I knew Ivey and I would both sign it. There wasn't any further conversation to have with his father or his family lawyer. There would probably be repercussions for the act, but nothing that we couldn't manage. If Ivey lost his job, his money, he could find a new one and he could have mine, but Ivey seemed sure that none of that would come to pass.

My father looked at his watch again and stood, waving us both off in the casual way he'd always waved *me* off. It was as much an acceptance into the family as Ivey was ever going to get.

"I promised your mother a date," he said.

"Let me know when you have the new agreement?"

Ivey stood and reached out to shake my father's hand a second time.

"Thank you for seeing it our way," he said, as my father accepted the gesture that almost felt like a peace offering.

"I don't think I had a choice."

"You didn't." I grinned at him, and his facade almost cracked. "Tell Mama I love her. And thank you."

Ivey and I headed for the door. My hand was on the handle when my father cleared his throat behind us. My heart skipped a beat, worried that he'd changed his mind, that I'd said the wrong thing.

"Come see her more," he said, softer than his normal voice. More tender. "If not me, her. She loves you."

I swallowed past an unexpected lump in my throat and nodded, unable to look back at him. Ivey pushed open the door and we stepped back into the sun-washed light of the house.

"Do you want to tell your mom goodbye?" he asked.

"She's always scarce when he's in work mode," I said. "But I'll....I'll come see her soon."

"It sounds like she would like that."

"Would you want to come?"

"Of course," he whispered, kissing the side of my forehead. "Let's get out of here now before your dad changes his mind."

I barked out a laugh and pulled Ivey out of the house, almost joyful from the relief of the conversation. He made an amused sound when we passed back by my mom's car, and I promised him he'd get to drive it next time we came over. If for nothing else, to let Kale know, and I would love and cherish any opportunity that came up to stick it to the other man.

"What now?" Ivey asked as we buckled in and I turned the car on.

"Well, that's one down. You have four to go. Or seven, depending on your luck."

"I'm not sure what to say to that."

"Three of my friends have partners," I explained, realizing it was the first time I'd really taken the time to tell Ivey anything about my friends. That it was the first time he'd really even been in Los Angeles with the intent to *be* with me. "The fourth does too, but he's in denial about it."

"Sounds like there's a story there," he said.

"I'm sure there will be."

I checked my phone, finding a thousand messages in the group text with said friends that I knew I'd never read. The only one that mattered was the most recent one from Rob with a Manhattan Beach address that didn't look familiar to me in the slightest.

"Everything good?" Ivey asked, reaching over and tapping the corner of my mouth. I realized I was frowning, and I angled my head to the side and nipped his finger between my teeth.

"My friends are in Manhattan Beach," I said, throwing the address into my nav. It populated with a straight cut though the city that was going to take us almost an hour. "It's a drive."

I sucked his finger deeper into my mouth, growling at the divine way Ivey's cheeks flushed when I swirled my tongue around his knuckles.

"Good thing you have tolerable company," he rasped, dropping his head against the headrest.

I pulled his finger out of my mouth and set his hand on his lap. His slacks were hot enough to catch fire, and I knew he was hard.

So was I.

"Tolerable," I agreed, giving him a pat before taking the steering wheel in both hands so I didn't do something that would push my luck like stripping him out of his clothes and fucking him at the mouth of my parent's driveway. "Ready?"

He shook his head, mouth falling into an easy smile.

"As I'll ever be."

We were halfway to Manhattan Beach when Ivey turned to me with a worried look on his face.

"What's wrong?" I asked, letting go of the wheel with my right hand so I could touch his face.

"What if they don't like me?"

"They will."

"But what if they don't?" he pressed.

"It doesn't matter to me. But none of them are as protective of me as Kale is of you, so I don't think you really have anything to worry about."

Ivey leaned against my palm and I fought the urge to pull over and hold him.

Pull over and fuck him.

God, the ways I wanted my husband.

"How, uhm…" His brow knit together, mouth twisting into a tight curve. "How submissive should I be? What's okay?"

"However submissive you want to be," I answered. "My friend Rob is dating another dominant man who gives him hell over getting on his knees. Archie worships the ground Owen walks on, but I don't think they lean into roles one way or another. I haven't gotten a read on Flynn's boyfriend because I've been with you. But it doesn't matter."

"I want them to like me."

I would have sworn he said that with a pout. I gave his cheek a soft tap, and he groaned, looking away from me and turning his attention out the window.

"They'll love you," I promised. "Just like I do."

I SHOULD HAVE BEEN MORE NERVOUS TO MEET DALTON'S FRIENDS, BUT there was something about the way his car stood out in the parking lot of the bar that balanced my nerves. He parked sandwiched between a Maserati and an Audi, where the whole rest of the parking lot was packed with mid-range models in various stages of disrepair.

"Where the fuck," he muttered under his breath, locking the car and frowning at the entrance just as a raucous group shout rang out from the open patio doors.

"Where have you brought me?" I asked, tucking my shoulder behind his and grabbing his hand.

"I think this is Grayson's turtle racing bar."

"Whose what now?"

"Rob's boyfriend," Dalton said, heading toward the dark brick building. "Are you sure you're ready to meet them?"

There was a vinyl sign over a window advertising a bucket of beer on special, flapping in the breeze.

"Absolutely."

It was easy to find his friends in the bar because, for as much as their cars stuck out in the parking lot, the group of men stood out more. Or at least four of them did. One of the youngest men was the first to see *us*, and he waved his hand in the air like if he hadn't notified us, we'd have otherwise missed them.

"Last chance," Dalton said softly. "They're a lot."

"Can't be more than Kale," I countered.

He snorted like I couldn't have been more wrong.

"Well, if it isn't Mr. Fox and his husband, Mr. Fox," the one who flagged us down said, twirling his hand in a rather dramatic flourish.

"There hasn't been any name changes," Dalton corrected. "But this is my husband, Carter Royce."

Fuck, I loved the way he kept Ivey for himself. It reeked of propriety and carried just as much meaning to me as our rings did. As a collar would have. But a collar—and a name change—were squarely in the middle of the list of things we probably should talk about at some point, even if we hadn't gotten around to it yet.

"This is Archie," Dalton said, pointing at the man in question and then working his way around the rest of the group. "Archie's boyfriend, Owen. This is Rob and Grayson, Flynn. Do you remember Barclay from school?"

"Never thought I'd see you again," Barclay said, giving me a respectable clap on the back.

"Life has a funny way," I agreed.

"Have you been well?" he asked, the downward tilt of his chin and the seriousness around the corner of his eyes making it clear he knew more of the story between Dalton and me than most.

"Yeah." I nodded, finding the word stuck in my throat. "I've never been better."

"Good." Barclay glanced at Dalton, who was speaking with the rest of his friends, even with his hand still held tight in mine. "So has he."

"I'm glad. What about you?"

Frustration flashed across his face and he took a deep breath, shoulders rising and falling like they carried the weight of a man distressed. "I'll live to fight another day."

"To fuck another day," Flynn said, shoving Barclay in the shoulder before smiling at me. "Good to finally meet you, Carter."

"Oh, God." I scrunched my nose, unaware of how much I hated my name until that very moment. "My friends call me Royce."

"Royce," he corrected. "How long are you in town for?"

"Forever, it seems. Or at least as long as he'll have me here."

A wide, bright smile split Flynn's face and he visibly relaxed. "That's good. We were a bit scared you were going to steal Dalton off to New York."

"I'm sure that's what my friends would have preferred," I said.

"Now they'll just have to live with it." Flynn's eyes sparkled with mischief, and he pulled his phone out of his pocket. Something on the screen caught his eye and his expression darkened before he returned his phone to his pocket.

"Everything good?" I asked.

He nodded, the moment passed. "My boyfriend is at work and he's being a brat."

"I can't wait to meet him."

"Rose is lovely," Archie said. "If not a little shy for my tastes."

"Everyone is shy compared to you," his boyfriend Owen said, elbowing him in the ribs. "It's impossible for you to stop talking long enough to let him even try to come out of his shell around us."

Archie pressed his hand against his chest, feigning offense. At least, I guessed it was pretend.

"I think you have me confused with Grayson," he said.

"I resent that." Grayson raised his beer bottle and slammed the bottom of it down on the top of Archie's freshly opened drink. The beer immediately began to fizz, shooting like a rocket toward the neck of the bottle.

"You resemble it, you asshole," Archie muttered before sealing his lips around the bottle just in time to catch the bubbles before they overflowed.

"Please ignore him," Rob said, extending his hand for me to

shake. "Archie brings out the worst in everyone, especially Grayson."

Archie flipped him off, mouth still consumed with swallowing down his beer before it splashed all over his hand.

"You two need a drink," Grayson said, shoving a bucket of beer toward us. "And a seat."

The group of them was clustered into a circular booth and the table was scattered with buckets of beer in various stages of use and an assortment of bar food that looked like it probably all tasted the same.

Delicious.

Rob and Grayson slid further into the booth, setting off a chain reaction that almost shoved Barclay out the other side. He braced himself with a foot against the floor and a curse under his breath. Dalton gestured for me to take a seat, and the two of us settled into the space that had been allocated for us. He took two beers out of the bucket Grayson had slid toward us, cracking the tops of both and slipping one into my waiting hand.

"This will be nice," he said. "Maybe."

"After how high-strung your father was, it'll be a relief."

"Did you two want to put a bet down?" Grayson asked.

"A bet on what?"

"The turtles," he said, like it was common sense.

"The what?"

"The turtle races," Grayson said. "There's honestly no real reason to be in Manhattan Beach besides the turtle races."

"It's one of his favorite things to do," Rob said, patting the top of Grayson's head. Grayson shoved his hand off, but the sparkle in his eyes made it clear he enjoyed the attention, however patronizing.

"I think we're fine for now," Dalton said to Grayson. "Don't want to test our luck just yet."

Four hours and an immeasurable number of beers later, the turtle races were finished. The owner of the bar, who was apparently a friend of Grayson's, assured us it would be okay to leave the cars in the parking lot overnight, so we did. Rob had invited everyone back to his house for a swim, but Flynn was eager to get home to his boyfriend, and Barclay's mood had worsened as the day went on and he also declined. Archie struck me as the kind of man to be down for whatever, wherever, so they piled into a town car and set off for Rob's house.

Dalton and I rode together back to his house in a comfortable silence that didn't break, even as we stepped into the quiet of his home. Before he could ask or, worse, tell me no, I went down to my knees and busied myself with the laces of his shoes.

"You're drunk," he murmured, threading his fingers through my hair and leaning against the wall.

"I still know how shoelaces work."

"You know what I mean," he muttered.

Lifting his feet one by one, I helped Dalton out of his shoes and his socks, then his belt, and his shirt.

"This is who I am," I reminded him, even if the words were a little slurry. "I can't turn it off just because I drank enough beer to sustain a small country."

"We should have nachos," he said, which I took to be agreement on my statement.

"I can make you some," I offered.

Dalton frowned, wagging his finger. "I love it when you're this way, Ivey, but I want to do things with you too."

I toed out of my shoes and pushed them next to his. "Nachos, then."

I was pretty drunk, and so was he. Prepping the nachos consisted of a lot of bumping into each other and the counter as we moved around the kitchen together. It wasn't just the alcohol, though. This was a new thing for us to do together. There were enough soft touches to last a lifetime, and I rested my chin on Dalton's shoulder while he messily dumped layers of chips and cheese into the air fryer bucket.

"Beans," he murmured.

"Don't go on nachos."

"Divorce," he teased, taking a few tries to get the bucket slid back into the air fryer. After he set the timer and the temperature, he turned and slid his hands around my waist and notched my body between his spread legs.

"You're cute when you're drunk."

"You've never called me cute." He squinted up at me.

"You've never been cute before," I said, brushing the side of my finger across his cheek. "You've been attractive and handsome, breathtaking, consuming…"

Dalton screwed up his face and covered my mouth with his fingertips. "Enough flattery. Just kiss me."

"Yes, Sir," I whispered, leaning in and slanting our mouths together.

The kiss was wet and sloppy. Dalton tasted like salt and lime and beer, and he dug his fingers into my hips as he slid his tongue deeper into my mouth. His hands dragged up my sides and then he held my face, the tone of the kiss quickly going from drunk and playful to drunk and serious. Our teeth clashed, and Dalton shoved off the counter, walking us both across the kitchen until my shoulders hit his pantry door.

With the upper hand, Dalton shoved his thigh between my legs, pressing hard and insistent against my erection until I whimpered into his mouth. I was hard enough to want him, but nowhere near hard enough to come. The shitty beer made my brain dance, and I let the kiss consume me until there was nothing left except the hot swirl of his tongue and the solid press of his lips.

"I love you so much," he whispered, kissing the corner of my mouth. "For so long, I wished I could go back and do it different."

"Vegas is in the past," I reminded him.

"No." He shook his head and looked up at me imploringly. "I mean, further than that. I used to wish I could go back and never date her."

I sucked in a breath and wrapped my arms around Dalton's shoulders, twining my fingers together at the base of his neck. Genevieve would always exist for us, if not together, then at least individually. We'd both come so far from where we'd been in college, but that wasn't something that simply went away with time. It just became easier to carry, if you were lucky.

Which we both were.

"But since you've come back into my life, I see the error of that. Not that I mean you're worth what she did." His mouth twisted, like he didn't like the words coming out of his mouth. "I mean, you're worth everything, but what she did—"

"It was inexcusable," I said with a nod. "And it's okay. I know what you're trying to say."

I understood it better than most would because it was a thought process I'd had myself on more than one occasion over the years. But even before I reconnected with Dalton, I'd started to see the way all the threads of my life weaved together to point me down the next path. From boarding school to college to Vegas and back home again. Everything that I did was built on something that had come before, and while being a survivor of abuse wasn't something I wanted to talk about, it was in the foundation of everything that had come after.

"I want to marry you." Dalton's eyes flashed with the clarity of someone far more sober than either of us was.

"We are married," I reminded him.

"I know, but...I want to do it the right way. I want to give you a big wedding. Do you want a big wedding?"

"I just want you."

"I'm yours." He grinned and hummed that soft and pleased sound drunk people made when they had been proven right about something.

"I don't want to have a big wedding," I told him, because I didn't.

Dalton dropped his face into the crook of my neck, head crashing against the cabinet behind me. He cursed under his breath, then smiled against the side of my neck and bit me.

"Tell me about your dream wedding."

The short hairs at the nape of his neck were soft against my fingers. He bit me harder, sucking a bruise into my collarbone.

"Just you and me." I moaned when his mouth popped away from my skin, wondering if I was still too drunk to come or not.

"Courthouse? City Hall?" He licked the teeth marks he'd left in my skin.

I'd have married Dalton anywhere.

In fact, I already had. And since there were a thousand choices and decisions that had brought me to him, I knew better than to change a single one.

"Neither," I whispered. "Let's go to Vegas."

The timer on the air fryer beeped at us from the other side of the kitchen and Dalton ignored it, smiling up at me like a devil, like a man possessed.

Like a man who owned me, heart and soul.

He grabbed my hand and raised it between us, again kissing the ring he'd put there.

"Let's go to Vegas."

I married Carter Emerson Royce IV on my third—and hopefully final—trip to Las Vegas.

Sure, we were already legally married and had been for going on fifteen years, but the vows meant so much more than they had before. The rings we put on each other's fingers represented far more than a legally binding agreement to honor and cherish. The responsibility that ran between us went far deeper than that. I could feel the promise of it in the weight of his fingers against my skin, the soft press of his mouth against mine, the quiet whimper when the plug in his ass started to vibrate in the middle of the ceremony.

By the time we got back to the hotel room, Ivey was sweating and trembling, his perfectly styled blond hair on the verge of falling out of place from how much he kept fussing with it. I'd turned off the vibrator at the end of the ceremony to give him a break, but judging by the state of him, it had acted more as a punishment than anything else.

Purely accidental, as his punishment was still yet to come.

I hung the do not disturb sign on the door and latched the deadbolt, then shoved him so hard against the wall the breath rushed out of his lungs. I levered myself toward him, forearm pressed against his throat and knee lodged firmly between his thighs. Ivey's hands hung loose at his sides and his cock thumped against my knee.

"My husband," I whispered, nipping at the underside of his chin.

"Yours." His lashes fluttered closed, like golden fans across his cheekbones.

"My cock-hungry pain slut."

He moaned, giving me a jerky nod.

I ripped off his belt and shoved down his pants, reaching back and giving the base of the plug a tug and a twist. I didn't pull it out, but I fucked him with it until his knees gave out. Once he was on the floor, a whimpering pile of man, I was ready to go.

"Undress me," I demanded.

His fingers didn't work, so he used his teeth on the thin, waxed laces of my shoes. I had to brace myself against the wall so the wave of ownership and pride that crashed over me didn't take me right down to the floor with him. How had I gotten so lucky? How had this man become mine?

Ivey pulled my shoes off one by one, then managed to get his fingers to work when it came to my socks. I helped him with my belt and he took control of the rest, taking my pants and underwear to my ankles before lifting up and starting at the bottom button of my shirt. My bow tie was already loose around my neck. I'd untied it in the back of the limo because the sight of Ivey with my ring on his finger and those words of commitment fresh on his tongue threatened to take the very breath right out of me.

One button.

Two.

Three.

He was eye level again, pushing my tux jacket and shirt off my shoulders and into the pile of clothes on the floor.

I gave him the same treatment, helping him the rest of the way with his pants and underwear, his shoes and socks. I kissed the tops of his feet because he was perfect and he deserved it. His shirt, his tie, his jacket, and we were naked together in the entryway of a penthouse hotel room in a city neither of us had ever wanted to see again, the rest of our lives right around the corner.

"Go into the bedroom," I told him. "On your stomach."

He tripped over our clothes, but recovered and scrambled into the bedroom. I palmed my cock with a strangled grunt, debating if I wanted to get off immediately so I could last longer or cross my fingers and hope for the best. The bed creaked from the other room as Ivey climbed onto it, and I bent over to dig around in the pocket of my jacket for the vibrating plug remote.

I turned it on and Ivey yelped.

Yeah, I needed to come.

Everything I needed for the night was waiting in the bedroom because, for as many times as I'd found myself unprepared with Ivey in the past, our wedding night was not going to be one of those times.

Ivey was on the bed like I'd instructed, cheek resting on a pillow and his eyes half closed. The flared black base on the plug was visible between the plush mounds of his ass, his entire body shaking from the vibrations of the toy. My cock leaked against my stomach, and I did my best to ignore it as I gathered my supplies. Setting the remote on the nightstand, I pulled my toy bag out from the closet and measured out four lengths of black rope.

"Spread 'em," I said, and Ivey buried his face in the pillows, splaying out on the bed like a starfish.

I looped his wrists with a Burlington bowline, fastening him to the headboard, then repeated the quick knots on each ankle. Ivey was so big his body sprawled across the whole bed, the tips of his toes grazing the edges of the mattress.

"Can you move?" I asked.

He wiggled his wrists and whimpered.

I snatched one of the decorative pillows from the chair in the corner and shoved it under his hips, lifting his ass into the air. He looked perfect like that, splayed out and on display, his ass halfway to ready for my cock.

"I wish you could see yourself."

I moved around the side of the bed and took the rest of my toys from the bag. I hadn't brought a lot because I didn't need a lot. I'd packed the paddle I used on him the first night at his apartment, a cane that I'd purchased after getting home from New York, and a small flogger with chevron cut rubber falls. I added a bottle of lube to the mix, then tried to gather my thoughts.

It was hopeless, I realized. I was too far gone.

Kneeling on the bed between his stretched legs, I took my dick into my hand and jerked myself off. It didn't take long until cum trickled out of my cock, splattering against his ass in hot stripes.

"Sir!" he shouted, louder than he'd ever spoken to me before.

I ignored him until I'd worked all the cum out of my cock, then I spanked his bare ass with my hand, smearing the cum around his skin.

"What?" I hit him again and again, until my cum had spread across his entire ass, already drying.

"A waste," he murmured, rolling his head across the pillows. "Inside me."

"You'll get plenty inside of you, Ivey." I spanked him again. "Don't you worry about that.

The plug vibrated away, and I traded my hand for the paddle.

It was easy to hit him when he was tied down and spread out, the way he most often was in my dreams. The only thing I loved more than the way he tried to swallow down his cries and stifle the spasms in his body was when he reached the point of not being able to do either. His ass was purple and pink by the time he got there, short gasps and cries falling out of his mouth with every impact.

I tossed the paddle onto the floor and picked up the flogger, giving a test strike against Ivey's right shoulder blade. He hadn't been expecting it, barreling so fast into subspace, and the misdirected snap of pain had him fighting against his restraints. I leaned over him, smoothing my hand over the marks left from the falls, lips pressed against his ear.

"Settle down, Ivey." I kissed the spot right in front of his ear.

He cursed under his breath, and I leaned back, swinging the flogger again.

He was more ready for it, and there was something indescribably sexy about that. The way he'd hurt for me, followed by the way he'd managed how to take the pain because it was a gift from me…fucking out of this world.

"I love you," I told him, spreading my window of impact across the rest of his upper back. His skin had already started to turn the most beautiful shade of pink with dark purple stars peppered around the space. "I'm so in love with you. My perfect fucking man. You're perfect."

I fisted my cock with my left hand and stroked myself with rough and awkward twists of my wrist while I rained down against his back with the flogger. I moved down to his ass, and the response from him was nothing but pleasure. A muffled whimper and his hips twisted against the pillow searching for friction.

He was vulnerable and he was close.

So was I, though.

I added the flogger to the pile with the paddle and reached for the lube, drizzling a generous amount down my shaft. I fucked my cock up and down the slit of his crack, against the base of the plug, pressing it deeper into him. His fingers scrabbled against the headboard, sweat racing down the curve of his spine to the dips above his ass that fit my hands like they'd been molded for them.

"P…p…please, Sir."

Ivey's face was smothered in the pillows and I fisted the back of his hair, yanking him up.

"What do you need, Ivey?"

"Inside."

I loved that he was reduced to single words, almost unable to articulate the way he needed me. That was the most perfect form of his submission, where he was truly beyond asking or demanding, when he was only there to receive what I decided to give him. It was a heady kind of power that made my chest swell with every breath. Letting go of my cock, I pulled the plug out of his ass. His hole was lubed and twitching, gaping as it chased after something to fill it. The absolute basest form of need. I traced the frilled pucker with my thumbs, and Ivey whined again.

"You want me inside of you?" I asked, sliding both of my thumbs into him.

The noise that left his mouth sounded like the most pitiful kind of relief, like an easement but not enough to really soothe the ache. My fingers were slick with lube and I pulled his hole apart, teasing the head of my cock in the space between. It would be a tight squeeze, but he wanted to be filled and who was I to deny him the most basic of pleasures?

"Ivey." I pressed my tip between my thumbs, making my intentions clear.

He nodded his head into the pillows, bearing down around me and making room for my fingers and my cock to ease into him.

"Sir." The single syllable came out a garbled plea, followed by, "Husb…"

I pushed my whole length into him.

"Say it," I demanded, pulling all the way out.

"Hus—"

I cut him off by slamming all the way back into him. He was tight and slippery, stretched from the plug and the lube, pliant from the pain and the pleasure.

"Say it, Ivey," I whispered, repeating the same withdraw and entry thrust. Each punch of my hips sucked the words right out of him, and I smiled.

I smiled for the way he tried, and the way he failed, and the way his cock leaked against the pillow beneath him.

"Husband!" he cried out, the single word choked with tears. "Husband. My husband."

"Damn right." I let my thumbs slide out of him and I started to fuck him in earnest. Short and hard thrusts, dragging the head of my cock over his prostate on every hot, slick slide. Falling forward, I braced myself against his shoulders, pushing him into the mattress with every snap of my hips. Sweat dripped into my eyes, but I didn't care. The only thing that mattered was Ivey. Ivey and his pain and his pleasure and his arousal.

A keening wail fell out of his mouth and his hole tightened down around the middle of my cock like a fucking vise grip. I went still and let his muscles try and milk me, reaching between him and pillow to see how badly he'd ruined the bedding. It was a mess, covered in sweat and cum. Positively ruined, like him.

"Do you have another?" I asked, bending toward him and nipping at his shoulder with my teeth.

He whimpered and I shifted, focusing on the task at hand, which in that moment was fucking him until he couldn't see straight. He thrashed beneath me and whined when it got too sensitive, and when I took the vibrating plug and forced it inside of him, alongside my cock, I got what I wanted.

Another orgasm.

It was strong enough to send me over the edge, the tightness of his body paired with the press and the vibration of the plug against my shaft, and we were coming together. My orgasm slammed into me with the force of a truck, body bucking madly as the first spurts of cum left my cock. I had Ivey so tight around his waist, I knew there would be finger-shaped bruises across the swell of his hips when we woke up the next day.

I must have blacked out, because the next thing I remembered, I was crumpled on top of Ivey's sweat-soaked back, cock still twitching with the aftershocks of my orgasm. The plug vibrated on the bed against my knee, and I threw it onto the floor because my skin was beyond sensitive from what had to have been a full-body orgasm.

Gingerly, I climbed off Ivey, sitting on the edge of the bed so I could undo the knots around his wrists and ankles. After I tossed the rope onto the floor, Ivey made a *harrumphing* sound, but didn't move. I brushed my hand across the side of his face, moving sweat from his eyes, hair from his forehead.

"Are you with me?" I asked quietly.

In response, he raised his eyebrows like he was trying to open his eyes, but his muscles wouldn't cooperate.

"I'm going to go draw a bath. Will you be good until I'm back?"

He answered that with a sigh that felt like a yes.

Climbing off the bed on shaking legs, I went into the bathroom and plugged the huge jacuzzi tub before turning the water on the hot side of warm. In the bedroom, the sheets rustled and I knew Ivey was coming back to consciousness. The hotel staff had brought up champagne and a fruit plate while we were out, but I didn't think Ivey had even noticed it when we got back. I brought the plate and the ice bucket into the bathroom, then went to get him from the bedroom.

I found Ivey sitting up, elbows resting on his knees, his expression dazed. He blinked up at me when I walked in, a tired and content smile spreading across his face.

"There you are," I said, coming to stand between his legs. He dropped his cheek against my stomach, and I worked my fingers through the wet strands of hair at the back of his neck. "Do I have a happy husband? The most content little sub?"

Ivey hummed and nodded, looping his arms around my waist.

"Let's get you into the bath," I said, curling my arms under his armpits and hoisting him up to his feet.

Ivey leaned against me with another happy moan, and I walked him into the bathroom and helped him down into the tub. I arranged myself behind him, then set two flutes of champagne on the edge.

"Did you want a drink?" I asked. "Some fruit?"

With one arm banded around his chest, I used my feet to keep his legs spread open and I plucked a strawberry from the fruit plate with my free hand. Reaching around, I dipped it into the champagne and traced the tip of it across his lips. Ivey dropped his head against my shoulder and took the fruit into his mouth with a moan.

He was still boneless, still at a loss for words. Ivey chewed slowly, and I slid my hand beneath the surface of the water and searched out his cock, which was far from boneless. He gasped when I tightened my hand around his length, giving him a slow stroke beneath the bubbling water.

"I can't," he rasped.

"Don't waste your energy speaking, Ivey," I warned. "Have a drink and relax, because you're going to come again."

He whined, pushing against the hold I had on him, but not enough to really do anything about it. Ivey was bigger than me and it would be easy for him to overpower me if he ever really wanted to, which he didn't. But he also knew if he told me to stop, I would. He wanted to be pushed to a third orgasm, and he trusted me to get him there, so I would.

I waited for Ivey to get his fingers around the stem of a glass and the glass to his lips before I touched him again. He grimaced, the muscles in his back hard and tight against my chest. His thighs trembled against mine, and I loosened the fist around his dick for the next stroke.

"I promise you fifteen unforgettable years," I whispered the start of my vows to him into his ear. He hummed, a moan and a sigh all at once before he swallowed some of the champagne.

"And fifteen after that, and fifteen after that," I went on. "I promise I will fight you and I will fight for you. I swear on my life that no one who isn't me will ever hurt you again."

That one had gotten a raised brow from the officiant, but the broad smile the words had drawn out of Ivey's mouth had silenced any potential protestations at the time.

In front of me, Ivey took another drink of his champagne, hips lifting when I set a pace with my hand.

"We are bound together, you and I, and I promise that you'll want for nothing as long as you wear my ring," I said, closing my eyes and recalling how perfect his face looked in the garish neon of the walk-up wedding chapel. "I vow to anticipate your needs, your wants, your desires, and I promise to satisfy. Each. And every. One."

I punctuated my favorite part of the vow with a flick of my

wrist around the flared tip of his cock. Ivey's breathing stuttered and he managed back another swallow of champagne, emptying the glass. He set it on the edge of the tub and went for another strawberry. He fumbled his hold on it, the piece of fruit splashing into the tub as Ivey grabbed my knee and dug his fingernails in with a pained gasp of breath.

"Just like that," I coaxed, quickening my pace between his legs. "You need this, Ivey. Come on. Come for me."

He cried out, bursts of cum spilling into the water as I wrung yet another orgasm out of him. His entire body seized and trembled between my legs, fighting hard against my hold and my hands, and I knew he'd reached the point of no return. Slowly, I unfolded my fingers from his length and smoothed my hand down the taut muscles on the inside of his thigh.

"There you go," I whispered, pressing wet kisses against the side of his face. "That was it. That was all. Look at you, making me a man of my word."

"I love you," he whimpered, pressing against my body until I let him turn and curl into my lap. It was nearly impossible in the water, but it was my favorite way to hold him after a scene and I wasn't going to deprive him of it now, not after he'd given me so very much.

"I love you," he said again, fingertips already pruned and splayed over my shoulder.

I smoothed my hands down his arms, trailing warm water back over his skin as I traced the outline of his muscles, his ribs, the bruises I'd just given him. Every star, every handprint, every stripe was proof of my vows to him made real. Every kiss to him, and from him to me, a promise. A promise for our future and for our past.

"We are bound together, you and I," Ivey whispered, pressing a kiss against my heart before finishing his final vow to me. "For fifteen more years…"

"And then together longer." I held him tight against me. "Until the end of our time."

ALSO BY KATE HAWTHORNE

Trophy Doms Social Club

Humbled

Edged

Praised

Bound

Shared

Giving Consent

Worth the Risk

Worth the Wait

Worth the Fight

Worth the Chance

All in Good Time

Necessary Space

Necessary Time

Duality

Dual Destruction

Dual Surrender

Dual Defiance

Two Truths and a Lie

A Real Good Lie

A Cold Hard Truth

A Matter of Fact

Room for Love

Reckless

Heartless

Faultless

Fearless

Limitless

A Very Messy Motel Brothers Wedding

Relentless

Secrets in Edgewood

A Taste of Sin

The Cost of Desire

A Love Made Whole

Secrets in Edgewood: The Complete Series

The Lonely Hearts Stories

His Kind of Love

The Colors Between Us

Love Comes After

Until You Say Otherwise

<u>**STANDALONES**</u>

Rebound

One for the Road

Daybreak - Vino & Veritas

Unfettered

Dreams

A Thousand Lifetimes

<u>**COLLABORATIONS**</u>

With E.M. Denning

Irreplaceable

Future Fake Husband

Future Gay Boyfriend

Future Ex Enemy

With J.R. Gray

May the Best Man Win

ABOUT KATE HAWTHORNE

Kate Hawthorne is a writer and author educator with over three dozen published romance novels spread across two successful and award winning pen names.

Known for stories that pack a figurative (and sometimes literal) punch, Kate has built a recognizable brand that consistently delivers emotionally charged and character driven happy endings for everyone.

Visit her website
http://www.katehawthornebooks.com

Sign up for Kate's newsletter
http://www.katehawthornebooks.com/extra

facebook.com/authorkatehawthorne
x.com/katewriteswords
instagram.com/kate.hawthorne
patreon.com/katehawthorne